SEEKING FORTUNE

A REGENCY INSPIRATIONAL ROMANCE

JOSIE RIVIERA

INTRODUCTION

To keep up on newly released ebooks, paperbacks, Large Print Paperbacks, audiobooks, as well as exclusive sales, sign up for Josie's Newsletter today.

As a thank you, I'll send you a Free PDF ... The Beauty Of ...

Josie's Newsletter

Did you know that according to a Yale University study, people who read books live longer?

5 STAR READER REVIEWS

Amazon Review by Kindle Customer

"The setting was beautifully described. The reader will feel a part of the workings at the estate, the gypsy camp plus the nearby village.

The period details were well researched.

The characters were multifaceted, interesting, colorful and intriguing.

The story contained hidden secrets, deceit, prejudice, conversion to God, forgiveness, friendship that leads to love. A wonderful entertaining book must read book.

A Very Highly Recommenced Read!!!"

Amazon Review by D. Keith

"Riviera weaves a wondrous tale. of love, betrayal, and forgiveness. Valentina and James are both lost in a work of grief, but God ordered their steps and they eventually find their HEA. This inspirational romance is suitable for all ages."

Amazon Review by Kindle Customer

"What a beautifully romantic story! I fell in love with gypsies when I first started reading romance. It was great visiting with them again in this book."

This book is dedicated to all my wonderful readers who have supported me every inch of the way.
THANK YOU!

PRAISE AND AWARDS

USA TODAY bestselling author

#1 First Place Golden Pen Award

CHAPTER 1

Si khohaimo may patshivalo sar o tshatshim.
There are lies more believable than the truth.
Old Romany saying

ngland 1811

"BURY ME STANDING, for I have been on my knees all my life."

Valentina Rupa bowed her head to hear her beloved mother's last words, to see the twitch of her eyes beneath her eyelids, the rise and fall of her chest beneath the thin blankets.

Her mother's breath faded, already settling into the bleak night, already gone.

Unearthly quiet filled their makeshift canopy. The dwindling light from the nearby campfires of their Romany tribe seeped through the canvas.

1

"*Daj.* Mother … don't stop speaking." Tears blinded Valentina's eyes, defeated her voice. She focused on her mother's lips, willing her to speak once more. What good did it do to be a *drabardi*, a powerful fortune-teller and healer, if she couldn't save her own mother?

Valentina's younger sister, Yolanda, stood beside her. Yolanda coughed violently, then wheezed.

"Please, Daj, it's not your time." Yolanda's hoarse voice faded to a whisper. "Her lips, she's breathing …"

"Nay, it's the north wind." Valentina peered at the oak tree branches bending against a biting gust, threatening to collapse their crude canopy. Wagon wheels creaked, groaning into the dirt, familiar sounds, yet so distant. Their mother had lived her entire life in the caravan, traveling from village to village. There was no other way for her. Only the way of the Romany.

The air hung thick and heavy, weighty against Valentina's damp cheeks. She didn't care, didn't bother to wipe them. She hated the weakness of crying. Crying meant loss and loneliness and defeat.

She glanced at Yolanda, noting her ashen face, the stoop of her slight shoulders. "Try to rest for a while."

"I'm not tired." Yolanda rubbed her temples. "Now that both Mother and Father are dead, we're orphans."

"I'll not abandon you." Valentina choked back her fears and crushing uncertainties. She was the older sister. She always took care of Yolanda.

With shaking fingers, she tucked the threadbare blankets around their mother's feeble body, smoothed the wrinkled fabric, and folded the ends back. Neatly, the way her mother liked it done. Tucked, smoothed, folded. Tucked, smoothed, folded.

"Daj, you starved yourself so we could eat. We'd have found the food we needed somehow." Her hands glided purposefully. "Why do the English treat the Rom as if we're animals?"

"Because this is the land of the English," Yolanda said. "They make their own rules."

Long shivers rippled through Valentina's body, a cadence of trepidation and doubt. In a single, deliberate breath, she blew them out.

The friends who'd discreetly stayed out of the way melted in now, coming from their wagons to gather around the deathbed. The sad cries of the caravan penetrated the dusk. Purple-lipped, the elderly, ragged men and women huddled together, stamping their feet to keep away the chill.

With the sleeve of her frayed cotton gown, Valentina wiped her eyes. Her hands were still wet from retrieving water from the river. She'd used the water to bathe her mother, an ironic Romany custom relying on her mother's willingness to go to her death.

Yolanda helped Valentina gather their mother's personal belongings and carried them to the campfire. The flames rose against the night sky and consumed the remnants of their mother's life—a well-worn apron, a silky fringed sash. Their people burned most possessions of the dead, believing the possessions were unclean and defiled the living.

Valentina skimmed her index finger across her mother's double-edged dagger and accidentally drew blood. Grimacing, she licked her finger. She didn't have the heart to destroy the weapon, so she thrust the dagger into its sheath and tied it on a cord along her gown's seam.

Then she slid her palm across the last treasure, her mother's yellow scarf, her *diklo*. Bringing it to her face, Valentina closed her eyes and inhaled. The scent of oak and jasmine, exotic and mysterious, flooded through her. She remembered her mother jauntily tying the diklo around her greying hair each morning.

3

Valentina knew she was supposed to take one small token before burial, instead she took two. She'd never been one to obey rules. She folded the yellow scarf into a perfect triangle and tied it loosely around her throat. It didn't match her faded scarlet gown, and that didn't matter.

Nothing mattered now except her sister.

Yolanda's pretty, round face contorted in grief as she placed small multicolored stones around their mother's body. Valentina inserted pearls in her mother's nose, a Romany custom to keep out all wickedness. Her hands wavered, and she avoided touching the body for fear of contamination.

Inhaling the fragrance of a drop of frankincense, she smoothed the spicy golden oil along her arms to protect herself against evil spirits. A shadow of skepticism crossed her soul, and her hands stopped. Maybe spirits didn't exist at all. They certainly demanded endless rituals, and in return granted … nothing. Glancing around at the eerie silhouettes dancing in the firelight, she dabbed a few more drops of oil on her wrists, just in case.

The men of their tribe had moved to sit in the grassy clearing on the forest's edge, the scent of sweet blackberry brandy filling the brisk October air. They'd stolen it from an unsuspecting Englishman in town. Several grizzled dogs lay listless at their feet.

Luca, the caravan's young leader, was the only man who stood. His baggy green pants were fitted at the ankle and billowed in the wind. He mourned Valentina and Yolanda's mother in a plaintive cadence and guided the elders in solemn chants. Although all the other young men had gone off in search of food and never returned, Luca hadn't deserted the tribe.

"I'll get more hot water, Yolanda, before we prepare for Daj's burial." Valentina retrieved her wool cloak and then hoisted a pot of water off of a smoky campfire. With her free hand, she brushed a strand of hair behind her ear, longing for a warm bath. However, custom prevented her from washing until after her mother's burial.

She made her way past the lamenters to the small tent the women shared. An afternoon rain had washed soggy leaves over the ground. One of the dogs lifted its head and sniffed, the thick fur around its neck bristling. A sudden crackle—somewhere a tree branch snapped.

Her senses sharpened. The last few nights she'd dozed while nursing her mother and had dreamed about a man. A rich man. A powerful man.

Scanning the dense woods, she sensed someone was watching. She had the gift of second sight, her mother had said, but Valentina shook the thought away. Besides, her tribe was far too secluded to be found.

* * *

YOLANDA LABORED through the night with a deep, raspy cough, while Valentina brewed a mixture of vegetable matter and barley water and fed it to her sister. Still, the cough persisted.

By morning, Yolanda's breathing came rapidly; her skin was pale. Curing Yolanda's chronic cough had been beyond their mother's skill, and Valentina's, also. With each day, Yolanda's condition had steadily worsened. Perhaps she had an infection.

Luca entered the tent. His brows furrowed as he studied Yolanda's sweaty face. "There's a gentleman who owns an estate in Ipswich, and a physician might live nearby," he said.

Valentina caught Luca's worried look and stood, deliberating.

"Perhaps the physician can prescribe a tonic medicine."

She squeezed Yolanda's chilly hands reassuringly. "If we leave now, we'll be back at the camp before nightfall. Daj's burial isn't until tomorrow. Are you well enough for the walk to Ipswich, Yolanda?"

"Aye, of course." If Yolanda wanted to portray strength, the effect was spoiled by the look of hesitation in her deep-brown eyes. And then by a violent cough.

The midday sun loomed by the time Luca led Valentina and Yolanda to the outskirts of a grand country estate with a vast two-story home made of stone and the surrounding land dotted with tenant farmer cottages. Through the tall boxwood hedges that screened them from view, Valentina spotted a thin boy skipping stones on the banks of a slow-flowing stream.

The refreshing autumn breeze had renewed her spirits. Although still saddened by her mother's death, she was certain her sister would soon receive the care she needed to recover.

Luca stepped over a fallen stump and remarked how the color was returning to Yolanda's pale cheeks. "The walk has done us all good."

Valentina smiled, appreciating his attempt to encourage them.

"After your mother's burial," he continued, "we'll head south toward the coast."

"Before the winter, hopefully," Valentina answered, guiding Yolanda past a low wooden fence. From the corner of her eye, she thought she glimpsed movement at the edge of the field they were skirting. For a moment, she froze.

"Luca—" Her voice rose in alarm as she saw two men running toward them.

"What are you Gypsies doing here?" one of the men shouted. His hair was silver-white, and as he neared, she could see numerous lines creased his forehead.

Valentina's hands flew to her chest. "We're—"

Yolanda's lips quivered as she pressed her elbows to her sides. "Please. We're not doing anything wrong." She coughed so hard her face flushed crimson.

"Are you trying to steal from us? You'll answer to Mr. Colchester." The silver-haired man fixed his gaze on the other man. "Aye, Roland?"

Roland, a rough-looking man with huge shoulders, nodded. "Aye, Geoffrey. Gypsies aren't wanted here."

Prickles made their way up the back of Valentina's neck.

There was no time to explain. She whirled and grabbed her sister's hand. Frantically, she scanned the field. *Where was Luca?*

Trembling, shaking, gasping, she tugged Yolanda back toward the forest. The undergrowth whipped at her ankles. Her lungs burned.

"We should've stayed at the camp. I don't need a physician." Yolanda's cough was incessant as she tried to keep up. "If they catch us …" She slipped and fell, bracing herself on both arms as she hit the ground. Her head went down, and she cried out in pain.

"Valentina!" Yolanda glanced at her arm, twisted at an odd angle, and blanched. "It hurts. The pain is throbbing. I can't run!"

Absorbed in her sister, Valentina allowed herself one gasping breath and risked a look over her shoulder. The two men—Geoffrey and Roland— were dashing straight toward them.

Valentina slid her arm around Yolanda's shoulders, assisting her sister first to a kneeling position, then gently to her feet.

Yolanda pursed her lips, her eyes darkened with pain. "My arm feels hot."

As she murmured assurances to Yolanda, the trees rustled

and Valentina peered upward. Luca had launched himself into the heavy branches of a tall, mossy pine. The limbs cracked under his weight as he braced his bare feet on branches on either side of the trunk, balancing with ease. Raw-boned and dark, he coiled and yanked a carving knife from his boot as the two men reached the women.

Valentina tried not to glance at him, fearful the men would see Luca and ruin his ambush. Before the men could speak, Luca vaulted to the ground and locked his muscled arm around Roland's throat.

"Romany men don't share, and no one takes our drabardi anywhere." His blade glinted in a shaft of sunlight.

Roland struck a heavy jab to Luca's chest and threw Luca onto the ground. His head bounced hard, his eyes closed. Then Roland turned to Yolanda, now sobbing from pain.

"I'll take the hurt lass to the house," Roland said to the other man. Without waiting for a word from either woman, he scooped Yolanda up and lumbered toward the estate.

Valentina took judicious note of Luca. He was breathing steadily, and his eyelids flickered.

Geoffrey extended his hand. "Come with us. Your sister is hurt and needs help."

She ignored his hand. "Is there a physician on the estate?"

"Nay, although he lives close by. He can tend to her arm come the morrow. I fear it might be fractured."

Come the morrow. Valentina scraped a hand through her heavy, tangled hair. They had planned to return to camp by nightfall.

Briefly, she squeezed her eyes shut. Her mother's body required a proper burial ritual. However, her sister's injury required a physician to attend to her.

Valentina glanced over her shoulder at Luca. His quick, reassuring nod settled her conflicting considerations. In a wordless exchange, he assured her he'd attend to her mother's burial.

Pushing up the sleeves of her scarlet gown, she straightened her shoulders, and her five-foot stature seemed to lengthen. She matched Geoffrey's swift strides, concentrating on Yolanda and the grand house that awaited them.

Daj would want her to focus on Yolanda's care, she assured herself. Come the morrow, they'd return to their caravan.

CHAPTER 2

Devlesa araklam tum.
It is with God that we found you.
Old Romany saying

James Colchester rubbed his eyes, struggling with the fatigue of numerous sleepless nights. As a commissioned officer, he'd fought another senseless battle in King George's name. Time he would've preferred to spend near his son. Once the battle in Spain had ended for the time being, he'd quickly returned home.

His son's excited squeals of laughter as he'd run into James' arms had been his reward for his efforts. Warmth moved his heart, lifted his spirit. Now, with the boy finally asleep on his lap, he forced his shoulders to relax, and he lifted a prayer.

"Thank you, Lord, for watching over my son and keeping him safe."

James shifted in the straight-backed chair. It pressed

unyieldingly against his sore muscles and was barely able to contain his long form and his little son's too. Despite his prosperity, he favored simplicity. His bedchamber contained little more than an unadorned fireplace, a clean bed, a wooden table beneath a woven tablecloth. He shook back an errant strand of hair, grown long from neglect. He'd haphazardly tied it back with a leather thong.

Geoffrey, James' steward, stepped into the room.

"Trouble, I hear?" James reached for his goblet of port wine set on the carved rosewood side

table beside him. "A Gypsy woman on the estate?"

"Two Gypsy women, sir. They're sisters. And one Gypsy man, who would've been more than happy to slit Roland's throat. Roland and I saw them near the estate this afternoon, a few hours before you returned. Roland was feeding the wild animals near his cottage while I was attending to one of the tenants. Anyway, when we confronted the Gypsies because we assumed they were stealing, they tried to run off. The younger sister injured her arm."

"And the Gypsy man?"

"He was no threat." Geoffrey shook his head, adding a dismissive hand gesture. "Aside from the one woman's injury, the both of them looked like they hadn't had a decent meal in weeks. That's why I brought them here."

"Tell Wiborow to have guest bedchambers prepared for them both, as well as a warm meal. I'll call for the physician come the morrow."

"I assumed you would and have already made provisions for the women when we arrived a few hours ago. The injured sister is resting. The other sister is waiting in the parlor. I wasn't certain if you wanted to speak with her before you retired." Geoffrey squinted at the sleeping child in James' lap. "Forgive me for not asking about your son sooner. How is he?" He sighed. "Poor boy."

"My son was born deaf. Rest assured, he isn't poor."

"Aye. I only meant—" Apparently thinking better about continuing, Geoffrey took a long breath and threaded a wrinkled hand through his sparse hair. He perused the sideboard before selecting a ripe pear. "May I sit?"

"Of course."

Geoffrey's heavy profile cast a stooped shadow along the candle-lit room. He angled his chair near the fireplace, grabbed a glass of ale from the sideboard and took a lengthy swill. He'd been James' loyal steward since James had inherited his parents' estate six years earlier.

"I overheard several servants speculating in the hallway," James said, "and they mentioned one of the Gypsy women is a fortune-teller."

Geoffrey leaned forward in his chair. "Aye. Some of the servants have gone to their camp to have their fortunes told by the older sister, I believe."

"Perhaps she is the woman who once read my late wife's fortune. 'Twould be a coincidence, aye?" James stroked the stubble on his chin, and adjusting his sleeping son on his lap, stretched his legs toward the warm fire. He was still chilled from the battle. Anxiety threaded his words, despite his attempt to disguise it.

Geoffrey stared at his tankard and didn't meet James' gaze. "After your wife's death, the entire manor fears another outbreak of influenza."

"May I remind you, Geoffrey, that living here in the country, we're much removed from this latest epidemic."

"I trust you'll make the right decision, Mr. Colchester, and settle our departure. Wales is your birthplace and you must be anxious to return." Geoffrey finished his ale. "My advice is to remove Jeremy from the memories of his sister and mother."

"Please don't mention my beautiful daughter and my late

wife in the same breath." Absently, James stroked Jeremy's pale cheek with his thumb. "'Tis not easy to travel with a son who hasn't been healthy. He might not be able to withstand such an arduous journey."

"Still, we should depart before winter."

James took a long breath. "Where did you say you found the Gypsies?" The chair prodded and poked into his back, refusing to bend. He shifted. Changing position didn't help. Nothing helped.

"At the edge of the property near the boxwood hedges. Roland spotted them, and I overheard the man say something about breaking camp and heading south toward the coast."

The coast. The sea. Beatrix. James closed his eyes against the sharp ache that clenched his stomach whenever he thought of his cherished daughter. He could still hear her sweet babbling voice echoing through the hallways.

He sank back in his chair, attempting to find the balance missing in his life, anything to ease the gnawing, ceaseless despair. What parents could ever recover from the death of their beloved child?

He should've heeded the fortune-teller's warning those few short years ago instead of disregarding it. He should've heeded it. He leaned against the stiff wooden back of his chair and briefly closed his eyes. If he had heeded the fortune-teller's words, Beatrix might still be alive.

Nay. The Bible warned about fortune-tellers.

He swallowed, tasting an agonizing thought. Really? Why? And where was God, then, because God hadn't listened to James' prayers in a long, long time.

He stood, lifting Jeremy. The boy wrapped his small arms around James' neck. His chest swelled at the love he felt for his son, constant and fierce.

"I may request a reading from this fortune-teller," he said quietly.

Geoffrey lowered his thick white brows and shook his head in an emphatic 'nay'. "Mr. Colchester, we are Christians. 'Do not turn to mediums or necromancers; do not seek them out, and so make yourselves unclean by them: I am the Lord your God.'"

James nodded. "Leviticus 19:31. I'm well aware of that specific Bible verse, Geoffrey." Cradling his son, James strode into the oil-lit hallway. He found Jeremy's nurse in the kitchen. "Elspeth, 'tis hours past Jeremy's bedtime." He placed the child into her outstretched arms.

Jeremy opened his greyish-blue eyes and stared up at his father. Tears pooled in the dark circles beneath his eyes. As James gazed at the innocent boy's innocent expression, a stab of pain pierced his insides. Jeremy's sweet face mirrored his twin sister, Beatrix. The same bubbly smile that touched people's hearts, the same joyfulness, the same hair color, as blonde as their late mother's.

"You'll be safe, son, I promise," James murmured.

"He's fine, Mr. Colchester." Elspeth's polite smile didn't go any farther than her mouth. The servants had been on edge for months, ever since James' wife had died.

Elspeth rocked Jeremy's slight body back and forth. "When your son realized you were gone, he dreamt those terrible nightmares again."

James smoothed the fine hair from his son's forehead. A deep gentleness surged, mingling with desperation. "Let's pray Jeremy's dreams will soon return to happier times." With a brief nod, James quickly left, striding across the pale blue carpet, heading for the parlor and the fortune-teller.

* * *

VALENTINA KEPT her gaze on the eight-foot longcase clock positioned on a side wall in the parlor. The hour was nearing nine.

Despite the fire burning in the parlor's fireplace, she rubbed her arms, chasing away the chill, her rings sparkling in the candlelight. She yanked her multilayered gown around her feet as she sat stiffly on a settee with scrolled ends and lion-carved legs. Her once vibrant clothes were now muted, matching her unwashed body and soiled appearance.

The door opened and she straightened, studying the tall, good-looking man who'd stepped into the room. His features were chiseled, his build muscular, and he strode across the carpeted floor with quiet authority. Beneath dark arched brows, his piercing grey eyes observed her with frank interest.

Her chin went up as she returned his gaze. "Bury me standing. *Prohasar man opre pirend.*" She repeated her mother's words in her native Romany tongue.

"I don't understand." He stopped abruptly and folded strong arms over his high-collared waistcoat. His face was hidden in the shadows, although the aristocratic lines were apparent. He was lean with broad shoulders, and she had to admit he was very handsome. And he was observing her with unconcealed interest.

"I speak the language of the Romany. My language." She wiped her palms along her gown, taken aback at the sweat on them despite the chill in the air.

"I'm James. James Colchester."

She blinked, startled that he'd used his given name.

Her dream came back in a rush. A rich man. A powerful man. He'd whispered to her when her sleep deepened and disappeared before she could reach him.

He stepped forward, his compelling gaze fixed on her face. "And you are?"

"Valentina Rupa." She stood, grimacing at the shooting cramp in her legs. She'd barely moved the previous day, kneeling at her mother's deathbed, and that had been followed by today's long walk and then by sitting for hours in this cold room. She trusted they wouldn't buckle and betray her weakness.

He must have seen her wobble, for he reached out and grasped her elbow. "I have been told that my men mistakenly assumed you were all trying to steal something—although I'm not certain what. In the confusion, you and your sister fled, resulting in your sister's arm being injured. Correct?"

She shook off his hand and didn't answer.

Annoyance flickered across his face. "Correct?"

"Aye. We came here seeking a physician for my sister's cough, and now she has two reasons to see one."

"I'm sorry she was hurt. We'll know more come the morrow after the physician examines her."

Valentina gave a cool nod framed in steel. "Where *is* Yolanda?"

"She is resting comfortably in one of the upstairs bedchambers."

"She is safe?"

"Safe? Aye, of course." His smoky gaze surveyed her. "And I believe you're the fortune-teller from the fair in Ipswich some years back."

"How would you remember me?"

"I remember your eyes. They glow like polished emeralds."

"I don't remember you." She surveyed his wealth of black hair, his self-commanding presence. "All gadje look alike to me."

Moonlight winked through the panes of the leaded windows giving an eerie golden glow to the room. "I want to see my sister."

"Let her rest."

Would he hurt Yolanda? Nay. His eyes were warm, his manner gentle. Still, she didn't know anything about him, except that he was a gadje.

Her gaze darted to the doorway. Perhaps she should find Yolanda and leave.

As soon as the thought formed, she headed for the door. James caught her from behind, one arm wrapping around her waist. The warm fabric of his muslin shirt slid against her bare arms. "Please. You have nothing to fear."

"You certainly are right." Shrugging off his hold, she swiveled to face him. "Because we've committed no crime."

His lips twitched, so subtle she might've imagined it.

She went on. "'Tis necessary that Yolanda and I finish the burial rituals for our mother." A tear slipped down her cheek and she attempted to discreetly wipe it away. "I must be assured we leave at first light."

"I'm sorry about your mother's death. 'Tis up to the physician, not me." James hesitated, then added. "Besides speaking to you, there was another reason I wanted to see you tonight before you were shown to your own bedchamber."

"Because your needs are more important than ours?

He frowned. "Of course not."

Men like him were only interested in themselves. Perhaps he had no intention of calling a physician. Perhaps ...The word *bedchamber* rang in her ears, and panicking, she ripped her mother's double-edged dagger from its sheath and raised the weapon.

With the swiftness of a trained soldier, he grabbed her wrist. "Give the dagger to me, Valentina."

CHAPTER 3

Te na khutshos perdal tsho ushali.
Try not to jump over your own shadow.
Old Romany saying

*V*alentina's hands wouldn't stop shaking. She'd never used a dagger before. Sweat broke out on her skin, dampening her gown.

James grabbed her other wrist and pulled her toward him. His hard thighs brushed against hers. "Valentina, drop the blade."

She breathed quick, thin gasps of air and met his furious stare. With a low groan, she released the dagger. It clattered to the floor and spun out of reach.

"I haven't hurt you or your sister, nor do I intend to, so there's nothing to fear. I'm a man of my word." He picked up the dagger and set it atop the wooden mantel. Then he lit a candle in an iron spiked candle holder and placed it beside the dagger.

"Please come here." He gestured toward a narrow ornate table in the corner of the room.

With a hard swallow, she eyed the dagger just out of reach. Then, with a lift of her head, she purposely walked ahead of him. She insulted him by doing so, although he wasn't aware of it. In the Romany culture, a woman never walked in front of a man.

He pulled out a heavy mahogany chair beside the table and beckoned her to sit. "I'd like you to read my fortune."

Her hands dropped to her sides. For a moment, she was at a loss for words. "You gadje think the Rom ways are mere superstitions."

"Aye, and my Christian beliefs also forbid fortune-telling."

"So why ask me?"

"At the fair, you demonstrated an astonishing ability to foresee the future." He avoided her gaze, his deep voice a monotone. Dragging up a second chair, he sat across from her.

"So that's why I've been waiting in your parlor for hours?"

"I apologize. I've recently returned home from a meaningless, violent war." He shook his head, then reached out his hands to her.

Valentina had gotten used to the gadjes' unfamiliar smells and filthy palms. She breathed the nearness of this man—a manly scent of earth and leather. His palms were clean.

"And if I refuse to read your fortune?" She focused on the cut-glass chandelier hanging from the ceiling to distance herself from his stare.

His fingers stroked hers. "I'm hoping you won't."

Valentina jerked her hands away. Smoothing her heavy dark hair, she was surprised she was suddenly self-conscious of her soiled appearance.

Her thoughts scrambled to understand his request. Perhaps she'd misunderstood him.

Perhaps she hadn't.

She shivered.

He stood and slipped off his waistcoat, an intricate black design woven into rich wool. So beautiful, the garment could fetch enough money in the marketplace to feed her tribe for months.

He draped the soft fabric around her shoulders. "You must be cold."

She glided the waistcoat between her fingers and opened her mouth to protest.

His mouth quirked and he shook his head, effectively silencing her. He rolled up the stark white sleeves of his shirt, revealing the solid strength of his arms. His gaze was steadfast and single-minded.

In frustration, she sighed. "Let me see your hands."

He set both his hands on the table and she bent her head to examine them.

"Does it matter which hand you read first?" he asked.

His nearness created a disconcerting tingle in her chest. The heat emanated from his body and melted on her skin.

"Give me the hand you write with."

Even if she were in the proper frame of mind to read his palm, 'twould be done under her terms and conditions. She preferred to do readings in her own setting—among her kinsmen or at a makeshift table set alongside a dirt road. Either way, she ought to be in control, not him. He gave her no choice about the setting for his reading, but there were other ways she could maintain control.

He turned his right palm up. Out of sheer habit, she lifted his hand and traced his lifeline, the most important crease on the palm. As she guided her thumb against the firm line, an unexpected flow of heat passed between them.

She dropped his hand. His fingers fell against her leg and

scorched through the fabric of her skirt. She grabbed the table to steady her nerves.

His dark eyebrows rose. "Try again?"

She picked up his hand. Complex and extensive lines shown on his palm, representing a wealthy and successful life. Very likely, considering his elaborate home.

Examining his long fingers first, she then traced the outer edge of his palm. "These tiny lines are your worries."

He lowered his head, examined his palm and frowned. "There are many."

A star shape embedded across his travel line indicated a crisis. Still to come? She hadn't seen a star on anyone's palm in years. She bent her head. Aye. Deeply embedded in his right palm. Danger. Sadness.

The head line began above the life line and spanned horizontally. Both lines were joined, signifying a strong sense of mind ruling over body. But the angle of luck, the space between the life line and head line, was small. The smaller the space, the smaller the luck. She glanced at his unreadable face and swallowed.

His voice, surprisingly heavy, interrupted her thoughts. "I'm pondering a move to Wales."

"Why?"

"To escape the influenza epidemic."

"Then go."

"'Tis not that easy with an entire household." He avoided her gaze and contemplated the elaborate longcase clock against the side wall, its weight-driven pendulum swinging back and forth. "Someone very dear to me is frail, and 'twould be difficult for him to travel long distances. Because of the danger of contracting influenza, we'd need to avoid main roads and larger villages, thus doubling the length of our journey."

"And you want to know what I think?"

Aye." He looked back at her. "Is it safe to remain in England until the spring? Or should we risk the journey?"

The urgency in his voice worried her.

He didn't believe in fortune-telling, yet he seemed to need assurance his household would be safe. Instinct told her to be careful. He was landed gentry; he was dangerous.

Should she reply impersonally?

She grazed her fingers over his calloused hands. Webs of jagged scars traced up his arms, reddened against his dark skin. Most likely, he'd fought in frequent battles. England was forever either signing a peace treaty or at war.

The length of his forefinger reached the bottom nail of the middle finger. This meant confidence and ambition.

His eyebrows furrowed. "Explain as you read."

Her gaze moved to his palms. She ran her finger along his heart line. His heart, intense and deep, swaddled her like a blanket.

"You're not explaining," he said.

"I'll speak when there's something to say." With a light touch, she drew a path down his palms. Several smaller lines showed death. She tried to keep her face calm, her manner subdued. Might this loss be from his past, or his future?

His travel line was more intriguing. A vivid square appeared, a sign telling her 'twas safe for him to travel. The danger reflected in the smaller lines meant any peril might occur in England.

She kept her gaze lowered. If he knew 'twas safe to travel, might he—despite his assurances—insist on taking her and Yolanda with him, perhaps to entertain him with more fortune-telling along the way. Then months would pass before she and Yolanda returned to their mother's gravesite and the caravan.

Valentina flattened two fingers against each eye and forced them closed. Charged silence filled the air.

Once, she'd told Yolanda she judged a person's character and secret desires by the lines she read on their palms.

Daj had taught Valentina the code of honor the Rom lived by—reveal what was probable

and say nothing more. Of course, Valentina embellished her readings to please the customer and make more money. So as not to distress them, she might omit a disturbing truth. That was all.

A wealthy man sat across from her. He was not a customer, though, and she would make no money. But he was a man with power over her.

The memory of his nonchalant words crowded her indecision. *"I'm unaware of your Gypsy ways and I'm sorry about your mother's death."*

Hollow condolences. Did he truly care about her mother or Yolanda's injury?

"Si khohaimo may patshivalo sar o tshatshim," she half-whispered.

"Speak in English," he said.

There are lies more believable than the truth.

Her mother's tender guidance intruded on her instinct to tell less than the truth. *Respect your gifts. Use them wisely.*

Valentina opened her eyes and focused on the magnificent painting of a horse hanging on the opposite wall. "Then all I can tell you from the lines I see on your palm is that I'm uncertain."

"Nothing else?" he prompted.

She fingered his waistcoat draped around her. A bitter taste lingered in her throat as she shook her head. By not explaining everything she'd seen, she was betraying the ancient gift passed down to her for safekeeping by her beloved mother and generations of Romany women before her. But this was the best way she knew to protect her and her sister.

23

"Thank you, Valentina." The warmth of his smile was reflected in his tone. His white teeth contrasted with his wind-burned skin. Minute lines crinkled around his mouth and the small freckle above his lips. As the firelight flickered across his face, she noticed the shadow of a dark stubble outlining his firm chin. "Thank you," he repeated.

She heard the desperation in his voice now, and sudden tears welled. He looked exhausted.

He needed time to regain his stamina, to rest after a difficult battle. There was no need to alarm him, no need for him to trek halfway across the country.

Besides, there hadn't been an outbreak of influenza in months.

* * *

JAMES EXHALED, quiet and slow. His hands trembled, ever so faintly, with his relief. He feared his son would be unable to fight influenza if it struck. However, they need not endure the difficult journey to Wales.

He closed his eyes and whispered a grateful prayer to God, along with a request to forgive him as the beginning of the Bible verse, Isaiah 8:19, nudged at him. "And when they say to you, 'Inquire of the mediums and the necromancers who chirp and mutter,' should not a people inquire of their God."

This was different, he told himself. With painful accuracy, Valentina had foretold Beatrix's death.

Still fresh in his memory, the early spring morning had been clear and cold. Despite his objections, his late wife Alyce had insisted on having her palm read by a young Gypsy woman at a nearby traveling fair. The reading had disturbed her—their daughter was in grave danger. He'd dismissed Alyce's concerns with a skeptical laugh, but then he'd locked gazes with the green-eyed Gypsy. He'd always remember her, those green eyes and those words that had predicted his daughter's death. Could fate have brought her to him a second time?

Valentina had given a quiet nod to confirm her prediction. Then she'd concentrated on her next customer's outstretched palm.

James rubbed his hands against his thighs to stop the familiar despondency wracking through him. Such strange Gypsy words Valentina had uttered, an enigma with her superstitions.

Aye, many people believed Gypsies were unscrupulous. Nonetheless, he'd gathered from the crowd milling around her that this woman held a reputation for being forthright.

The smoldering fireplace cast the room in subdued shadows and veiled silhouettes, while Valentina continued to bite her full bottom lip. Her cheeks were flushed, the color rising with each word she'd spoken. Her nerves showed. 'Twas doubtful she'd read a man's palm in his own home before.

Despite her ragged appearance, her exotic features and spirit fascinated him. Coal-black hair tangled around her face, disheveled and caked with mud. Loose tendrils softened the strained expression on her heart-shaped face.

He stood. "Valentina, would you care to bathe?"

Her small chin lifted. "I can't." Her proud Gypsy nose gave her an air of integrity.

"So 'tis true? Gypsies don't bathe?"

She stood, shoving back her chair and plunking her hands on her hips, accentuating her small waist. With a flourish, she shook off his waistcoat and flung it to the floor. Her stormy gaze flared with outrage. Thick black lashes cast a sooty outline under her wide-set eyes and olive skin.

"You believe my people don't wash?"

He was wise enough not to answer that. "The servants will heat water and bring a tub to your chamber."

"They may heat the water, but I will not bathe. And I've no interest in seeing my chamber. I prefer to sleep outdoors." She took a step, apparently attempting to brush past him, but then her eyes closed and she slumped.

James caught her in his arms as she fell. She might not be as tough as she appeared.

He held her, enjoying the fullness of her warm body, knowing he should let her go.

He drew his lips together and inhaled. Even in her filthy state, her skin smelled subtly of forbidden spices. Attraction heated through him, toward her, a Gypsy woman, a woman who showed no fear. His grip tightened under her arms in an attempt to keep her upright. She'd had an exhausting night, on top of the recent death of her mother.

As abruptly as she'd fainted, her eyes flew open. She tore from his grasp. "Don't think you can touch me whenever you please, because I won't allow it."

He held up his hands, not knowing where to put them. He liked to keep his hands folded behind him. However, she made him feel like he should be clasping them together, begging for a morsel of understanding.

"Presently, you're not in your caravan. Here we are considerably civilized and we bathe often." He softened his tone and dropped his hands to his sides.

Her small tongue moistened her lips. "'Tis the Romany custom to wait until after our mother's burial to bathe."

"Surely, you would agree you need a bath. Let me show you to your chamber."

Stains of scarlet spotted her high cheekbones at his suggestion.

An unexpected burst of wind blew open the door, extinguishing the candle in the iron spiked candle holder and darkening the room. The burning scent of wax shriveled the air.

Valentina frowned, looking as apprehensive about the unexpected draft as he. As the last curl of smoke disappeared, she seemed uncertain. But then her glare, set to challenge, regarded him with rebellion.

"I will go to this chamber, but I will not bathe."

CHAPTER 4

Te bisterdon tumare anava.
May your names be forgotten.
Romany saying

"Your bath will be brought up to you, although you should be made to fetch it yourself." The scathing pronouncement from the housekeeper, Wiborow, came down the stairs and collided with Valentina's scowl.

Valentina focused her attention on the pinpoint flame of the beeswax candle Wiborow carried. The candle shed little light as Valentina climbed the staircase behind the servant. When they reached a landing, Wiborow opened a door leading into a spacious chamber.

"Mr. Colchester requests you sleep here for the night."

Valentina blinked at the richness of the canopied bed in the center of the luxurious room. Lustrous draperies in powder-blue silk were tied with heavy gold rope, exposing matching sheets. Snowy white pillows crowned the head-board underneath a silver-white canopy. A dancing fire flared in the grate of the carved stone fireplace.

Awe veered to anger. Anger swelled to outrage. No doubt, Mr. Colchester wanted to remind her of his affluent lifestyle compared to the squalor of her ragged caravan. The realization kicked at her like a starved dog groveling for a bone. Her chest constricted with hurt, with loss.

"'Requests?'" she repeated with sarcasm.

"Your sister is asleep." Wiborow's stance indicated she'd physically force Valentina to stay in this room. Her thin eyebrows drew together in a scowl. "Someone of your station should be more appreciative of Mr. Colchester's kindness."

Someone of her *lowly* station? Valentina clamped her mouth shut, biting back her retort.

Wiborow marched to an ancient trunk tucked in the corner of the chamber. "You should have everything you need for your bath." She rummaged through the trunk, spilling the scent of rarely used linens into the room, and pulled out a fine cotton nightdress and dressing gown.

Valentina flicked a glance toward the rattling coming from the hallway. A freckle-faced servant with a mass of red hair tumbling down her shoulders carried two lit candles through the open doorway. A half-dozen flustered house-maids followed, hoisting a large tub and buckets of steaming water. They poured the water into the tub, then pulled a screen around it to close off the drafts.

Wiborow glowered at the red-headed servant. "Clare, set the candles on the mantel. Be careful. You are so clumsy of late, you're constantly bruising yourself."

Valentina guessed Clare's age to be close to her own and offered a tentative smile. In response, Clare clasped her freckled hands in prayer, her fingers pointed upward.

Valentina recognized the mistrustful sneers, the furtive squints, the raised brows. She'd seen it on most English faces whenever her caravan settled at the outskirts of a new town. The despised gadje had formed their opinions before the Rom even arrived, although they were eager to have their fortunes told. And she was eager to take their shillings in return.

Disdainfully, Wiborow sniffed. "I'll fetch clean clothes and discard your wretched gown."

"My clothes are also at fault?" Valentina considered her once colorful scarlet gown, now mud-spattered and torn. With the determination of a proud woman, she forbade herself to cry as the servants departed.

The house quieted a few minutes later.

She stepped to the half-open window and peered down. A night breeze lowered the clouds, sending a faint wind across her face that made her tremble. Mr. Colchester would be pleased if she bathed, believing she'd abided by his request.

"*Te merel amaro kuro o lasho,*" she began, intending to curse his horse. Then she closed the window and rested her head in her hands. No use in cursing an innocent horse.

Pivoting, she eyed the clear water of the tub and tucked her hair behind her ears. The scent of the clean water and soap tempted.

Valentina untied her mother's diklo, allowing the bright scarf to unravel and float to the floor. She secured it into a knot under the carved foot post of the bed, then stripped off her filthy clothes and immersed herself in soapy water up to her chin. Surely, the Romany spirits would understand that she had to bathe at some point.

Warm water lapped her skin, and the fragrance of pine and mint wafted from the rosemary soap. She erased the torment of the night by scrubbing her hair until her scalp was sore, then settled back into the soapy water. Her over-wrought nerves calmed. She closed her eyes and dozed.

Two bold knocks awakened her. A pucker-faced Wiborow tromped into the chamber carrying a bundle of clean clothes and crisp linens. Clare accompanied her, toting a tray, and thin odors of cooked cabbage and carrots streamed through the chamber.

Valentina glimpsed Mr. Colchester leaning in the door-way. He still wore his white muslin shirt, black pants, and suspenders. He folded his solid arms across his chest, a bemused expression on his face, before averting his gaze from hers.

Valentina's heart thudded in degradation as she covered herself with her arms, thankful for the screen that shielded most of her. "Get out of my chamber." In furious rebellion, she tipped up her chin and glared.

"I believe the chamber is mine," he countered.

She took a deep breath and dunked beneath the bath water. When she emerged, gasping for breath, he and his servants were gone, and the chamber door had been closed.

* * *

THIRTY MINUTES LATER, James knocked on Valentina's door.

He waited.

"Surely you can't be speechless," he said after a full minute of silence. "Are you finished with your bath?"

"Aye."

"May I come in?"

"Aye."

He opened the door and stepped inside. Fully dressed in the clean clothes set out for her, Valentina sat on the edge of the bed.

"I didn't wash to please you," she said.

"Somehow this edifying bit of information doesn't surprise me."

Was she aware of how provocative she looked, the seductive allure of her plain gown? Her emerald eyes slanted at the corners and gave the appearance of a tigress's eyes—points of yellow flickering in the center of a green pool.

He moved forward, his footsteps muted by the thick royal-blue carpet. All that separated them was three paces and his sharp breathing.

Standing, she eased back toward the wall, but she slipped, her bare feet apparently still wet from the bath. He caught her, a pleasant pastime he seemed to excel in lately.

She struggled upright. "Don't touch me."

"Once again, I'm attempting to save you from dropping to the floor." Despite his authoritative tone, he raised his hands and retreated. Somehow, she managed to make him feel like a criminal in his own home.

"Yolanda is sleeping?" Those warning sparks again in those huge emerald eyes.

"Aye. A servant checked on her a while ago."

He couldn't help focusing on Valentina's lips, moist and inviting in the shimmering candlelight. Her glowing skin and lyrical voice reminded him more of a wayward angel than an angry Gypsy.

She backed up, twisted and frowned at the wall behind her, and then turned back around to face him. "What time are we leaving come the morrow?"

There it was, that innocent question reeking of a demand.

"We've discussed this, remember? As soon as the physician examines your sister's arm."

He could've given a number of clearer responses, although he couldn't think of what they would be, so he added, "A fortnight ago, there were reports of highwaymen along the roads. The danger is too great for women traveling alone, which is why I'll ride back to your camp with you."

For a moment, he thought she might cry. Why? He was only trying to help.

He extended one hand. "I'm truly sorry about your mother's death."

Quiet vulnerability wrapped around her small form, along with a tinge of sadness. "Your sympathies ring hollow. If Yolanda and I don't return to our tribe come the morrow, the Rom spirits will bring disaster."

"Tell your impatient spirits you can't risk your or your sister's life for them, and you'll return to your caravan soon."

"You're arrogant to imagine you have the right to plan my life."

"I'm not planning your life. I'm simply planning your safe return to camp." He should grab her by her shapely shoulders and shake away the droplets of water still clinging to her neck from her bath. But the corners of her lovely mouth had turned down, and he couldn't lift his hands.

He regarded her empty tray of food neatly set by the door. "If your sister requires a lengthier recuperation, you're both welcome to stay in my home for as long as you'd like."

Somehow, the idea of her living in his house lifted his mood. He had the distinct feeling she thought just the opposite.

She blasted him with a mutinous expression. "Whether we stay a week or a day, you won't be bedding me."

For a split second, his breath was suspended. Smiling stiffly, he scratched the coarse stubble of his whiskered chin. "I'm a Christian man who follows the Lord's teachings, which doesn't include bedding a woman I've known for less than one day." He compressed his lips and studied her. Her slim body had filled out since he'd last seen her years before. He hadn't expected the breathtaking woman who stood before him, so close that the warmth of her body touched his skin.

Nay. Involvement with a woman wasn't his forte. His failed marriage was proof of that.

He gave himself a firm mental shake and pushed desire far from his thoughts. Valentina had come to him for help because of her injured sister. In a moment of impulse, he'd asked her for a palm reading.

His conscience whispered a reminder. He had no reason to encourage her and her sister to remain any longer than was necessary for Yolanda's recovery.

But his conscience always had been a nuisance.

Still, he enjoyed Valentina's jaunty rejoinders, and the softness that came over her fiery expression when she spoke of her mother and sister.

Averting his gaze from her face, he stared into the fading embers of the fire. As he turned back to her, an unexpected spark cast her features in a bright cinnamon hue. Her demeanor had changed, neither demanding nor challenging.

"We won't be needing anyone to ride with us to our caravan, and we're certainly not afraid of highwaymen."

He inhaled the scent of black pepper and exotic spices, and his leather boots propelled him forward, one step, two. Her lips reminded him of the full coral lips he'd once admired in a fine painting, too beautiful to be real.

"I've always wondered—where do your people wander?" he asked.

"Wherever there is food and relative safety from the English."

Despite himself, he grinned. She spoke with all the haughtiness of a newly crowned monarch.

"Valentina, the English are not the ogres you believe."

"If you lived in my caravan, you would think otherwise."

Her fringe of black eyelashes fluttered like an agitated bird. Truly she was an exotic, enchanting, exquisite creature.

He moved another step closer. The idea of kissing her had nothing to do with reason.

Women. Dependency. Relying on someone else for happiness.

Nay. Never.

This could be different. He'd never felt so attracted to a woman.

He closed the distance between them and tenderly pushed a wayward tendril from her cheek. "Valentina, I—"

"I told you not to touch me." She jerked away from his hand and drew a lengthy, suffocated breath. "Now get out."

She was right.

"I apologize. I overstepped my boundary."

In his own house.

She scoffed.

"What I meant was …"

Perhaps he could speak as a reasonable man if he were speaking to a reasonable woman.

She lifted her face toward the ceiling as if she'd already dismissed him. Him, the man who was attempting to care for her and her sister so they wouldn't starve.

Moonlight streamed through the window, outlining Valentina's perfect form, her crossed arms, her high chin.

Reining in his annoyance, he strode out of the chamber and slammed the door.

* * *

THE FIRE in the grate had burned low and gave little heat. Chilled to her toes, Valentina wrapped her nightdress closer around her. She lit two candles, placed them on either side of

35

the mantel, and then settled into bed. With a lengthy sigh, she rolled to her side.

She wouldn't allow any man to get too close. She'd learned *that* hard lesson years before.

Troka, an ungainly man with yellowing teeth and perverted urges, had stunted her yearnings before her breasts had ever bloomed. Even now, she remembered the stench of his sticky bear-claw hands closing over her mouth. His groping fingers had probed her young body, her flat chest and slim hips. His threats of hurting her family if she didn't submit had killed the last of her screams.

Much later, Luca had found her, disoriented and rambling, wallowing in the sludge of tears and dishonor. He'd spoken in a deceptively calm tone, brought her back to the caravan and had kept her secret all these years. They had forged a silent agreement. When her explanations to her family of where she'd been had sounded guilty, Luca had merely nodded. A good friend, her protector, adding credibility to her feeble story.

Every man, barring Luca, was the same. They wanted things done their way, on their terms.

And she'd vowed, as a rock had settled where her heart had once been, that what she'd endured one muddy night years before would never happen again.

CHAPTER 5

I chatski tsinuda de tehara, vai de haino, khal tut.
The true nettle stings from the beginning.
Old Romany saying

The following morning, Valentina pulled herself awake from a restless sleep.

She changed into a soft olive-green percale gown from the trunk and tied her mother's yellow diklo around her throat. She cleaned her teeth, combed her fingers through her clean hair and scurried into the long hall and down the wide staircase.

Following her nose and ears, she found her way to the smoky, bustling kitchen.

Without meeting Valentina's gaze, Clare handed her a slice of warm buttered bread topped with spicy apple preserves.

Valentina set the bread on the table. "Has anyone seen my sister? Is she awake"

"She's being looked after." Affected by a slight lisp, Clare whistled over the words.

Valentina followed Clare through the pantry and outside into the herb garden. "'Tis morning and Yolanda and I are supposed to leave."

Wiborow appeared at the doorway and screwed her lips into a knowing smile. "You'll see your sister in a short while, at the midday meal. You should know that the only reason he's tolerating you Gypsies is because of Beatrix."

"Who's Beatrix?"

No reply from either servant as they headed back into the kitchen, leaving Valentina in the herb garden.

Expelling an exasperated breath, Valentina grabbed a handful of parsley. A whiff of freshly tilled dirt met with her nose. Bright autumn days colored in golden leaves normally gave her strength. Not today. Today her throat ached with loss, with loneliness for her sister's absence, for their mother's death.

She chewed on the parsley stem and eyed the wide variety of herbs— tarragon and wild mustard, stinging nettle and foxglove—used to enhance all manner of food, as well as remedies for ailments. Deciding to avoid the kitchen, she walked around the house and reentered through the marbled front foyer.

A housemaid, cold malice imprinted on her ruddy face, pushed up the sleeves of her gown as Valentina walked past. "Gypsies are dark because they never wash," she declared to no one in particular.

Already, the English's ignorance was showing, and Valentina hadn't walked five steps.

She raised her head, and her gaze collided with Mr. Colchester's. He wore a coal-black waistcoat over a white linen shirt, the sleeves emphasizing his solid arms. A faint light shone in the grey depths of his eyes. "Good morning, Valentina. The midday meal will be served soon."

"Aye, so I've been told." He either hadn't heard his maid's comment, or he'd chosen to ignore it. "By the way, your herbs are sorely uncared for."

"Are you interested in tending to my herbs?"

His quiet inquiry checked her in midstep. "Perhaps in a thousand years."

He scanned her face and her gown, taking his time. "I prefer the Gypsy clothes you wore yesterday," he said with a relaxed smile. "They suited you better."

She knew his teasing voice was meant to charm. And it did. She stiffened her resistance.

"This gown is from your house," she answered, "not mine."

"I didn't realize you had a house."

"A home doesn't need to stay in one place. It should move with you."

He peered around at the chairs covered in cream silk brocade, the expensive paintings in elaborate gold frames, the terraced courtyard beyond the bow windows. "I cannot imagine taking all my belongings wherever I go."

"Because you have everything a man could ever want in a lifetime."

His gaze held hers. "Not everything."

Her mind groped madly for another subject. She took a deep breath, but only inhaled his scent of leather and horses and worn saddles. "I assume you intend to keep your promise, Mr. Colchester."

"Which promise?"

Her gaze wandered to the prominent freckle above his lip. Spurred by impatience for noticing, she shrugged in mock explanation. "To allow my sister and me to leave, assuming the physician agrees."

"You've always been 'allowed' to leave. Somehow, I don't believe anyone could keep you anywhere for long without your consent, anyway. And your sister should be downstairs shortly. Perhaps we should wait for her in here."

He escorted her into the dining room, where servants were carrying in food. He spoke to some of them, who paused in their duties to answer, and he listened attentively while they spoke. Yet Valentina was still the recipient of suspicious looks, and the servants' malice increased her anxiety about seeing her sister again and then finally leaving.

"I haven't seen Yolanda since last evening," she said when Mr. Colchester turned back to her. We've never been apart this long." She scanned the hallway, wondering how many more minutes it would be before she saw her sister again.

She glanced back at Mr. Colchester, trying to be upset at him, although when she searched her thoughts, there was nothing to be upset at him for. He wasn't guilty of anything except genuine kindness.

He escorted her to a chair that was to the right of the head of the table. "One of the reasons I wanted you both to dine with me is to silence any wagging tongues, to dispel any tales that you're a witch disguised as a Gypsy."

She studied the mahogany table, sunken with food and drink, and chewed her bottom lip. "Thank you. You've been most generous. Although you're still a gadje."

"Somehow, I'm guessing you're not complimenting me."

"You're a stranger to the Romany because you are an English—"

"Valentina, I didn't recognize you! You're wearing such a rich-looking gown!" Yolanda's melodious voice sang from the hallway.

Valentina whirled. There Yolanda stood in the doorway, precious and pale, her ebony hair falling in a cluster of waves around her face. Her injured arm was wrapped in a sling.

"You look beautiful." Valentina raced to Yolanda and embraced her. "Are you all right?"

"Aye, except my arm hurts. A physician was supposed to be called in, although 'twas determined to summon a bone setter instead. My forearm was set without too much pain, although it still throbs."

Valentina raised her brows. "And your cough?"

"Definitely better."

"Now all you require is time and rest and food in order to heal," Mr. Colchester said.

"I slept in a wonderful bedchamber last evening." Yolanda gestured to a basket of fresh, yeasty rolls on the sideboard. "The food is in such abundance here, and I bathed. The water was actually warm and smelled of lavender. Do you think the spirits will be furious about my bath?"

"I hope not," Valentina murmured.

"Mr. Colchester is so generous."

Sighing, Valentina quickly steered Yolanda away from Mr. Colchester's wide smile and to a corner of the splendorous blue and gold dining room, grateful for the noisy clatter of the silverware as the maids began serving. "However," she whispered, "he has a misguided fear for our safety."

"I've spent my first night in luxury. And the bone setter said I wasn't strong enough to travel for a few days because of the fracture."

Worry filled Valentina at her sister's words. The scent of cooked game and salted vegetables, which had been enticing, now overwhelmed her. She was jostled from behind as a servant stepped past her, carrying a platter of baked ham.

"There are robbers among us who'll steal the clothes off yer back," he muttered.

Valentina scowled at the thick-jowled servant, his ruddy cheeks, the unflinching distrust in his watery blue eyes.

41

Yolanda squeezed Valentina's hand before she could speak. "Don't let ill-informed people upset you."

Before the servant could scurry away, Mr. Colchester joined them. His sharp glare, packed with a frown, froze the servant in place. "Valentina and Yolanda, I apologize for his ignorance," he said clearly.

His concern touched Valentina. However, these people lived and worked in his home. Shouldn't they know better?

"Englishmen can never understand a Rom's suffering," she replied.

"I am from Wales."

"Still, you wouldn't understand." She blinked back unexpected tears. To cry in front of a gadje shamed her.

"Help me understand." His words, tender as a breeze in the stifling dining room, held an empathy she hadn't expected.

For an answer, she took her sister's uninjured arm and returned to the table.

Once Mr. Colchester had seated them, Valentina on his right and Yolanda on his left, he sat and lifted his wineglass. "I'm pleased you're reunited with your sister. Even though I'm a gadje—which surely means I'm honest and agreeable."

Valentina ignored his attempt to lighten her mood, preferring to examine the gleaming silver spoon beside her plate.

"Perhaps an apology is in order for your attack on my good character?" he added.

She glimpsed his chiding smile, although she felt like she was drowning in shame. Hadn't he realized she'd been crying?

She pushed back her chair and stood. "And perhaps dining with you wasn't such a good idea."

He stood as well. "Please stay. You haven't tried the venison, nor the potatoes." He placed one hand lightly on her shoulders.

Before she was able to pull away, a little boy entered the dining room and marched determinedly to Mr. Colchester. He tugged on the man's waistcoat with one hand and held a squirming flat-nosed puppy with the other. Although the boy didn't speak, he made his intentions known. He pointed toward a window, back to himself, then out the window again. He had the innocent face of a cherub and an oddly familiar grin. Valentina had the urge to scoop him up in her arms.

Mr. Colchester released her and crouched to eye level with the boy. "Jeremy, 'tis too cold for you to play outdoors."

The boy's face puckered, and he aimed his gaze insistently toward the doorway and the foyer beyond.

Mr. Colchester tenderly touched the boy's cheeks, then tousled his hair. "Perhaps for a short while you can play outside. Elspeth will fetch your cloak and boots." He signaled to a woman who stood in the doorway, and lowered his tone as he directed, "Be certain Jeremy stays near the older boys and supervise him at all times."

The boy clapped his hands and set the puppy on the floor. The puppy bounded away, Jeremy on its heels.

"Who is that little boy?" Valentina asked. "One of the tenant farmer's children?"

Mr. Colchester granted her a broad smile. "Jeremy is my son."

She grabbed the back of her chair in astonishment.

Of course. The boy was a miniature version of his father —the same silvery eyes, the same smile, the same slim build. Except the boy's grey eyes were specked with blue, as blue as a robin's egg. And his skin was pallid, the dark lines hinting at a recent illness.

"I didn't realize you were married," she said, surprised she could speak.

"My late wife, Alyce, died several months ago."

Valentina heard his voice as if he were speaking through a thick fog.

"She contracted influenza," he was saying. "The finest doctors couldn't save her."

His wife had died, and her death explained the tiny lines creasing his palms, indicating sadness. Memory of the previous night's fortune-telling left a bitter taste in Valentina's throat. "How old is your son?"

"Six. He had a twin sister. My daughter Beatrix."

Had.

"*You should know that the only reason he's tolerating you Gypsies is because of Beatrix,*" Wiborow had said.

Valentina's breath caught. "Is Beatrix here?" She scanned the room, absurdly expecting to spot a little girl about Jeremy's age.

"She died."

If Valentina hadn't been watching Mr. Colchester so closely, she would have missed the wave of grief sweeping over his face.

She swallowed. Her vision blurred. "How?"

"She went wandering." Briefly, he closed his eyes. "Jesus said, 'Let the little children come to me and do not hinder them, for to such belongs the kingdom of heaven.'" He opened his eyes and met her questioning stare.

"And your son is—"

"Deaf."

No wonder the boy hadn't spoken.

"He cannot hear your laughter," she said softly, half to herself. "Nor a bird chirping, nor his puppy barking."

Mr. Colchester's gaze flashed a warning. *No pity.*

No one could fault him for his protectiveness. He was a

widower, trying to do his best to raise a child on his own. And he was proving to be a far more complex man than she'd originally assumed.

She surveyed the dining table, laden with more food than her tribe could eat in a week. Chunky loaves of brown bread, sharp and pungent wedges of cheese, ripe apples and pears. An overabundance of plenty while her mother had starved herself to death to preserve their family and tribe's meager amount of food.

Her gaze skated back to Mr. Colchester. His nods to the maids were courteous, his laughter to an earlier joke genuine. Yet he'd lost his daughter. And his wife.

A man who feared influenza. A man who loved his son.

Hardships on his palm. She'd dismissed them, although the lines had demanded attention. That she could do that fortune-telling again …

"Our king balances his peace treaties with a war now and then." From the kitchen, Geoffrey's gravelly proclamation rose above the servants' voices.

"I wondered if my knees were still attached to my legs after crouching in the dirt all those miserable soaking nights," Roland's voice added.

"The king has brought prosperity to England and—" Geoffrey gasped. The sound of a shattering wine glass sounded from the kitchen.

"Geoffrey's choking on a slice of pear!" a servant shouted.

James jumped to his feet and reached Geoffrey first. He delivered several back blows between Geoffrey's shoulder blades.

Both Valentina and Yolanda shot up. Despite Mr. Colchester's efforts, Geoffrey was unconscious.

"I'll get some herbs from the garden," Valentina said.

From the kitchen, Mr. Colchester met her gaze. "Go."

Yolanda grasped Valentina's gown and slowed their flight as they raced through the kitchen and into the herb garden.

"There are stinging nettle plants growing here." Valentina bent among the spindly plants and dug through tarragon and wild mustard.

Wiborow marched into the garden and elbowed Yolanda out of the way. Her tiny eyes narrowed, her withered face appraised. "Do you enjoy gardening?"

Valentina met Wiborow's gaze. "Aye. I'm a Rom."

"And my sister is a natural healer," Yolanda added.

Valentina yanked the spiky nettles from the ground, pricking her finger on the needles. She raced back to the house and steeped the stinging needles in tepid water, creating a sour brew. Steadying herself, she carried her potion into the kitchen. Yolanda and Wiborow followed.

Valentina settled beside Geoffrey and Mr. Colchester. Geoffrey was groggy but breathing normally. Carefully, she placed the potion to his dry lips.

Roland hovered over her. "If you harm Geoffrey with that witch's potion, you Gypsy—"

Valentina jumped at his shouting, spilling the brew over her fingers.

Mr. Colchester silenced Roland with a slight raise of his hand, but a shadow of apprehension creased his brows. Beads of sweat formed above his tightened lips.

"Don't be alarmed," she said to reassure him. "This brew will calm Geoffrey."

He nodded his assent for her to continue.

Geoffrey's weathered skin had taken on an ash-colored hue. She allowed him seconds between each sip to catch his breath, closing her eyes and chanting in Romany. "*May angle sar te merel kadi yag.* Before this fire burns out," she translated, "please spare this man from any pain today."

"I like the English words better." With a slight smile,

Geoffrey opened his eyes, crinkling the creases above his white brows. "Now allow me to walk out of this room upright as a man."

"I'll assist him." Deftly, Mr. Colchester brought Geoffrey to his feet, and Roland helped him out of the room.

"What happened?" one of the assembled servants whispered to another.

"The deer meat is rancid," the other servant answered.

"The meat is perfectly fine, you dolt," said the third. "Geoffrey's an old man and his body is weak. But if you were paying attention, you'd know he choked on a pear."

Mr. Colchester turned, seeming to concentrate on every speculative word. When his gaze reached Valentina, his expression was grateful. "Thank you, my Gypsy *cariad,* for helping me tend to my dearest friend."

"I'm happy to do anything I can. Geoffrey is a gracious and considerate man."

"Aye."

The room quieted.

Mr. Colchester turned to the gathered. "Let us pray for my steward's full return to good health. With God's grace, he'll recover admirably."

He spoke to them all, although his admiring gaze remained on Valentina. His silver eyes, mesmeric and burning, drew her to him.

CHAPTER 6

Saka perkero charo dikhel.
Everybody sees only his dish.
Old Romany saying

*T*wo hours had passed since the midday meal.

Everywhere she went, Valentina heard the servants in the house murmur that she was a sorceress. After all, she'd helped Geoffrey using herbs and Gypsy chants.

And didn't they understand? If she were a sorceress, she and Yolanda wouldn't have been forced to steal and beg all those years to stay alive.

When she stepped into the kitchen, hoping for a cup of tea, overweight cooks peered up from their kitchen tasks and smiled, all of them red-faced from the heat of the ovens. A friendly nod from Clare proved both welcoming and troubling. Formerly snobbish servants started rushing into the kitchen, vying with each other for her attention as they went into excruciating details about their dizziness and aching bones, asking for some remedy, some relief. The same servants who'd avoided her since she'd arrived.

For the next half hour, she patiently explained how to brew medicinal teas using dandelion root, flaxseed, water and honey for dizziness and digestion. For pain relief, she recommended a mixture of lemon balm, coriander, nutmeg, and vodka.

She kept up her descriptions of the simple ingredients required for the cures until all the servants' questions had been answered. Speaking with them she felt emboldened, no longer angry at them for being English, and subsequently, inexplicably guilty for thinking otherwise.

They went back to their tasks and only Clare remained. "Thank you for helping us," she blurted.

Valentina eyed the young girl's curly carrot-red hair and fair complexion. Clare looked so unlike the robust, olive-skinned Romany women Valentina had grown up with. Despite being a servant, Clare reminded Valentina of a pampered flower.

So why *was* she helping the English? Valentina asked herself. She certainly shouldn't trust them because she'd only known their cruelty, one of the causes of her tribe's deprivation.

She shook her head, chiding herself for her prejudice. If she expected to drive a change in their views toward the Rom, shouldn't she be the first to steer the change in the right direction, becoming more tolerant of their culture? Didn't they have their own explanations for their viewpoints? Weren't there other options besides hatred toward other people because of differing beliefs?

But if the English got too close, they might force her to care about them, their lives, their heartaches, their illnesses, a small voice pointed out.

And so what? Was that so wrong, to take down these boundaries?

With Clare beside her, she walked to the wide entry doors leading to the front lawn. As she'd spoken with the servants, her gaze had milled the hallway, searching for a glimpse of Mr. Colchester's reassuring smile.

Valentina fastened a borrowed wool pelisse over her gown, tucked her yellow diklo beneath the collar, and secured a bonnet over her unruly hair.

Seeing Wiborow bearing down toward them, Clare jumped and started away. Valentina stopped her with a quick question. "Clare, do you know where Mr. Colchester is?"

"He looked in on Geoffrey earlier and is most likely at church now. He attends service daily."

Stepping outside, Valentina peered at a sizable gold cross dwarfing the steeple of a distant parish church. The front lawn greeted her with the scent of oak trees and acorns and a crisp midafternoon sun. Fragrances of tart olive soap and burning wax filled the air. She embraced the day and took a heartening breath.

Glancing to a nearby outbuilding, she saw Yolanda engaged in watching a woman weave sheep's wool at a loom. Standing near her was a heavy-set blond man who, judging by his attire and well-muscled arms, was a blacksmith.

A smile touched Valentina's lips. As a Romany should, Yolanda had fit easily into her new setting.

Jeremy's giggles drew her attention. He was chasing his golden-brown puppy around the grass in a carefree circle. The puppy concentrated on chasing its short tail, a comical twitch of intent on its squared-off jaw. Jeremy stopped and bent his head between his knees, then collapsed on the ground. His little face flushed with exhaustion, his slim body heaved with the exertion of catching his breath.

Valentina hesitated. They met each other's stares, hers

watchful, his gleeful. He extended her a hearty wave. The sweet gesture warmed her insides, and she grinned and waved back before walking over to her sister.

"How is your arm?" she asked when she reached Yolanda.

The blacksmith nodded to them both and walked away.

"Better," Yolanda said, and then frowned. "Valentina, I'm sorry I'm delaying our departure. Daj is waiting to be buried."

"I'm certain Luca is taking care of everything. He'll bury Daj with the dignity she deserved."

"But Luca was injured—"

"Knowing Luca, he wasn't hurt for long. Besides, you need time to relax and eat proper food. Soon you'll be recovered from your cough and your arm will be strong again."

"I like it here and Mr. Colchester said we could stay as long as we want." Yolanda clasped her hands loosely and gazed at the ground. "I miss Daj, I mourn her, but she'd want us to stay, wouldn't she?"

"Aye. Knowing our caring mother, she certainly would. And far better you convalesce here, where you can heal properly and be well-fed."

Yolanda swallowed a relieved ripple of giggling. "I'm so happy you agree."

With a buoyancy she hadn't felt in weeks, Valentina hugged her sister and then set off to explore the estate. As she wended through gardens and lawns and beyond, to where acres of harvested fields stretched as far as she could see, tenant farmers treated her to admiring stares. Others peeked from behind the safety of doors open just a crack. A few men with leathery faces greeted her by name and dipped their hats respectfully. Besieged by her confused emotions, she murmured inquiries about their health.

For one of the men's hand inflammation, she recommended a poultice of bark powder and warm water, advising him to wrap his hand in a linen bandage for a couple of days. To aid in helping another man's wife to sleep better, she suggested lemon balm water mixed with a teaspoon of honey.

Leaving the farmland behind, she pulled her pelisse more tightly around her shoulders and made her way to the edge of the woods. Stone walls bordered a path that grew narrower with every step. Her sturdy leather boots pinched her feet as she navigated up a sloping pasture. Normally, she ran barefoot, but Mr. Colchester had had the boots delivered to her chamber that morning.

However, he wasn't here. She tugged off the offending boots and threw them into a sparse field. She'd find them later and sell them. They'd fetch a good price in the marketplace.

Cool, black soil wedged between her toes. She found another meager footpath concealed by slippery leaves and avoided a shy cow with moist brown eyes in a bordering pasture.

All this land. If only she had no boundaries and could truly go wherever she pleased. Oftentimes, a Romany's life was restricted to camping on the outskirts of villages.

"Enjoying the view?" Mr. Colchester's soft inquiry came from behind her. She hadn't heard him approach, although when she spun to face him, he was so close she felt the heat emanating from his skin.

She stared at his white shirt showing beneath his black waistcoat and cloak. Always the well-dressed, urbane and thoroughly handsome gentleman.

"Must you constantly emerge when I least expect?" she chided.

"I'm not one of your spirits, appearing and reappearing on a convenient whim."

She glanced at the weather-beaten rocks lining the top of

the hillside. The wind picked up, and the branches of the pine trees swayed restlessly. With a slight shiver, she pressed her elbows to her sides.

Amusement shone in his gaze, then speculation. "Surely a brave woman like you can't be afraid of heights?"

"I'm not afraid of anything."

"Not even me?"

She shook an invisible piece of soil from her pelisse. "Especially not you."

"In any event, you're safe and under my protection." He watched her. Shielding. Safeguarding. Warding off imagined and unimagined harm. Harboring a warmth for her under a veiled expression she recognized as desire.

Instinctively, the armor around her heart rose. "Has church let out already? I assumed English vicars droned on for hours."

"I prayed quickly and added an extra 'Glory to God' for you. Would you like to join me at service come the morrow? I'll introduce you to Richard, the vicar."

"Many Romany tribes attend church. Not mine. We chant to the spirits."

"Does it help? All that chanting?"

The painful slice in her chest reminded her that the spirits hadn't helped her mother to survive. "Sometimes, when I was a child, chanting gave me peace," she said softly.

"You might find such power in prayer you'll want to accompany me one day."

She sidestepped him. "How did you find where I was?"

He glanced over his shoulder. "You left a pair of boots in the last field."

"I don't need boots." She wiggled her toes in the crisp grass and returned his smile. "And I don't want them."

His chuckle was so boyishly appealing, she could hardly

believe he was the same man who ran this vast estate with such obvious, if relaxed, authority.

"I understand a number of servants and villagers spoke to you about cures for their illnesses," he said.

"I explained several simple herbal cures. However, my knowledge is limited, even as a drabardi, so please don't ask me too many questions."

"I know a drabardi is a highly respected healer in your culture. And although I'm sorry about your sister's injury, I'm assuming you'll be staying on until she recuperates?"

She agreed, but added, "I won't be a pigeon held captive in your fancy cage forever."

"On the contrary, you're an exotic bird and a most welcome guest who can come and go as she pleases."

She retreated and leaned back against the trunk of a blackthorn tree. 'Twas too fine a day to quarrel. Scanning the distant view, she spotted a river meandering through the outlying forest, rising and spilling into the tended fields. A sprinkle of sheep and cattle dotted the pastures.

"Your estate resembles a make-believe kingdom. 'Tis a mystical *paramitsha*." Assessing his casual stance, she wondered at his skill in appearing always relaxed, no matter the surroundings. A realization struck her with a tinge of regret. He was everything she'd always dreamed a man should be.

"Wales is my favorite home," he said. "Rough, untamed— so different from England."

Like you. He didn't voice it, although the words hung silently in the air around them.

"As you can see," he went on, "my home here was built on a cliff. 'Twas where Beatrix died." He drew a sharp breath and turned away, touching the corners of his eyes. "The memories of Beatrix are so poignant." He faced her again. "Just promise you'll never venture near the edge."

"I promise." A high cloud obscured the sun, and a breeze ruffled the hem of her gown. The softness in his voice contrasted with the hard lines of his face, and his quiet words made her pulse stall, thus slowing her speech. She gravitated closer to him. Sympathy poured from her spirit, drawn by his sorrow and the sweet little girl who had captured his love.

"Our home quieted without both children." His infinite silver eyes filled with grief. And a silent flicker of vulnerability that touched her heart.

He'd exhibited a tenderness toward Jeremy that few men showed toward their children. Her stomach knotted and she inhaled, unable to fill her lungs completely with pure air. She'd never marry, never bear children, because no decent man would want her. She was considered *marime* to the Rom, soiled because of the rape. A wave of shame swelled through her.

The branches of the blackthorn tree rustled, and two blackbirds sang from their elevated perch.

She whipped around and stepped blindly away from him.

His hand caught her arm. "You'll be staying for a while longer, then?"

"Aye."

"Good." He pulled her a fraction nearer, until her nose almost touched his chest. He lifted her chin and studied her face for several long seconds. "Your heart is beating like a startled bird. I'm simply a man who wants to protect you."

She focused on a yellow leaf wafting to the ground before glancing uncertainly at him. "Then may I ask you a question?"

"Of course."

"Beatrix died at a young age?"

"Aye." He stared at a point somewhere beyond her. "'Twas an accident that should never have happened."

"I'm so sorry."

His expression filled with overwhelming grief. "My late wife had left Beatrix alone. We were forewarned our daughter might be in grave danger, but we disregarded it. Beatrix never recovered from the fall, and our home became empty without both children running about."

"Your wife … The death must have been agonizing for her to accept."

"Perhaps." A muscle worked in his jaw. "We had Jeremy, of course."

"Your son is adorable."

"He's very special. He requires a considerable amount of care because of his deafness."

Unexpected tears flooded her eyes. "My tribe adores children, as do all Romany. My kinsmen are kindhearted."

He touched her cheek, catching a teardrop with his forefinger. "Do Gypsies marry before having children?"

She jerked back and plunked her hands on her hips. One minute he was wiping her tears, the next he was asking if the Rom bedded each other before marriage! "My culture isn't immoral. All Romany are expected to marry."

His quiet reply stopped her from continuing. "Lately, all my thoughts are about you and your fascinating culture. I meant no disrespect. Please, am I forgiven, Valentina?"

"Aye." She accepted his guarded apology and couldn't help a grin. "Have you ever eaten roasted hedgehog, by the way?"

"Not unless the animal disguised itself as a cooked peacock."

"'Tis a favorite dish at our Romany weddings."

"Perhaps you can prepare one for me." His whole manner changed to brushed velvet, languid and smooth.

"I'm not known for my cooking skills, only my abilities with herbs."

Several seconds ticked by.

"How old *are* Gypsy women when they marry?" he asked at last.

She flicked an unmanageable wave from her forehead. "Many are betrothed at fourteen."

"And you are older than this?"

"I am one and twenty."

His expression sharpened on her. "Are there many suitors waiting for you at your caravan, Valentina?"

She looked up at the branches above her before gesturing to the two blackbirds preparing to take flight. "I've had little time for courtship. We begged for food, for clothes, whatever we needed." She cleared her throat and grimaced. "And we steal."

He grabbed her trembling hands. "Your secret is safe with me. I'll always protect you."

She met his gaze. "I need no protection from a gadje."

"A gadje who is intrigued by your traditions. Please continue."

She drew a quiet breath and pulled from his grasp. "Romany marry only Romany, or our entire line is polluted."

A disquieting image of a baby flickered through her mind. A baby she'd never seen, with light olive skin and gleaming grey eyes. A baby girl, she knew instinctively. She held still in expectation of a closer look, but the baby vanished from her thoughts.

"There are people in my household who would disagree and think quite the contrary," he said, "believing my blood would add merit to the Gypsy line."

"Your *proper* blood? To be fair, I've seen worse-looking proper gentlemen than you." She shuddered. "Far worse."

He threw back his head and laughed. "And I've seen far worse looking English and Welsh women. We now share a common bond, as do you and your indigent Gypsy suitors."

"Fancy words, Mr. Colchester."

They shared a smile.

He turned her face up, forcing her to focus on his lips, so close that their breaths merged. "Valentina, around you I'm a driven man, a bee drawn to a perfect flower. You can add me to your list of suitors."

"Mr. Colchester, surely you're—"

"Please call me James."

"Or shall I call you a rogue, because you believe you can seduce me with shallow verses?"

"You should insert one of your Gypsy swear words between breaths. 'Twill add credibility to your insults."

His confident gaze held her spellbound, and she could feel the warmth tinting her cheeks.

Forcing herself to look down, she smoothed her gown. "You believe you rule everything and everyone around you."

"On the contrary, I try to live by the wise words in Luke 6:31: 'Treat others the same you want them to treat you.'" Again, he lifted his hand and touched her cheek. His rough, firm hand. "I didn't mean to upset you. Talking about my daughter, my son, led me to thinking about children and family."

She attempted a smile. "Please don't apologize."

His gaze, ever perceptive, probed hers. His hand burned like molten steel against her skin, and she was utterly at a loss to speak, to move, to think, because she was melting.

He bent his head and his lips lightly grazed hers. His eyes turned a slate-grey as he watched her, reminding her of a shadowy dusk and secret, shared evenings. Silver needles and silken threads kept her body from moving.

"We should leave before it gets any later." With a sigh, he took a step back and extended his hand. "Let's walk back together. I'll show you some of the outlying farms."

She accepted his hand, and he laced his fingers through hers. Together, they began their descent down the hill. As he guided her in the direction of the main house, he explained the workings of the land, which was divided into forests, pastures, and cultivated fields. After a few minutes, he gathered her hand and placed it in the crook of his arm.

They strolled beside the river, and she studied him from the corner of her eye. Impressively fine-looking and commanding, he owned more acreage than she thought any man, any one person, could ever own. Seeing how comfortably he strode through his idyllic setting reminded her she didn't belong here. Whom did she think she could fool?

He paused to discuss some matter with a tenant farmer, and as he laughed she went over her earlier decision. She and Yolanda would stay. Yolanda needed to build herself up after the past few months, when she had gotten so sick and the entire tribe had verged on starvation. Moreover, as the day waned, she knew Luca and the elders were attending to her mother's burial.

Strengthened by her decision, she smiled at Mr. Colchester as he returned to her side. He seemed taken aback, then quickly returned the smile. Their excursion led them to the stone church. As Valentina studied the ivy-covered stonework, she wondered what her life would be like with a man like him. The deflating breath she took quickly returned her to reality.

As she turned to regard the swelling hills they'd just left, their peaks stretching to the canvas of a darkening sky, a small figure walking across one of the tenant farmer's acreage stood out.

Yolanda.

Valentina's forehead puckered with wariness. Her sister wandered alone.

Although her injured arm was still suspended in a sling, she swung her other arm freely, obviously in good spirits. Now where could she be off to?

"Do you not like what you're seeing?" Mr. Colchester asked, interrupting her thoughts. "Are you in need of my prayers now that we've arrived at the parish church? Perhaps the vicar will join us."

"The vicar is most likely inside praying for *you*, because you didn't pray long enough today. If I ever need prayer, I'll call upon Maximilian."

He quirked a dark eyebrow. "Considering the pious pope has been dead for some time, you might need a vicar, instead. I'll leave a Bible in your chamber this evening. Can you read?"

"Of course I can read. Do you think I'm illiterate? Your ideas about the Rom are sadly lacking in substance." She bit her lower lip. "Bury me standing, for I have been on my knees all my life," she said quietly.

He leaned against the wall of the church and regarded her with compassion. "'Tis a sad saying."

The gentleness in his deep voice pulled the air from her lungs. "'Tis the life of the Romany."

"I cannot ever imagine you on your knees, Valentina."

"There are hardships you cannot imagine, Mr. Colchester."

Starvation, desperation, ever-present grief as members of the tribe died, or simply left for a better life. She knew she'd told him too much, knew there was so much more she wanted to tell him.

His gaze reached hers—sobering, offering a quiet understanding.

She heard a sudden intake of breath, not knowing if the sound was his or hers.

"Call me James," he reminded her softly.

James. She mouthed the name silently, allowing the *J* to waft on her tongue. Calling him by his name felt familiar and easy.

Temptation prodded, but reality doused her with a reminder of her place in society. A Romany beggar. She blinked and turned to admire James' grand house. The reflected sunlight off the glass-paned windows blinked back at her.

* * *

RECALLING with effort where they were and that plenty of servants and tenants were around, watching them, James stepped away from the church and offered his arm again to Valentina. High time they returned to the house.

Her words had peeled off layers of buried feelings despite his decision never to care again about any woman. His disastrous marriage had cured him of love—the endless heartache, the affection that hadn't been returned, and betrayal.

The plain bonnet Valentina wore accented her oval face— and her bewitching eyes and enticing smile. Tears fluttered on her thick black lashes. She refused his arm, instead wrapping her wool pelisse closer around her body and walking on to the main house.

The day had begun bright and sunny. Now the air was bitter, the oak trees bowing to the insistent north wind, the sun beginning its descent.

Romany have no homeland. We are nomads.

He shivered. The icy chill of the wind went right through his bones.

CHAPTER 7

Na daran, Romal, wi same sam Rom Tshatsh.
Do not fear, you Gypsy men, for we are Gypsies too.
Old Romany saying

*S*everal days after her outing with James, Valentina
retreated to her chamber for the afternoon. As she
gazed about the room, it never ceased to amaze her, the
riches James was accustomed to: the exquisite silk wall
coverings and drapes, the elegant mahogany furniture, the
sophisticated books and expensive artwork. She wandered to
her bedside table and picked up the Bible he'd left for her.
She'd begun reading the Psalms each day, which James had
recommended.

"'Tis a collection of poems from the Old Testament," he'd
explained. "Some call Psalms expressions of the heart."

She particularly loved Psalm 8:1: "O Lord, our God, how
excellent is thy name in all the earth! who has set thy glory
above the heavens."

The previous afternoon, when she'd strolled with James in the rose garden, she'd discussed that particular psalm with him.

The brilliant blue sky had been spotted by puffy white clouds, and they'd walked to the gazebo nearby, sitting across from each other on wrought iron chairs, sharing a pot of tea. Though the cool breeze of late October carried the lingering scent of roses, Valentina had been glad for her short, fitted jacket.

A quarter of an hour went by swiftly while they'd exchanged contemplations about the Bible. James had enlightened her about several facts, explaining the sacred book had been written over a fifteen-hundred-year span by many authors. Pausing, he'd asked her what she thought was the main theme of the Bible.

"God? Salvation? Heaven?" Thoughtfully, she stirred her tea. "What do you believe?"

He gave her a meaningful look. "I believe the theme is hope and salvation, and the promise of the Kingdom of God."

"Sometimes I feel as though the words in the Bible were written directly for me, acknowledging the troubles I face," she said. "Although, how would God know the hardships of the Romany, or understand the terrible things we do in order to survive?"

James took her hands in his, nodding with his usual astuteness. "If your mind is troubled, the Psalms will give you comfort, as well as practical advice. God assures us we were created to live forever with Him. Every day is a struggle. Just try to live in the peace God promised."

She sighed and scuffed at a stone with her lace-up boot. "My reality hasn't been peaceful, and I've never thought of myself as a good, righteous person. I've been pushed into a difficult life—pressured to do things I knew were wrong."

"Perhaps because of the way you've lived, your expectations are unrealistic. Be kind to yourself. You're a brave woman. As well as kind and compassionate and honorable."

She averted her gaze, her mind replaying the pickpocketing, the robbing, the begging, the busking. She certainly didn't feel honorable.

He gazed down at her, and then he kissed her, long and tenderly. So, this was what it felt like, she thought, to be kissed with such affection by a kind and gentle man. With him, she felt respected and protected.

When he lifted his head, he murmured, "While you were being pushed into dishonor, God was pulling you in another, more honorable direction. His sacred hand has always been on your shoulder, guiding every aspect of your life."

Remembering that conversation—and the kiss— Valentina stood by the window in her bedchamber clutching her Bible and admiring the now-familiar view of James' estate—the sprawling, flowering vines glancing around a stone wall, the sun-dappled gazebo where they had enjoyed that afternoon tea, and thatched cottages outlining the fields.

The late October day was glorious—which was how she thought of the hours spent with James every day. Their time together had an otherworldly quality, tarnished only by the frequent reminder that one day soon, she'd be leaving and returning to her life as a Rom.

She stretched out her hand to trace the cool glass of the window.

Where was the elusive peace God promised? She'd never experienced it. Conflicts and reprimands dwelled within her heart, disturbing any serenity she sought. To add to her disagreeable opinions of herself was one plaguing thought— she'd omitted telling James everything she'd seen when reading his palm. Aye, she'd once regarded reading palms as a game, yet he had had the right to hear the truth.

A light rap on her door brought her thoughts back to the

present. Reluctantly, she placed the Bible on her night table and hurried to the door.

"I need your help." Clare's smile was angelic as she stepped inside Valentina's chamber. "My aunt Dionise is in a bad humor. She complains her bones ache in the cold weather, and I'm concerned."

After a few moments of deliberation, Valentina replied, "I use all types of plants for treatment, mostly found in the forest. The Romany call your aunt's condition *prikasza*." She pulled on a woolen cloak. "Illness isn't natural, and 'tis the reason why your aunt is irritable."

"I've lived on Mr. Colchester's estate since I was a child and know the grounds like the hairs on my legs," Clare said. "I've finished my chores for now, so I'll help you find whatever plant you need."

For more than an hour, the women scoured the woods adjoining the main house and gathered rotting chestnut leaves. Back in the kitchen before the preparations began for the evening meal, Valentina boiled her tonic in a heavy kettle on the wood stove, which Clare had taught her how to use. She closed her eyes to visualize the recovery and speed the healing. She ladled some of the tonic into a bottle for Clare and handed it to her. "Your aunt must drink this tonight."

As she spoke, Roland lumbered into the hallway. He paused at the kitchen doorway and sniffed. "What am I smelling?"

"Boiled chestnut leaves," Clare teased. "'Tis one of Valentina's Gypsy remedies."

"I wouldn't tolerate a Gypsy woman's tainted brew." His enormous hand grabbed Clare's wrist. "Besides, I want to be fit for tonight. Meet me at my cottage."

Clare lightly swatted his hand. "You're hurting me."

He shrugged. "Sometimes I don't realize my strength."

Valentina kept her voice matter-of-fact. "Most men never do."

He grabbed an apple out of the fruit bowl on the table and bit into its green flesh. "Men are free to take whatever pleases us." Gathering a handful of apples, he deliberately dropped several, sending Clare on a scurry through the kitchen to retrieve them.

Valentina bent to recover an apple that rolled under the table. When she lifted her head, she gaped. Hatred had found a comfortable place on Roland's unsmiling face.

"I've worked for Mr. Colchester's family my entire life," he said. "And if there's one type of woman he loathes, 'tis a deceitful one. You don't git any further than Wednesday if you think I don't see your intentions. You want to steal everything he owns. When he realizes this, you'll no longer be welcome."

A swell of sadness sent a rush of heat to Valentina's face. The combination of Roland's bad breath and apple made her eyes smart. "Mr. Colchester stated that Yolanda and I are welcome here." Her voice stayed steady as the sweep of Clare's skirt came into view.

Roland dazzled Clare with a smile. "I'll find you later."

Clare fixed a shiny-eyed gaze at his hulking back as he left the kitchen. Her hands gripped the bowl of apples before she set it on the table. "I wish he'd take more notice of me."

Valentina pinched herself to keep from shaking sense into Clare. "He's noticed you."

Because he apparently lusted after every female within one hundred miles.

Clare massaged her wrist. "At present, he's besotted with Lowdie, the new servant from Wales."

Valentina studied Clare curiously, since Clare did care for the brute. What kind of woman wanted a callous man?

"Can you help me with your Gypsy magic?" Clare asked. "I want to win him back before I lose him completely."

The delightful idea of bringing Roland to heel prompted Valentina's smile. "I know the perfect charm and 'twill bewitch him."

The spell might force Roland to care about Clare and not hurt her, soundly worth the effort. Valentina squeezed Clare's hand, concerned for the young servant who expected so little of herself.

"Do you know where he sleeps?" Valentina asked.

Clare blushed and nodded. "He's Mr. Colchester's game-keeper, and he sleeps in the gamekeeper's cottage."

"When he's asleep, snip a lock of his hair. Carry the lock at all times, and you alone shall hold his heart."

"He thinks I'm another stone on the wall. I want him to love me."

"After this spell, he'll be entranced with you. 'Tis a Romany hair charm and extremely effective."

Clare smiled, and Valentina lowered her gaze to mask her own mischievous grin. Definitely, the charm reaped benefits for all.

* * *

AT THE END of the evening, Valentina sank onto her bed. The household had quieted at last. She picked up the Bible and pondered Psalm, 31, which was quickly becoming her favorite psalm. She read aloud verse 24: "Be of good courage and He shall strengthen your heart, all ye that hope for the Lord."

Could this passage give her the hope she'd been searching for? Should she take responsibility for her future, look within herself and to the God James spoke about?

She prayed quietly, and in the space of a few minutes, she

felt calmer. She put her hands behind her head and fell asleep.

Hours later, a low growl prodded her awake.

"Valentina?"

She rubbed the blurriness from her eyes and peered into the night shadows. The figure of a man hovered above her, and she could clearly see the outline of a strong nose and high forehead, and the glint of one gold earring in his ear. Even in the dark, his fiery dark eyes glittered.

Valentina threw off her blankets. "Luca? How did you find me?" He leaned down, and she gave him a welcoming hug. Smoky scents of firewood and raw brandy greeted her, so recognizable she sobbed out loud.

"I've watched the estate for days," he said.

"I'm so thankful you're well. Daj is buried?"

"Aye. Your mother's funeral was honorable. You and your sister would have been proud."

She choked back tears she knew he'd loathe. Still, one slipped down her cheek and she wiped her face against the coarse wool of his cloak. "At first, I feared you were hurt when we were taken."

He gripped her hands and settled them on her lap, then stood and shook back his silky black hair. "My head ached for two days, but I'm fine now." Grabbing a candle from her bedside table, he strode to the fireplace and used the ashes flickering in the grate to light the candle.

"How did you get past all the servants?"

"I scaled the wall." He placed the candle on the mantel. "Get your wrap. We're leaving." His eyes shone with a wild, bright fire. The candlelight revealed the harsh creases near his mouth and the line of his unyielding jaw.

Fully alert, she sat upright. "You want me to leave with you? Now?"

"Aye. The caravan is preparing to depart. We'll travel south where it's warmer."

"I can't go anywhere without Yolanda."

He nodded. "We can return for her come the morrow and then catch up to the caravan." He pulled her from the bed and guided her to the open window. She shivered in the cold as he pulled a thick coil of rope from his cloak.

Valentina reeled. "Nay. Absolutely not."

Luca gripped her forearms and searched her face. "When have you ever been afraid? Trust me."

She drew a breath. "There are safer ways to leave than flinging ourselves out the window. All I have to do is tell James—"

"James?" Luca dropped his hand and paced. Small steps. Incessant. Irritated. After a few moments, his cool smile returned, a brilliant camouflage he employed whenever he grew annoyed. "Come."

Accustomed to his thinly disguised commands, she nodded reluctantly. He'd never directed his anger at her. Nonetheless, she'd seen the result of his wrath when someone opposed him. He'd brutally beaten many an opponent.

He looped the rope around her waist. "Kick your legs when you swing too close to the wall and hang onto the rope as I lower you."

She picked up her wrap, set it back down. "This isn't a childhood prank we can laugh about afterward. Be sensible for once."

"I'm the leader of our tribe. 'Tis your duty to obey my decisions or the spirits will be enraged."

"Or *you* will be enraged."

His face reddened. His shoulder muscles tightened.

She inhaled a jagged breath. Deliberately, she stared at his forearms, tough and lean beneath his ragged shirt. "You go.

Yolanda's arm was injured and she's still recuperating. We'll catch up with you as soon as she's able to travel."

The smile he offered was cheerless, and without speaking he wound the rope around the oak bedpost and secured a knot.

She trembled as she stood beside him, following his fingers as he fixed the knots securely. She had learned to rely on him, although a disturbing tempo, beating disaster, drummed along her spine.

Thinking at first she'd imagined the indistinct shrieks from the hallway, Valentina swung around as her chamber door swung open.

Wiborow blasted in like an enraged hobgoblin. "I knew I heard a man's voice." She gaped at Luca. "Who—"

Valentina quickly stepped in front of Luca. "He's a friend."

Her hair disheveled and nightclothes askew, the housekeeper's eyes rounded to twin full moons. She spun and bolted from the chamber, her piercing scream sounding an alarm. "Gypsy bandits. They're attacking! Come to Valentina's chamber quickly!"

Luca grabbed the rope. "We must try now."

"Nay." Valentina gripped his arms. "Listen to me. I'm not going."

She felt, rather than saw, his wave of impatience. All his reactions poured from his skin—a fierce, primitive emanation of power in a sleek, panther-like body. She wanted to protest, although her mouth was too dry.

Footsteps pounded down the corridor.

"Valentina, what are you doing?" James' voice ripped through her chamber.

She whirled. "How dare you charge in here?"

"In my own house?" He untied the rope from the bedpost and flung it to the floor, then stared past her at Luca.

This couldn't be happening. Luca was here, in her chamber, and it looked like she was leaving with him. James would never forgive her.

James' fists closed at his sides. "Were you *both* trying to get yourselves killed?"

Luca pushed up the sleeves of his shirt. "I don't take orders from a worthless gadje."

Valentina's body grew clammy with sweat, her gown sticking to her legs.

James' gaze was riveted on Luca and a sharp dawning of understanding lit his eyes. "You must be Valentina's Gypsy suitor." He motioned to a white-faced Wiborow and a scowling Roland to stay in the doorway.

Luca's nostrils flared. "Why are you keeping my Romany women?"

"*Your* women?"

Valentina drew in a ragged breath. "Mr. Colchester, please, don't."

James didn't turn. His muscles hardened beneath his rumpled shirt.

"Don't defend me." Luca directed a hard stare at her before glaring at James. "I can take care of myself."

"Luca, you need to go. You're outnumbered." Valentina moved closer to the two men. They glowered at each other with controlled, frightening rage. Her chest tightened in dread.

"Fight me, Mr. Fancy Gentleman." Luca enhanced his threat with a short, cynical laugh.

Valentina could predict Luca's actions as surely as she had five fingers on each hand. He wouldn't fight if he thought he couldn't win. He'd taunt, assess, and bide his time until he had the advantage. Nevertheless, he'd never win against James, because the tenant farmers and servants were everywhere, and Luca wasn't invincible.

She spoke through a throat that refused to allow a full

breath. "Mr. Colchester, I'll never forgive you if you hurt my friend." The air closed, the defeat heavy. "Please ... James."

Invisible tension rippled the muscles in James' back. He never moved, never turned.

"How often, Valentina, have you asked me for a favor using my given name?"

She jammed her fists against her thighs. "I'm asking now."

James raised his arms and stepped back, the abrupt crack of the floorboard jarring the silence. "Roland, haul our vagrant clear of the grounds."

"Mr. Colchester—"

"Do as I ask, Roland." James' voice lowered to a murmur as he turned toward Valentina. "And tell this man not to come here again."

"Luca." She drew a long, quavering breath. "Go quietly. Yolanda and I are all right."

Skewered by the men's glares, she gave a disparaging laugh. In her heart she knew she served one role. She was a possession to both these controlling males. Nothing more.

Roland stepped forward and jerked Luca's arms behind him. "Your Gypsy face isn't wanted here. Don't you remember that lesson from last time?"

Luca nodded reassurance to Valentina as he strode from her chamber. "I'll alert the others. We're traveling to the coast, near Brighton." His gaze was cold, his voice ominously soft.

She didn't reply. There were no "others" to alert. Their tribesmen were elderly, frail, and powerless.

After the door shut behind Luca, James twisted to face her. Anger flickered in the depths of his grey eyes. "I thought you and your sister were happy here."

"We are. I had no idea Luca would show up in my bedchamber." She scowled at him with what she hoped was a perfect balance of fury and defiance. "If you're waiting for me to apologize, you'll be waiting until the spirits sprout wings."

"If you attempt another foolhardy idea that might get you killed, you'll wish *you* had wings." He strode three paces forward. "I was alarmed. I reacted too quickly."

"You mean overreacted."

"All I could picture was the rope around your waist, and you attempting to climb down from the window." He whispered a word he'd used before—cariad—although she didn't understand what it meant.

"I'm not that foolhardy anymore."

"If you fell …" He rubbed his thumb across her lips, not making the slightest attempt to veil the flame in his eyes. He kissed her eyes and nose before finding her mouth, slowing and deepening his kisses.

Her rigid muscles relaxed. She couldn't pull away. She *had* to pull away.

Shamelessly her body didn't listen and ignited. His tongue outlined the corners and creases of her lips before moving slowly into her mouth. A sweet, searing, mindlessness flooded her veins as her tongue responded to his plunging and probing. When he lifted his head, she gasped, weak and confused, surprised to feel his heart thrashing as wildly as hers.

After he'd left her chamber a few minutes afterward and she'd found her balance again, she stared at the door. She could still feel his tender embraces, and the taste of his hard, firm lips moving against hers.

CHAPTER 8

Feri ando payi sitsholpe te nayuas.
It was in the water that one learned to swim.
Romany saying

*V*alentina relived the scene with Luca countless times, denying her rush of relief when his reckless plan had been thwarted. Why had she questioned him? He was a part of her tribe, her past, her heritage.

With each passing day, she couldn't shake the awareness that she and Yolanda were growing more and more content. However, was it so wrong to enjoy a soft, cushioned bed and well-cooked food? And aye, she'd begun to look forward to her daily outings with a tall grey-eyed gentleman who warmed her entire body with his slow, devastating smile and recklessly good looks.

Every morning, she sought Yolanda's company for support and comfort. Yolanda was as loyal to Valentina as nobles had been to King Henry.

Two days after Luca had visited Valentina's bedchamber, she and Yolanda sat in the middle of Yolanda's bed, underneath a bright lavender canopy. The bed was piled high with plump apple-green pillows. Although not as grand as Valentina's chamber, Yolanda's chamber boasted well-appointed cherry furnishings and a stone fireplace.

Valentina rested against several of the pillows. "We'll leave when you're completely healed, Yolanda. Perhaps before Christmas."

Yolanda stared out the window before flicking an unfocused look in Valentina's direction. "Luca gave Daj an honorable burial. There's no urgency to leave anymore."

As hard as Valentina blinked, she realized her complaisant sister had uttered the last words she'd ever expected. "How else will we ever see our tribe again?"

"You go if you miss them so much." Dressed only in her linen chemise, Yolanda rose to stand near the window. As she pushed the bottom pane open a crack, a whiff of crisp autumn air cooled the chamber. "I want to stay as long as Mr. Colchester will have us."

Valentina fumbled between bewilderment and resentment. "Have you forgotten? Under the pretense of all this finery we are Romany beggars."

Yolanda twirled the ends of her wavy brown hair. "I like being taken care of. I like eating white bread instead of brown. I'm tired of freezing and going hungry and endlessly wandering."

"Since when?"

A smile broke over Yolanda's face. "Since I began seeing a wonderful man."

Valentina snatched a pillow and playfully tossed it at her sister. "You've always stated there was no one suitable for you in all of England."

"Several fine-looking, gracious men live on this estate."

"And who is this one particular fine-looking, gracious man?"

"His name is Reginald. He's one of Mr. Colchester's blacksmiths."

"I know who he is." Valentina chewed her bottom lip until it burned. "He's a large brute of a man who ought to keep his affections to himself. There's no sense in becoming attached to someone you'll soon be bidding farewell."

"Reginald is very interested in our customs. He asks all sorts of questions."

"He uses our customs as an excuse to get close to you." Valentina tucked her legs beneath her and tapped her fingers together. "Remember, he's a gadje."

Yolanda couldn't have looked more defiant than if she were playing the role of a two-year-old child who wouldn't eat her supper. "You're not my mother or my father, and you cannot force me to agree with you."

Yolanda was a follower. What had happened to her sister? The answer came from every corner of the chamber—where they sat, where they ate, where they slept. They'd lived in James' beautiful home and grown accustomed to finery they hadn't even imagined.

"Seeing Reginald isn't a good idea. 'Tis my responsibility to steer you away from people who will cause you heartbreak."

"Reginald makes me happy."

A short-lived happiness if influenza ever threatened James' household.

Valentina scraped back her hair. Now where had that thought come from, and with it, the churn of anxiety in her stomach?

Abruptly, she stood and padded to the window. "There's something I must tell you," she whispered in a strained voice.

Yolanda's doe-like eyes took on more fear than they could

hold. "You haven't used that serious of a tone since Father died. What is it?"

Valentina exhaled a lungful of agitation and eyed Yolanda's soft white chemise, the fine pin tucks accenting her sister's tiny waist, dark hair pulled back in a ponytail and caught in an embellished velvet bow. Her delicate sister deserved happiness, not anguish. Besides, Valentina no longer believed in Rom spirits, superstitions, and fortune-telling.

"'Tis nothing." She blew out a breath and gave Yolanda's slim hands an encouraging squeeze. "Reginald must be very important to you."

"Aye. He is." The cheery fire in the fireplace made Yolanda's complexion glow radiantly.

As the days passed and November neared, Valentina monitored Yolanda closely.

What would she do if anything happened to her sister? She was so young, so inexperienced. Valentina feared her sister wouldn't be able to stop Reginald, such a burly man, if his passion became too … passionate.

Whenever Reginald and Yolanda were together, Valentina waited for a sign that her sister needed protection. She'd be there. She'd be ready to aid Yolanda in any way she could.

But Yolanda's smiles came more easily. Her steps were lighthearted, her laughter downright exuberant. And the sign never came.

CHAPTER 9

Bi kashtesko merel i yag.
Without wood the fire would die.
Old Romany saying

On a soggy day in early November, Valentina spent the afternoon tilling soil in the herb garden. Several of the herbs had died as winter approached, although the whiff of a forgotten mustard seed carried on the light breeze.

"I'd wondered where you'd wandered today," a resonant, familiar voice teased.

She dropped the shovel and sent overgrown weeds tumbling.

"Spying on me, as usual?" He sat astride his horse, and her gaze wandered admiringly up the polished black boots covering his well-muscled legs. His thick wool waistcoat scarcely concealed the hardness of his body, nor the male strength brewing just beneath his polished exterior. Although she'd given herself innumerable lectures not to be affected by him, her disloyal heart sang each day as they walked the grounds of his estate or enjoyed afternoon tea or supper with Yolanda. She knew the servants and tenants objected to her being with him, knew that society expected her and James to be chaperoned, although everyone kept their displeasure to themselves.

"I'm attending to some unpleasant tasks today," he said. "I've feuded with my neighbor, Mr. Wellsey, for years. I'm hoping to put an end to our disagreement once and for all."

"In the garden?" she goaded, hoping for a rise. He'd purposely sought her. The thought tickled her with an unexpected smile.

"I'll be riding over to his estate."

She tightened the yellow diklo around her throat. "Will you return by this evening?"

"Aye." His eyes darkened. "Will you miss me?"

"Perhaps."

Their laughs came as one. He looked disgracefully handsome sitting atop his horse, the superb animal pawed fitfully at the ground. The white markings on its smoky-black coat were well defined, and the one on its head resembled a star. Similar to the star she'd seen on James' hand when she'd read his palm.

Her chin quivered.

"Anything wrong?" He leaned down and nudged a stray wisp of hair from her face. The light touch of his hand curved to her cheekbone.

Her breath caught. "Nay."

He laughed, the hearty, good-natured laugh now so familiar to her. "Surely you'd never lie to me?" He dismounted and coiled the horse's reins around an oak tree, then strode to her. He lowered his head, his lips stopping an inch of hers. "Don't run off with your Gypsy suitor while I'm gone."

She saw the craving in his eyes. Now she couldn't breathe at all. "I have no Romany suitor, nor any suitor."

"You have no suitor *yet*."

"I want no suitor *ever*."

"A distressing thought for any male within fifty paces of you." He swept weightless strokes up her back, a subtle gesture of possessiveness that opened a door to emotions that she intended to keep closed.

Before her mind became a blank, she asked, "Do you know what I wish for?"

"A suitor? Shall I list the reasons why I am best?"

"Absolutely not."

"I insist." His mouth inched closer. "We can begin with your assessment of my kissing."

Inwardly, a gala of feelings erupted. Her mind screamed caution, her mouth screamed hunger.

"'Tis the first step in your assessment," he continued. "Say *very well* and kiss me back. Fortunately, 'tis a skill which takes considerable practice."

Enticingly forbidden, she gloried in the pleasure of his firm mouth on hers, and her arms wrapped around his nape. He cuddled her, the insistent pump of his heart solid and reassuring, his fingers stroking teasing pathways along the inside of her arms. "Shall we continue with another rehearsal or a full recital?" he murmured.

In a haze, she almost nodded before her foggy brain skidded to a halt and reason reared. "You're outrageous," she said shakily.

"I'm simply drawn."

"To herbs?"

His knuckles brushed her cheekbones. "To one particular Gypsy woman who's beautiful and intoxicating."

Keep him at a distance. She resisted the tremor that shook her resolution and groped for a subject to break the attraction spinning between them. One issue James never wanted to discuss was his son's deafness.

She fell back a step. "May I tell you a story?"

A look of forced patience spanned his face. "Now?"

"Aye." She hesitated and bit her bottom lip. "Many years ago, a little deaf girl lived in a neighboring tribe."

"Really?" he drawled. "And?"

"We treated her the same as all the other children, although we always made sure she was looking at us when we spoke." The moment of quiet affection they'd shared dissolved, and she rushed her words. "However, when the girl grew into her teens, we all noticed there were many random things she hadn't understood, things we took for granted along the way."

"Communication takes constant effort." James offered a cool nod. "Elspeth, Jeremy's nurse, spends half her time trying to get his attention."

"Other than deafness, all children are the same. The only difference is language."

Warily, he contemplated her. "I give Jeremy the same love as I gave Beatrix.

"Aye, because you're his father." Valentina laid a hand on his sleeve. "May I make a suggestion?"

She felt his arm tighten, although he shrugged uninterestedly. "Of course."

"Allow Jeremy more freedom. Presently, his puppy is his only companion. He's a little boy who wants to play with other children."

"He's deaf. He's not like other children." James' features became unreadable. "I appreciate your suggestion. However, as you've said, I'm his father. I know what's best for him."

She let out an exasperated huff. "You don't always know what's best."

From the corner of her eye, she noticed Yolanda cross the

lawn and head toward the river. Yolanda shaded her eyes as she looked in their direction, and then shied away.

James gestured toward Yolanda. "You might consider thanking me like your sister does instead of passing on your opinions concerning my son."

"How can I thank you when you're a gadje?" Valentina's face heated, her breath sputtered. "Luca and I were starving when we left camp to find a physician for her. No one cared."

Wearily, James sighed. "You insist on punishing me for your difficult past instead of focusing on the present. Is there no place in your heart for gratitude?" He turned abruptly and strode toward his horse.

She waited. He might turn one last time. He always did, usually accompanied by a teasing smile.

Instead, he uncoiled the reins and mounted the stallion. Without a word, he jabbed his heels into the horse's flanks and broke away.

Disappointment deflated her chest as her anger subsided. He hadn't exhibited any joy when she'd voluntarily touched his sleeve, hadn't supported her suggestion by lightly squeezing her fingers.

In utter exasperation, she swung toward the main house, believing she imagined Yolanda's cries for help.

Nay, it couldn't be.

There. Again. The echo of a muted scream, coming from the river.

Valentina stopped. The air was motionless.

Another cry. Yolanda.

She clutched her gown and ran toward the river, tripping over the broad roots of an oak tree, passing by an old stone wall. She gulped back a horrified scream as she reached the bank. Yolanda was flailing, up to her neck in water.

Not daring to look away, Valentina snapped off a brittle tree branch and darted toward the water. She stretched the branch as far over the water as she dared without plunging in.

"Yolanda, reach for this!"

Yolanda struggled to grab the branch. Her head tilted back, her nose hardly visible above the water. Then she disappeared beneath the current as she was swept downstream.

Fright swept Valentina's whole being. Yolanda couldn't swim and neither could Valentina.

Terror had to be swallowed.

She lifted the hem of her gown and rushed into the river. Icy water blackened her world. The swift undercurrent whipped her heavy gown around her ankles.

"Valentina!" James's shouts penetrated the weighty depths.

Desperately, she kicked and broke through the water's surface.

James. Their gazes met. He stood on the riverbank, pulling off his coat, preparing to jump in the river. The cold water sprayed and splattered. Crests of water, smelling of fish, roiled to her chin.

A moment later, his strong arms were around her. He lifted her from the river and onto the muddy bank.

For several seconds, her voice wouldn't emit a sound. Sobs blocked coherency. "Yolanda ... drowning ... Must save—"

"Yolanda? In the water?" His tone held firm. "Stay here."

Nodding her head up and down like a marionette yanked by an invisible string, Valentina pinched her lips together to stop her teeth from chattering. Her soaked gown clung to every crevice of her body, sending an army of bone-chilling shivers down her spine.

James dove beneath the surface, up for air, then back

underneath. Swallowing a sob, Valentina clung to a single hope. James would never let Yolanda drown.

Still sitting on the ground, she stared at the sunlight glinting off the water's surface. The water stirred. Quieted. No churn. No ripple.

Her chest heaving as she tried to draw air into her lungs, she wiped her cracked lips with her sleeve, hunching with her nose to the ground. A lone green sprig grew near her feet. She snapped it by the root and sniffed a tinge of spicy basil. Unspoiled and alive, the smell of hope. Basil was the most dependable of herbs, flavorful and sweet, her mother had said.

Still holding the herb, she came to her feet. She studied each swell of water, assessing the golden-brown sheen coating the surface.

"Yolanda! James!" Her mind screamed louder than her voice.

Too many seconds had passed. The water calmed, the surface a white froth of foam.

She closed her eyes, fell to her knees, and prayed. One night after the evening meal, James had read from the book of Matthew, 21:22, and she'd memorized the passage because it spoke so true: "And whatever you ask in prayer, you will receive, if you have faith."

"Please God," she whispered, "hear my prayer." She kept her eyes closed, kept whispering the same prayer. "Be my guide. I don't want to feel lost and alone anymore. Meet me here in my darkest sadness."

Opening her eyes and scanning the river, she saw James first. He swam toward the riverbank towing her sister's limp body.

Valentina doubled over to put distance between herself and her impending grief. Then she ran to them both, clutching Yolanda so tightly she knew she'd leave finger imprints on Yolanda's skin.

"Is she dead, James? Nay, please nay," she sobbed.

"Trust me." Laying Yolanda on her back, he compressed his hands on her ribcage and bore down. Water spurted from Yolanda's mouth.

Valentina sank to the ground, welcoming each gasp, each cough, each sputter, because it meant her sister would survive.

"Why would Yolanda venture so close to the river when she couldn't swim?" she murmured through relieved tears.

"I'll ask you the same question." James raised Valentina's chin and wiped her damp cheeks. Distress sparked his eyes before they narrowed. "Can *you* swim?"

Valentina sniffed. The foul smell of the river clung to the insides of her nose and throat. Coarse silt stuck to the roof of her mouth, and she had no choice but to swallow.

"Can you swim?" he asked again.

She couldn't carry the burden of almost losing her sister, so she leaned against his chest.

"If I weren't afraid of water, I would have learned how to swim."

"You cannot swim," James repeated, searching Valentina's wide emerald eyes. Sheer trepidation shone back at him. "And yet you decided to dive into a raging river to save your sister."

He examined Yolanda, relieved at the color returning to her face. Keeping her within his sight, he shifted to Valentina.

She was watching her sister as well, but her expression was distant. "I didn't think. I wanted to—"

"Save her? You cannot swim. Of all the insane acts of ..." *Courage* came to his lips.

He enveloped her in his arms, her wetness molding to his

drenched shirt. With her hair smeared around her lovely face and her eyes bright with fear, she resembled a frightened fawn. Only the overpowering impulse to protect her kept him upright.

He clasped her nearer, swaying from side to side, absorbing her. "You exquisite, foolish woman."

She muttered a peculiar foreign word, followed by the force of sobs quaking against his chest. He couldn't release her. He gathered her so close she became a part of him.

He bent his face nearer her lips. "Why are you cursing me?"

"I'm not." Her voice broke. "Although I should."

He wiped the stream of tears off her cheeks. Sopping wet and trembling, she was the most divine creature he'd ever seen. He cupped her face with his hands. "Because I saved you?"

Brokenly, she cried, "Because lately you seem cross with me."

He was cross? Odd, he didn't remember. Of course, that swaggering Gypsy man appearing in her chamber a few weeks earlier hadn't helped his thinking of late.

He closed his arms around her, breathed in her achingly fiery scent, and felt her hammering heart.

She huddled her trembling body close for another few moments, accepting his warmness, but then she broke free to tend to her sister. Yolanda was shivering badly and just as frightened as Valentina. As he picked up his discarded waistcoat and laid it over the girl, he knew he would protect Valentina with his life.

He lifted his head at muffled hollering in the distance.

"Our help is rallying," he told them. "When we return to the house, Yolanda, you should be checked thoroughly. Hopefully, your fracture hasn't worsened. I'll call on the bone-setter to be certain."

She whispered her thanks as he picked her up and carried

her to his horse. He settled her in the saddle and then veered back toward Valentina, helping her onto the horse as well, in front of Yolanda.

"Thank you, James." Respect illuminated Valentina's gaze. Her words were pure, filling his heart.

"'Tis not difficult to thank me. You don't have to *ask* for my help, you merely have to *scream*."

A weak smile curved her lips. She wrung out her hair with quivery fingers. "Why did you return?"

"I heard your shouts. Thank God I found you."

Briefly, she closed her eyes. "I loathe feeling helpless."

"You're safe now."

"I prayed. I hoped that God was listening, that I was in His presence. I thought that couldn't happen unless I was in church, but I felt He was here."

"You don't need to be in church to be in the presence of God."

They continued on in silence, until her delicate brows pulled together and she glanced down at him. "Now you'll be late for your meeting with Mr. Wellsey."

"Another time, perhaps." James sifted through his thoughts, trying to recall why he wanted to meet with Wellsey. Nothing of importance came to mind. Nothing was important except Valentina's safety and the safety of those he loved.

Loved.

He shook his head. The thought just came. Had it been sitting there, idly, all this time, waiting for the right moment to admit how much he cared for her?

Impossible. They'd only known each other a short time. Love was a mindless, romantic concept that had no place in his life.

"I never learned how to swim, but I couldn't allow Yolanda to drown," Valentina was saying. "I'm sorry I placed you in so much danger."

Touched by her fearlessness in the face of danger, he raised his hand. "Please don't apologize."

His fear for both women's safety evaporated as he reflected on the past few minutes. Valentina was soaked and exhausted. Yet she'd sought the security of his embrace when she'd been most frightened.

"You are an exceptionally brave woman," he said.

Her uneven laugh floated through the fields. She flecked a dismissive wave toward herself. Twisting, she inspected every nick and bruise on Yolanda's arms before meeting his gaze. "You saved us both. Thank you, James."

He might have lost her.

A shudder rattled his gut. "You would have done the same for me."

"Who wouldn't risk their life to help someone?"

Staring ahead, he couldn't control the tremor in his voice. "Apparently not you, cariad," was all he could manage. "Apparently not you."

CHAPTER 10

Te xav to biav?
May I eat at your wedding?
Old Romany saying

Two weeks later, after Jeremy had finished his studies with his tutor, Valentina gaped at his smiling face across the black and white checkerboard. "You trounced me again. How did you succeed in winning this time?"

After a fortnight of playing checkers with the quiet boy, Valentina welcomed his enthusiastic giggle. She came around to him, lifted his arms and twirled him round and round and round. Perfectly terraced lawns sped by in a blur. Their whirling world came to a tumbling halt when they both rolled to the ground.

"I … am … a … win-ner." Jeremy laughed, his cheeks alive with color.

She pulled him upright, unable to contain her joy at

hearing him speak. He chuckled at her tickles and comical gestures as she admitted defeat.

His tiny hands hugged her neck, his fingertips barely touching. *"Mam?"*

The Welsh word for mother.

With a pang and a nod, she embraced him. "I'll do my best to be your mam for the time I'm here." She stretched her legs out on the lawn, cuddling him on her lap and scanning the expansive lawn.

James and several other men had ridden off at daybreak in a flurry of horses' hooves and high spirits, intent on hunting red deer and wild fowl. The sudden swoop of a falcon signaled the men's return. In tandem, Jeremy and Valentina lifted their gazes to the graceful bird soaring and diving with the wind. Kenelm, a falconer, strode from the barn and followed the bird's flight with his gaze. The falcon flew to rest on his gloved hand.

Jeremy wiggled out of Valentina's arms to greet the bird. He raced across the lawn, his rapidly growing puppy following his lead. Valentina imagined Jeremy's twin sister, Beatrix, running across the lawn beside him. The thought made her throat knot with grief and her grin die away. James had endured so much sadness.

Yolanda, a warm shawl wrapped around her shoulders, stood in the doorway of one of the outbuildings. She spoke with an elderly woman who sat inside at a spinning wheel, spinning raw wool into cloth, holding the yarn away from the wheel on her loom to add a crink.

Valentina smiled with amused consideration. Why her sister was interested in such a tedious task as weaving, she'd never understand. But then Yolanda's interest shifted as a heavily built man tromped over to her.

Reginald. He wiped the blackened hairs on his arm with a piece of cloth from the loom. Whatever he said made her laugh, and she gave her shiny hair a shake as they glided toward the pear orchard arm in arm.

These were the times that Valentina's hope strengthened, when the day bloomed optimistic and full of promise. And, of course, there were her daily hours spent with James.

The previous day, he'd guided her to a clearing that boasted a spectacular view of his home. Carved chimneys braced either end of the daunting manor house, the splendorous pitch of the high roof soaring toward feathery white clouds. The numerous farmers working the farmland completed the halcyon picture. The English countryside was so beautiful, she'd murmured, although a rush of homesickness had evoked sadness. If only her tribe could find this sort of peace and not continually struggle to survive.

"What can God possibly do in my life?" she said to James, turning away from the view. The life she did not deserve. "He'll never forgive all my sins."

"Have you repented?"

"Aye."

"Then do your best not to sin again."

She bit her lips to stave off the grief. "I'm a Rom, and I've done terrible things in more nameless towns than I can remember."

"The future is more important than your former ways, Valentina." Lightly, James kissed her temple. "Don't judge what God's going to do in your lifetime by what happened in the past. Your life is bigger than just a nameless town. The rest of your story is still unwritten and, best of all, God knows your ending."

She nodded, experiencing a sense of peace. Spending time with James, listening to him, she'd begun to see herself in a new light—not as she used to, ashamed for doing whatever it took to feed her family. Now, she'd begun to believe God had placed her on this landed gentry's estate for a reason, and she was right where she belonged—with James, a truly good man, a man of God.

And she was beginning to feel deep affection for James. He felt it too. His attentive gaze, his judicious expression, spoke louder than words. Whenever their conversations became too pensive, he'd tease her until she responded with a quip. He'd laugh with her, his handsome features enlivened by his good humor. She wanted to deny the attraction, knew 'twas impossible for them to be together.

A thunderbolt of activity broke her thoughts as James rode his horse out of the woods at a breakneck gallop. Immediately, her pulse began to thrum. He appeared so in control of his swift, powerful horse.

He brought his horse to a halt near the rail by the stable and dismounted. The horse balked and shied clear of the falcon. "'Tis merely a bird, Albern." James stroked the horse's sweaty mane, calling his horse by name.

Jeremy ran back to Valentina. Hand in hand, she and Jeremy wandered closer to the stable.

The falcon is tame, Valentina told herself, keeping a distrustful gaze on the black falcon and its magnificent wingspan. "The Rom are fearful of owls." She caught Jeremy's attention, dropped her hand and pointed to her lips. "Falcons, hawks, and owls are all predators." Bracelets jingling, she added a flap of her hands to imitate flying.

"Pre … da-tor?"

"A predator is—" she emulated a man on horseback—"a hunter."

Jeremy nodded that he understood and gave her and James a quick hug before skipping away in the falconer's footsteps.

Glad the falcon was gone, Valentina turned to James, only to find him regarding her with some amusement. He must have noticed her wariness around the bird.

"The Rom are fearful of owls," she muttered.

"Now why would Gypsies be afraid of a harmless owl?" he asked.

Valentina sucked in a swift breath as he stepped closer. Beneath his hunting jacket, his white shirt was open at the collar. His weather-darkened face showed a slight shadow of a beard, and his hair was damp from the hard ride of the hunt.

The bright noonday sun enhanced the lines of amusement playing around his mouth, and his eyes glinted with a mischievous sparkle. In a desperate attempt to ignore his charismatic grin, she focused on his skittish horse. "Your horse and I share the same feelings about birds of prey. We realize these birds are untrustworthy."

James handed a stable boy his horse's reins, then caught her hand and urged her to walk with

him. "Why are you fearful of an innocent bird and little else?"

"A falcon is a predator. So are owls. To the Rom, an owl's cry is very bad luck."

"Really?" Leisurely, he picked a dry leaf off her hair. His long fingers backcombed several strands, beginning at her scalp and ending with each loose wave tumbling down her back.

Her cheeks heated, her heart skipped, her arms riddled with pinpricks. "Surely there isn't a whole tree in my hair?"

His smile broadened. "An owl is a useful bird."

"The owl's hoot is a foreboding omen, an inevitable sign of trouble and sadness. Their cute, heart-shaped faces are a trick to fool the person who doesn't know any better."

"Aye, looks can be deceptive."

"If you believe an owl is harmless, you're shockingly blind."

"I assure you, I'm not blind." His gaze roamed over her face. "Shall I tell you about the woman standing before me?"

A delicious shiver coursed in her belly.

"I see a mysterious woman—"

"As usual, Mr. Colchester, you're not listening." *Move,* she commanded her rooted-to-the-ground feet.

"James, remember?" He slid his hands up her arms, his roughened fingers prickling her sensitive skin even through the sleeves of her coat.

She rolled her tight shoulders and pretended not to be affected by his burning, weightless strokes.

"Have you chosen to forget where we are—in full view of your son and falconer and grooms?" She cast a pointed gaze in Jeremy's direction. Beside the barn, the boy huddled in concentration near the falcon and Kenelm.

James raised his hands in an innocent gesture before placing them back on her shoulders. "My son isn't interested in us. A bird is indeed more fascinating."

"I can assure you that everyone who works for you is very interested."

"They're too busy to be concerned with me."

In fact, several servants had paused in midtask to watch them. Not stopping to explain, Valentina twisted away from him and dashed toward the stables.

James caught up with her as she entered an empty stall. With a kick, he closed the heavy door behind them. She waited, her back to him, keeping her gaze on thick bales of fragrant hay piled alongside the walls.

His arms circled her waist, his breath rousing her neck to gooseflesh. Her face brushed against his wide shoulder as she turned. Dreamy intimacy was all she knew, coupled with the heady awareness he wanted to kiss her.

"I thought of you today." The quiet tenderness in his tone stopped her breathing for a moment.

"You thought about me while you were hunting?"

His grey eyes changed to the color of raindrops on a drizzly day. "Aye. Whenever we're apart, I think about you."

When he spoke in silvery, discreet tones, Valentina forgot where she was, who she was. And when he added his languid, reassuring smile, her reasons to stay away from him dissolved. She examined the natural strength in his face, the set of his stubborn chin, and the temperamental freckle above his lips.

He brushed his mouth over hers, coaxing her lips to part. She closed her eyes and savored the sensation. The erratic beating of his heart coupled with her own.

She stirred.

His arms wrapped protectively around her and rested his jaw on her temple. "Don't move," he

murmured. "I like having you near me."

The sharp scent of leather and horses filled her nostrils. Streams of sunlight shone through a crack in the stable's outer wall, exposing floating dust laced with straw.

In an impulsive gesture, Valentina smoothed his hair in place, sliding the glossy texture between her fingers. She wiped the sweat off his moist forehead, his dark brows. She rubbed the back of his neck where the hair was crisp, full. and black.

It would be so easy to fall in love with him.

* * *

JAMES KNEW every last person on his estate was by now aware that he and Valentina were alone in the stable, but he didn't care. She fit so nicely along his body that he loathed moving, delighted she was letting him hold her for so long. "I don't see nearly enough of you," he said. "You're either weeding your herb garden, making who knows what kind of healing tonic in the kitchen, or caring for my son."

With his finger, he outlined the fullness of her lower lip.

Before Yolanda's near drowning, Valentina had been the delightful core of his shameless imagination. Lately, she brought out an affection in him he didn't recognize and couldn't analyze. His exquisite, willful Gypsy woman.

The past few mornings, he'd pondered and prayed, and he'd reached a decision. He'd grown tired of living alone and of rearing his son without a mother. A good, caring, selfless mother. Valentina displayed every one of these traits.

He'd made up his mind days ago. Nay. He'd made up his mind weeks ago, before the scare at the river. He'd continuously encouraged Valentina to remain with him on his estate, unable to understand his consuming interest in her, his need to protect her. Certainly, her sister's injury had restricted her travel. However, the women could have returned to their caravan at any point. And they hadn't.

His fingers traveled up her temples. "You're attentive to Jeremy's needs—much more so than my late wife."

"I've heard that Alyce was beautiful."

"Her interests centered only on herself. Not her daughter. Not her son." James searched Valentina's flushed face and attempted to read her thoughts. Perhaps if she had her own family to love and nurture …

He smiled. Certainly, his days would never be dull. Nor his nights.

He examined the small marking behind her ear. "Have you always had this birthmark? 'Tis in the shape of a horseshoe."

She forced away his hand. "I cover the birthmark with my hair. My mother said a horse kicked my father when she was pregnant with me and it left this mark. 'Tis disagreeable."

"There's nothing disagreeable about a spot that resembles a horseshoe."

Her grin was immense. Her light laughter took him back to happier days. She'd lived a humble life and bore her suffering with grace.

"Romany women believe in the stigmata," she said. The smile fled from her face. "However, the Rom asserted that the mark proved I was a *shuvani,* one of the wise ones."

His mind calculated his options. They could continue to live in England, as discreetly as he could manage. When the threat of influenza subsided, they'd move to his remote estate in Wales.

He used the birthmark as an excuse to kiss her there. "Does this 'stigmata' mean you're a witch?"

"'Tis said all Romany women are witches, which gives us the freedom to mold ourselves into any setting. A mocking gift to the Rom, to fit in everywhere and be wanted nowhere."

"You can be anything?"

"I can *be* anything." Her gaze sparked caution. "Not *do* anything."

His heart surged at the delightful idea of spending the rest of his life with her.

He raised her hands to his lips and kissed the inside of each palm. "Valentina, will you be my wife?"

* * *

VALENTINA JERKED BACK. The hay on the stable floor spun. She bent her head to conceal her confusion. No man had ever asked her to marry him, certainly not a gadje. She couldn't believe she'd heard him correctly, for the question had no home in her consciousness. James had no reason to want her—perhaps only as a servant. Yet he was offering her his name.

How could she ever dream of staying with this man when her sins against God ran as bottomless as the river? She wasn't enough, with all her failures, her scarcity of purpose other than survival.

James had often advised her to rely on God's grace and forgiveness.

Wasn't God's grace enough?

Aye, it should be. She could accept James' offer and abandon the idea of returning to her tribe.

Inwardly she shook her head. *Nay. She wasn't worthy of a man like him—landed gentry, a virtuous, respectable man.*

She gazed at the rough-hewn wall behind him. Her blurred vision changed the wooden boards to a sheet of washed-out brown.

James was watching her. "Surely you, of all people, can't be tongue-tied."

She averted her gaze. She didn't fear telling him about the rape. She feared his reaction. His admiration and respect for her would be gone. His eyes wouldn't glitter with amusement when they sparred.

And then, there was the half-truth she'd told him when reading his palm.

She swallowed a worn-out gulp. "First, I must speak to you about something."

Why had she assumed, with complete and utter foolishness, that she wouldn't have to explain her recklessness? Now she'd pay for it tenfold by losing his trust.

His hands held hers, gentle yet firm, heating her fingers. "You'll enjoy everything my wealth can provide, although we'll need to be discreet and cannot wed until we reach Wales."

She contemplated the conviction in his clear grey eyes.

Tell him. Her lungs weighed heavy, her breath came rocky. Heavy guilt at deceiving him berated her.

His lips touched hers. "I haven't asked you to witness my execution. I've asked you to marry me."

"A Gypsy wed to a Welsh gentleman," she hedged. "'Tis unthinkable."

He grinned. "Eventually, your tribe will come to accept me."

He'd sidestepped any declaration of love. Men in his position weren't concerned by such an impractical notion, although a small part of her had hoped he truly cared.

"And my son adores you." His hands slid up her arms and caught her shoulders. He was all male. His skin smelled of horse and sweat, and his lips were so enticing. As if hypnotized, she locked her fingers around his nape and gave in to the attraction.

He seemed to sense the moment she surrendered. With an effort that seemed to drain the power from his body, he stopped the kiss and leaned against the stable wall. His uneven breath told her that he, too, struggled for control.

"Your people will never respect me as your wife," she said.

He arched a brow and waited a beat. "We'll travel to Wales when the weather warms."

"I'm a Rom. I belong with my tribe and cannot leave England."

"Not anymore. Now you belong at my side."

At his side. As his wife.

She swallowed hard and locked her gaze on a chipmunk crawling through the dry straw at her feet. If she stared into James' eyes she would say aye, aye, aye, and press her face against his heart, pleading forgiveness for deceiving him with a half-truth.

Although she wouldn't do that, because she was a coward. She'd always been a coward.

She drew a heavy sigh. "I must return to my caravan where I'm best suited. My people are nomads and I'm one of them."

"You'll have a new life with me." For a second, susceptibility rang through his tone before the expression on his face veiled any further emotion.

A tremor quivered her lips where his fingers still rested. Ironically, she gripped his upper arms to stay afloat, the man who made her feel adrift in the middle of a murky river.

"You don't need to give me your answer yet," he said softly, despite the resolute, unreadable glint in his eyes.

Perhaps, just perhaps, she shouldn't start with herself when she gave a response. Perhaps she should start with God, and then the man she was falling in love with.

CHAPTER 11

Kon del tut o nai shai dela tut wi o vast.
He who willingly gives you a finger will also give you the
whole hand.
Old Romany saying

A film of smoke had been in the air for days.

Valentina leaned against the trunk of a wild cherry tree, the gummy tree wounds sticking to her back. She watched as the farm animals were butchered, one by one. Dried and salted meat would be ready to eat throughout the dreary winter months ahead. The tenants called November *blood month* for good reason. The smell of blood permeated the tiniest pores of her skin.

Groups of servants salted ducks by the smokehouse, reminding Valentina of the elderly women in her tribe. Romany women toiled day and night, similar to these women, fiercely clinging to their traditions and beliefs.

Valentina's thoughts drifted to James. Until the spring thaw, she would stay at his home. Traveling in wintry conditions was too difficult, and it might take her weeks to catch up with the tribe. Yolanda could decide at that time whether or not she would accompany her.

She shook her head. In truth, she knew much of her decision wasn't based on the difficulty of traveling, but on not wanting to leave James.

Only yesterday, during one of their daily walks, she'd given him advice on a decision concerning one of his tenants. Despite those walks, she'd recently felt his aloofness. He held her at a distance, his polite smile a wall she didn't have the courage to broach. Always, he was the elegant gentry, superbly dressed in grey tailored trousers and matching waistcoat, the master of all he appraised.

Sometimes, she thought she'd imagined that day in the stable. He'd never wanted her as his wife. Why would he? Then, she'd catch him watching her, his face displaying an affection that took her breath away. And she knew he'd meant every word and was waiting for her reply.

* * *

A MONTH PASSED. Except for Yolanda, the spacious upstairs hallway was deserted on an unusually warm and sunny December afternoon. The servants were all busy with their chores.

Wrapped in a gown of fine royal-blue wool, a smiling Yolanda made her way to the stairway landing humming a Christmas carol, "The Holly and the Ivy." She looped her linen undersleeves to create ruffles at her wrists. Her arm sling had come off a few days earlier.

"Will you help me decorate the hallway with Christmas

decorations?" Absently, she handed Valentina a bough of fragrant holly.

"Aye." Valentina smiled as she accepted the bough. "As long as you answer a question which has plagued me for weeks. Why did you venture so near the river the day you nearly drowned?"

Yolanda lost her smile and stopped singing. "I tripped. 'Twas slippery because of the rains, and I wasn't thinking."

"You weren't thinking," Valentina repeated, "because you were daydreaming. Most likely about Reginald."

"Aye, I think about him all the time. Are you still planning to return to the caravan in the spring? If so, you must realize 'twill be without me."

Yolanda said the words so nonchalantly, Valentina dropped her bough. These past few weeks, her sister had grown into a young woman with a mind as willful and exasperating as a newborn colt.

She wove a bough through the banister. "I see how attentive Reginald is toward you. Nonetheless, your involvement with him shouldn't continue."

"You spend hours with Mr. Colchester and I don't insist otherwise." The delicate lilt of Yolanda's challenge was encased in a tidy point. "Rumors about you two fly faster than falcons. He cares a great deal about you, and I doubt you notice anyone else is about when he's near."

Valentina expelled a breath and regarded her sister solemnly. *Now or never,* she encouraged herself. Taking a few seconds for composure, she set the holly branches aside and pulled Yolanda to sit with her on the carpeted landing. "I have two secrets to confide, both of which you must promise never to breathe a word to anyone."

Yolanda leaned forward. "You have my word." Her cheeks shone tanned and dusty in the patchwork sunlight filtering through the stained-glass window directly above them.

Valentina opened her mouth twice before she waded into the uncomfortable silence.

"Mr. Colchester has asked me to marry him," she finally said, surreptitiously watching her sister. She tried to fix a calm expression on her face, although the warmth moving up her cheeks was fast giving her away.

Happiness shone in Yolanda's velvet-brown gaze. "Valentina, that's wonderful."

"I'd never consent."

"Whyever not? Daj would approve because Mr. Colchester is a respectable and decent man. He can protect and properly care for you."

"Are you forgetting he's a gadje?"

Besides, Valentina silently rationalized, what was the point of caring for him if she was leaving in a few months? Wasn't that what the Rom did? They never stayed anywhere for long.

Yolanda arranged the holly branches in a neat pile and stood. With that determined march to her steps Valentina knew so well, Yolanda tromped to the stairs.

"Yolanda, where are you going?"

"I'll not listen to your excuses." She shook her head, wisely, as if she were an elder dispensing wisdom, then stepped back to Valentina. "He isn't the type of man to accept nay for an answer, though 'tis little wonder you're cautious. 'Tis said his circle of friends reaches to London."

Valentina visualized James looking impressively handsome in formal black evening dress, comfortable and smiling among the most elite members of London high society. No doubt the gentlemen invited his friendship, and the women longed to be held in his arms.

In a mist of glossy brown hair, Yolanda knelt beside Valentina. "You've turned pale. Why?"

"A man like him ... he'd never want me as his wife after ... If he knew—"

"You spoke of two secrets and marrying him is one. What is the other secret?"

Valentina sank her face in her hands. "Sometimes, I pretend it never happened. If I don't think about it, perhaps it will go away."

"Nothing goes away. Worries only fester unless you unburden yourself." Yolanda gave Valentina's fingers a short, emboldening squeeze. "Talk to me. Please."

"I don't know where to begin."

Conceivably, if her sister heard the wretched truth, she'd understand, and Valentina badly wanted to confess to someone. Exhaling, she tried to piece the explanation together. "The first night we arrived, I read his palm and—"

"And most likely you embellished your reading, the way you always do."

"Thank you for putting it so kindly." Valentina's eyes watered. She clasped her hands together on her lap. "You remember how frightened we were. All I had in my mind was finding you, returning to Daj and our tribe. So, when he requested I read his palm, I told him a half-truth."

"What did you say?" Yolanda's voice held a slight tremor. Slowly, she stood, pulling Valentina up along with her.

Valentina reached out to touch her sister, then drew back and hung her arms at her sides.

"He wanted a reply to his question about traveling to Wales to escape the influenza epidemic." Harder and harder to keep down, the familiar taste of remorse rose in Valentina's throat. She swallowed and focused on the gleaming wooden staircase. "I thought 'twas a silly game, he couldn't possibly believe anything I had to say. I was so angry ... so, I assured him he'd be safe in England."

"Isn't he a Christian?"

"Aye. Although he'd just returned from battle, and he's always so concerned about Jeremy."

"Perhaps he was seeking reassurance because there's so much hysteria whenever influenza is mentioned. He may have been desperate."

"A man like him would never feel desperate. He has a strong faith in God."

"Perhaps his faith faltered. Perhaps he felt overwhelmed because of his past sorrow and losing Beatrix. Everyone chatters about how hard he grieved when she died."

Valentina lowered her voice. "When I read his palm, I saw small lines of danger and a square on his travel line. Nonetheless, I told him *not* to travel to Wales."

"Why did you tell him that?"

"He seemed to want to hear something that would make him feel confident in his decision to stay here."

"Well, there's a simple solution. Tell him exactly what you've told me. We both know fortune-telling isn't true."

"I can't. Too many weeks have passed and I wouldn't know how to begin." Breathing frayed, anxiety raw, Valentina refused to sob. Crying, as she'd learned, solved nothing. Only determination and resolve brought about any results.

Outwardly, she held her stomach.

Inwardly, she screamed one silent question. *What should I do?*

Although she already knew and her sister was right. She would confess her half-truth to James. She was brave, she was fearless. Hadn't he told her those were the qualities he admired most about her? He didn't want her meek and timid, fearful of his anger.

Through James' faith, she was becoming a faithful follower of God. "'Whoever conceals their sins does not prosper, but the one who confesses and renounces them finds mercy,'" she whispered, adding, "Proverbs 28:13."

"I don't understand the Bible," Yolanda said.

"I'm beginning to understand it."

Valentina stood, solidly, at the ready.

She was through with false superstitions. Aye, she'd studied the Bible on so many evenings, alone in her chamber. That was the easy part. Now 'twas time to apply the Bible's teachings.

CHAPTER 12

I phuv kheldias.
The earth danced.
Old Romany saying

*E*yebrows arched like two broken arrows, Wiborow marched into Valentina's chamber the following afternoon.

"Choose a gown to wear for the Christmas Eve banquet this evening," she said. "Mr. Colchester ordered these gowns from Ireland for you and your sister." Two servants hoisted a trunk into Valentina's chamber, and then Wiborow led them back into the corridor.

"Ireland!" Yolanda's infectious enthusiasm spilled into the room, while Valentina scurried to open the trunk and sort through one extravagant gown after another. Amidst a kaleidoscope of taffeta and silk, Valentina fingered the fabric of each gown, the exquisite Irish lace. They were beautiful, the craftsmanship of the highest quality.

An hour later, prompted by Yolanda, Valentina chose the simplest gown of pale lavender with a square-cut bodice. She folded the others away, reflecting on how many starving Romany children could be fed with the cost of even just one gown.

She flattened the chosen gown over her curves, the silk fabric draping fetchingly over her full bust and rounded hips. Over the gown, she laced a see-through tunic in a vivid shade of lush green.

"Do lavender and green match?" Yolanda teased.

"Only at Christmas. I'll wear Mother's diklo to complement the colors."

Yolanda chuckled. "Yellow?"

As she stood, Valentina flashed a bright grin at her reflection. Inhaling deeply, she turned to the night table and reached for her hairbrush, sweeping it through her shiny black hair until her hair crackled. She fastened a pearl clip at the crown and let the unruly curls twist in ringlets down her back.

"We're Romany women," she said, satisfied with her appearance. "The starker the clash, the better."

Yolanda chose a pearl-dove empire-waisted gown lined in rich black velvet. She wrapped a glistening golden net around her hair to match the trim on her gown. Assisting Valentina with folding away the furs and lace strewn on the floor, Yolanda beamed. "We're wearing gowns made for royalty, in a gentleman's home, on the most festive night of the year!"

"Our tribe wouldn't recognize us."

"'Tis generous of Mr. Colchester to invite even his servants to the Christmas banquet."

"Aye." In some quiet place in her heart, Valentina reflected on the knowledge that this was James. This was his nature. He was strong and dependable and true to his word. Despite his position, he treated his servants and tenant farmers with respect. He showered Jeremy with care, and always made time for his son. And he was respected by all who knew him.

Of course, he was so handsome, with thick arched brows and dark lashes framing his grey eyes, his angular jaw and tousled raven-black hair. Although, 'twas what was within—his noble spirit and kind ways—that really mattered.

And tonight, she decided, after the Christmas banquet, she would tell him about her deceit and ask his forgiveness. She'd planned to speak about the fortune-telling incident after her conversation with Yolanda, but the right opportunity never presented itself.

No more excuses. Tonight was the night.

A few minutes later, the women stepped into the elegant ballroom and were greeted by a blast of heat from the blazing Yule log.

Scores of candles illuminated gleaming copper urns filled with greenery and splashes of red ribbons. A feast, resplendent with roasted peacocks, pheasants, swans, and partridges, more meats than Valentina had eaten in her lifetime, lined the side tables. Yolanda accepted a cup of wine from the ever-present Reginald.

Despite the fluttery feeling in her stomach, Valentina quickened her pace across the cream-colored carpet. Never had she worn a gown as grand or attended an affair as brilliant. She lifted her head and breathed in, her gold hoop earrings brushing against her shoulders. Hesitant, she searched the crowd for James.

He caught her gaze and rose to his feet. With courteous nods to the men surrounding him, he strode to her. His possessive gaze captured hers, pinching her breath and gripping her heart.

"You look beautiful tonight, cariad."

"Thank you." She bit back her exclamation of admiration.

James wore a variegated purple velvet waistcoat, edged in gold, offset by wine-colored breeches and low black boots.

The evening promised exhilaration, a night overflowing with magic. An enormous gemstone chandelier hung from the ceiling in the grandiose room, and the display of the ladies' vibrant gowns was reflected in the mirrored walls. The hum of laughter buzzed to a fever pitch, and expectancy hummed through Valentina's veins.

James tucked her fingers in the crook of his arm and guided her past a dozen carolers singing "Greensleeves," holding the final note for several beats. He waited for the exuberant applause to subside, leading Valentina to the far end of the room and curving one arm around her waist.

"Can you dance?"

"About as well as I can swim. And you cannot dance with me." She shook out the skirt of her lavender gown and stared past the wave of colorless faces. Well-balanced on a raised platform, the carolers opened their mouths into perfect Os, the horn player positioned the mouthpiece to his lips, and the music commenced with a lilting chord.

"You are the most exquisite woman in this ballroom tonight, and I can dance with whomever I choose." Genuine pride flashed in his eyes.

"You can't dance with a Gypsy woman. People will talk."

"Other people are not my concern." He swooshed her through the first few bars of an elegant dance, then effortlessly eased her onto a small outdoor alcove.

Although James had ignored his guests as they danced, Valentina had noted the contemptuous English faces. Distinguished nobles raised their eyebrows slyly, hiding their distaste beneath lively conversation and tinkling laughter.

The ballroom had shrunk, and Valentina was grateful for the cold air that greeted them on the alcove. Memories of her Romany life, so humiliating when compared to James' elegant life, came back in a rush. Mere inches separated her from James, but those inches contained two lives of enormous dissimilarities.

With a toss of her chin, she loosened the diklo, for it cut off her breath.

"Am I exquisite because I'm dressed in your fancy English clothes, Mr. Colchester?"

"My name is James." For a moment, his gaze narrowed. Bending his head nearer, he brushed his lips across her ear. "You are exquisite in anything you wear, although I like your Gypsy clothes best." His breath ravaged her sensitive earlobe and heat warbled down her neck.

The musicians played louder, the singers bursting to a climax, and James whirled her around the tiny space of the alcove. His well-muscled body glided with surprising grace as they danced, and his fingers tapped the rhythm of the lighthearted tune on her forearm.

She tried to follow his lead, although the alcove spun. "Please, you're dancing too fast." She laughed with pleasure and held his shoulders to keep her balance.

"Am I?"

The teasing affection on his face made her smile. "You must be the envy of every landed gentry because of your dance expertise and nimble tongue."

"Dancing is one of my hidden talents. Will you dance in my arms until sunrise now that you've discovered my secret?"

"Will I need to dance every dance?"

"I have other talents that I'll share with you when we grow tired of dancing." He challenged her with a gaze as intent as his voice. Bending his head, he smiled down at her as if she were very, very precious.

She met his gaze. "Thank you for a wonderful evening," she said quietly.

Two striking women in billowing floral percale and jeweled accent brooches swayed by the open doorway. They greeted James with deferential nods. Their behavior toward Valentina was prudently disguised behind false smiles, although gossip and malice couldn't be far behind.

Slowly, Valentina's self-assurance faded. Against her will, hot tears burned the back of her eyes. People's opinions shouldn't matter, but this night was magical. Everything mattered.

"I'll never be accepted into your world, Mr. Colchester," she murmured.

"Aye, you will. I give you my word." His slow, reassuring grin rendered her helpless. He gazed at her in a way he never had before—as if he would never let anyone hurt her.

A tingle warmed her body. The closest she'd ever come to happiness beckoned. This persuasive gentleman with his impeccable speech and refined manners wanted her as his wife, not as a lowly servant.

The instrumentalists added a drummer and bell player to their ensemble and slowed the tempo. Valentina gave a resigned sigh at the intricacy of the dance steps as James continually guided her.

"For a man of your height, you dance superbly and never miss a beat," she said.

"Take two steps to the right, not left, and follow my lead."

"All this effort to dance in a circle and begin again in the same place. My tribe dances to gay violins and broken tambourines. This type of dance is restricting."

He tightened his arms around her and drew her closer. "And you're a woman who doesn't like to be restricted."

Jeremy scampered past the door to the alcove. He spotted them and offered a quick wave in her direction.

Valentina touched James's sleeve. "Your son doesn't want to be restricted, either."

"So you've said."

Despite James' attempts to guide her, Valentina shuffled to the left. "Sorry, I think I stepped on your foot."

He grimaced before the sides of his mouth tugged up. "Not a problem, I have two."

"I hope I don't take him away from his studies."

"My foot? 'Tis quite intelligent and dances this particular dance quite well."

She covered her mouth to stifle her laughter, then placed her hands back on his shoulders. "Not your foot. Your son."

"Aye, of course." His low chuckle vibrated through her fingers. "And, nay, you don't take him away from his studies. He receives excellent instruction from his tutor every morning, so he can spend his free time with you. He'll begin formal schooling in a couple years, where he'll study Latin and mathematics."

"And then he'll be able to spend more time with other children."

"Perhaps."

She dragged her gaze from his and stared at the display of sugar confections the servants were arranging on a sideboard. The carolers burst into a rendition of the "Boar's Head Carol", and James led Valentina back into the ballroom. Then he hummed, loudly.

During the carol's refrain, he dispatched a servant standing close by. Placing one goblet of wine in Valentina's hand and taking another for himself, James resumed his humming, effectively discouraging any further conversation. By the fourth verse, his melody bore little resemblance to the original Christmas carol. Undeterred, he tapped his foot in time to the pounding drumbeat. On the other end of the room, Yolanda danced with Reginald, learning each new dance with self-confidence. Her dark hair bobbed through the crowd, and Reginald assisted when she missed a cue.

After the dance, they wandered to the tables to enjoy the feast—sumptuous supper meats, roasted thighs of turkey and raisin-filled festive breads.

Valentina shook her head. "I've never known a man so stubbornly opposed to ideas that weren't his own."

"Perhaps the lovely woman I am with is more stubborn."

"Now you can hear again?"

"If the musicians added a fiddle and triple harp, I'd sing all night, reliving my younger days in Wales." Youthful charm lit his expression over the rim of his goblet. "Truly, I like to sing, almost as much as I like to dance."

"Remind me to give you singing lessons," she teased.

"Remind me to give you dancing lessons."

The carolers began singing "Away in a Manger", and James and Valentina joined in. His rich baritone melded with her soaring soprano. Spicy sweet heat lulled her senses, her limbs warmed by the wine. She wanted to shout to the world how splendid she felt standing beside this tall, competent, refined gentleman.

When the song ended, his tone dropped to a whisper. "Valentina, there's a matter we must discuss. And you need to heed my words carefully, because your response means a great deal to me."

"There's something I need to tell you too." She meant to take a sip of her wine but was suddenly too nervous to drink it.

"May I speak first?" he asked.

"I hope you're not displeased by my singing."

"You sing like an angel. A Gypsy angel." He shook back his slightly unruly hair. His skin was tanned from all the time he spent outdoors with his son and the farmers. "We need to discuss a simple matter regarding my name. Please, please, always call me James."

"I will try."

"And I will continue to remind you, cariad." His eyes deepened to the charcoal grey color that always sent her senses into a tailspin.

She curled her fingers around her goblet and breathed in the heady scent of sweet wine. "I'm relieved the dance is over … *James.*"

"Good. I will reward your efforts by spending my days teaching you how to—"

"Dance," she finished.

His expression held a note of suggestive promises. "Once we are wed, I will fill your nights with dances and dreams." He held up a forefinger before she could protest. "Because if my memory serves me well, there is an offer I've made in a stable that awaits your reply."

Her brows drew together as she focused on his striking face. If only her hands would stop trembling. Her instinctive response was to ask him to hold her, so that she would be aware only of his strong muscled body protecting her while she shouted the answer he wanted.

Aye. Aye. Aye.

Aye, she would marry him.

Aye, she would cherish his son.

Aye, she would love him.

Her intrusive conscience snickered a rebuttal. *Not until you tell him the truth about the palm reading.*

"James, I—"

"Give me a moment."

She watched as he crossed the ballroom to refill their wine glasses.

Among his friends, James presented the perfect portrait of an urbane gentleman. This refined, undeniably attractive man had teased her about his foot and hummed an entire Christmas carol to her a short time ago. Wrapped in her musings, she misinterpreted the significance of Geoffrey standing beside a messenger boy by the doorway to the ballroom.

James unrolled the sealed paper the boy handed him, and his expression changed in a series too rapid to note, settling on acceptance.

"'Tis a dispatch for me to depart for war under Viscount Wellington," he announced, turning to his silent and stunned guests and servants. "The Portuguese are planning a siege against the French in Ciudad Rodrigo, Spain, and require British support."

"Tonight?" Geoffrey asked.

The messenger boy nodded.

Tonight?

Panic exploded, quashing Valentina's security. Her heart raced to keep up with her feet.

She hastened into the lively kitchen and leaned against the sink basin. The partridge roasting on a spit in the open fire made her heave. She bunched her hands together to fight off the nausea.

She was still there when Isabel, the head cook, raised her floury face and nodded in her direction as James strode through the kitchen. He'd already changed into his riding clothes—black breeches and a slate-colored hooded cloak—and emanated controlled authority and an aura of command.

The warm rush of pleasure surging through Valentina had nothing to do with the heat of the kitchen. He'd come to seek her. Her handsome, sophisticated gentleman.

To appear as if she hadn't noticed his arrival, she turned and started to clean the dirty mushrooms in the sink. His booted footsteps tap-tapped, tap-tapped, across the kitchen floor, and he stopped directly behind her. "I didn't realize mere mushrooms held such appeal." He leaned forward to drum his fingers along the edge of the sink.

She kept her hands in the dirty water.

"Turn around. I must depart."

His breath teased the back of her neck. Sweat trickled down her armpits. She glanced behind, taking in his broad chest, his muscular shoulders, his ever-present composure.

She jerked her hands from the water and wiped the grainy soil on her lavish gown. With an attempt at a smile, she swung around to face him.

"Promise you'll miss me when I'm away."

She hesitated and swung her hair away from her face. Her stomach was sinking. Her throat was swelling, the taste sickly sweet. "James, I ..."

His features darkened. Slowly, he ran his palms over her arms. "Aye?"

Her insides were shattering. "Another war awaits. Please be safe."

"We'll celebrate the holiday when I return."

"James, I am ..."

I am frightened for your welfare. Never in all her careful planning had she imagined *he* would leave his home before *she* did.

He nudged her into the dimly lit hallway. "You'll miss me more than I imagined. That brings me great pleasure." Boldly intimidating, his fingers outlined her lips in a deliberate, circular motion.

She tried for a flippant response, although when she went to speak, her voice failed altogether.

She cleared her throat. "I'm sorry you're forced to leave on Christmas Eve."

His nod was agonizingly tender and heartening. "I know these wars well enough, and I'll not be away longer than thirty days. Promise me you won't do anything foolish in the meantime. No jumping in rivers or leaping out windows."

She offered him a faint smile.

"Promise me." He cupped her chin, lifted her face and kissed her forehead.

Her throat tightened. "I promise." Her feelings were so conflicted, she truly considered

begging him to stay and bawling her fears into the smooth folds of his waistcoat.

"'Tis settled, then. Will you extend a proper farewell to seal our agreement?" He stroked her

back, calming her uncertainties. A fire kindled, spreading through her limbs, a curlicue flame.

Ineffective Romany endearments came to her lips, one resounding above the others.

Ves'tacha. Beloved.

She lifted her head to receive his kiss. His moist, solid mouth demanded a response. She relinquished control, because he would be leaving, because she had no control when he was near anyway. She stood on tiptoes and wrapped her arms around his neck.

"Tad." A familiar little voice carried through the hallway. James' lips trailed over Valentina's forehead, and she whirled as Jeremy came into view. She attempted to wiggle from James's grasp, but his grip stayed locked on her forearms.

Jeremy ran to his father and grabbed his leg.

James looked down at his son. "I must travel to London and will return soon." He released Valentina, crouched beside Jeremy, and hugged him. "Until then, I leave you with someone I trust."

"Then you will go on your way in safety, and your foot will not stumble," she murmured.

He gazed up at her. "Proverbs 3:23?"

"Aye." She stared at them both, one hand arrested on her lips, the other bunched at her side.

James stood. "You'll care for my son while I'm away?"

Jeremy beamed up at her with a whimsical smile and held out his arms. "Mam?"

Valentina blinked, recovering from James' surprising announcement. She would've taken care of Jeremy regardless. With one arm, she lifted Jeremy's slight body and steadied him on her hip.

"He can teach me how to play checkers better, although most likely, he'll still win."

James grinned and slipped on his tan riding gloves. A moment later, he was gone.

And her confession would have to wait.

CHAPTER 13

Ma-sh-llah!
As God wills!
Old Romany saying

A fortnight after James' departure, Roland sauntered into the kitchen while Valentina was preparing a poultice for a cook who'd burned her arm. He stretched his thickset arms over his head, exposing his fleshy, hairy stomach. "The weather is brilliant and I'm in the mood for a good, rousing fight."

Recalling the mass of rumbling clouds she'd seen earlier, Valentina wondered what brilliant weather he was referring to. The sun hadn't shone for days, and a stark wind blew tree limbs to the ground in defeat.

Clare sliced a loaf of finely ground white bread and handed him a thick slice. "Tobias and Geoffrey are overwhelmed with their responsibilities. Mr. Colchester has been gone for over two weeks."

With a barmy smile and a wink, Roland kissed Clare's cheek, as if they were privy to a secret.

Valentina ducked her head to hide her smile and reached for her cup of morning tea. The house droned with anticipation of an impending wedding between Clare and Roland. No purple bruises had appeared on Clare's arms of late, and the old ones were fading. Hopefully, Valentina thought, the beatings had ceased.

At midday, though, Roland trudged back into the kitchen and complained of a severe headache, quaking so violently the words came in spurts. He refused the food Clare set before him.

Clare threw off her linen apron and guided him to the servants' quarters in the attic, and then ran to fetch Valentina, who was reading in her chamber. As they covered Roland with heavy quilts, he started coughing.

Nay. The breath in Valentina's chest fluttered, as if a host of bats awoke in a cave with nowhere to fly. She felt Roland's forehead. Too warm.

"He never gets sick," Clare said. "What could possibly be the matter?"

Doubt swamped Valentina's body, and she wiped the sweat from the back of her neck. "He may be unwell," she said tentatively.

Of course, he couldn't be. And even if he was unwell, certainly 'twas not influenza.

She offered to stay with Clare and sit with him, and by midafternoon his thirst was unquenchable. His reddened gaze darted restlessly. "I need to sleep …"

From her perch on a high stool by his side, Clare flung off his quilts and cooled his feverish skin with wet linens. "No sleeping. I'll sing to keep you awake."

Day turned to night. Roland's condition worsened. In between charming English songs and cheerless ballads, he sputtered a last, erratic gasp and died.

Valentina's feet turned to lead, and she imagined the planks holding the floor together would cave from the weight of the burden she carried.

Clare wailed to the agitated servants hovering near. "Wake him. Please."

"He's departed to meet his maker," Wiborow said, her voice stale and strained.

Her face expressionless, Lowdie wrung her apron. "Clare, Roland favored you over all the other women." Her Welsh brogue sounded soft and utterly unconvincing.

"He died so quickly. What ailed him?" another servant asked, her question ringing as a clarion.

Valentina squeezed her eyes shut, frantically attempting to calm her worst fears.

Isabel, the head cook, swayed back and forth, her glassy blue eyes confused and afraid. "It could be influenza."

The innocent conjecture created an immediate hush to a room that had previously shrieked anxiety.

Panic-stricken faces turned toward Clare, Roland, and then Valentina.

Sweat beaded on her forehead. "Don't be alarmed." Her voice fractured. "I will—"

What would she do, exactly?

She jostled past the servants and staggered down the stairwell and toward her chamber.

Her heart thrashed so violently, she couldn't catch her breath.

'I leave you with someone I trust.' James' words to his son resounded in her ears.

He depended on her to protect Jeremy. She groped along the wall to her chamber and slid to the floor just inside the doorway. And then she prayed until the indigo evening crept to midnight. When Valentina glanced out her bedchamber window, a surly mist had settled over the rooftops of the tenants' homes, and winds ghosted across the lawn.

* * *

BEFORE DAWN, Yolanda burst into Valentina's chamber. "Roland died?"

"Aye." Valentina jerked upright on her bed. "I've been praying."

High color stained Yolanda's cheeks. She studied Valentina as if she were a strange being whom she no longer recognized. "When Mr. Colchester returns, tell him everything. You should've told him before he went off to battle."

"I intended to, although he left before I had the chance." Valentina flung off the bedcovers, stood and breathed deeply. Walking over to her sister, she smoothed a wisp of hair escaping one of Yolanda's plaits. The tang of fiery black pepper and garlic no longer clung to Yolanda's hair. Lately, Yolanda smelled of lavender and fine wine, the scents of an English woman living in a gentleman's home.

Yolanda jerked from her touch. She grabbed a bright-pink pillow, squeezing until it lost its shape. "You may not believe you have a gift, but I do and I'm frightened."

Suddenly aware she hadn't seen Yolanda at all the previous evening, Valentina asked, "Where were you last night when Roland died? Were you with Reginald?"

"Aye." Yolanda straightened to her full length of five feet. "And I love him."

* * *

THE JANUARY DAYS passed in eternal droplets, splatters with no beginning nor end. Night after night, Valentina rocked

Jeremy to sleep. She sang Romany lullabies from her child-hood, each song a reminder of a long-ago life.

"Your father will come home soon," she assured the boy each night he snuggled his head in the crook of her arm. She enunciated clearly, encouraging him to focus on her lips so that he might understand her words. And then she prayed with him. James had said he wanted Jeremy to understand God was close and always available.

She'd begin their prayers by thanking God, then pointing out things in Jeremy's chamber that Jeremy was thankful for. She'd end with, "Heavenly Father, we come to you needing your healing hand. Guide us toward health and wisdom. In your name we pray. Amen." With a warm hug and kiss, she'd tuck Jeremy into bed and wait until he was asleep.

* * *

On the Monday of the third week since James' departure, Valentina spent the afternoon digging through the garden, the herbs brief and coated with snow. The sun was setting when the hushed sound of men's voices came toward her. Tobias, a footman of medium build with brown hair and light-framed spectacles, strode toward her with Geoffrey. She regarded Tobias as friendly, dependable, and honest.

"Geoffrey is taking a small group of men and riding toward London, then on to Spain," Tobias told her. "We're summoning Mr. Colchester back to Ipswich."

"Thank you, God." Valentina breathed her first relieved breath in weeks.

When the house quieted that night, she retreated to her chamber and sat on the bed. Her thoughts were of James, always of James. She could still see the pride in his gaze when he'd danced with her at the Christmas banquet, his playful smile, his genuinely thoughtful way of listening to her when she spoke. He could have chosen any woman as his wife. Yet, he had chosen her.

Clutching her diklo as a drowning person gropes a lifeline, she whispered the words she would say when next they met. "James, I made a mistake, and I need to be honest about something I did that was very, very wrong. I'm sorry and take full responsibility for my rashness. Please forgive me."

She followed the imagined scene to its inevitable conclusion.

At first, he might be at a loss for words. He'd look down, or away, or he might study her,

his gaze unfocused. Eventually, despite her explanations, his posture would stiffen and he'd refuse to respond. And then he would dismiss her from his life.

She leaned back against the headboard and squeezed her eyes shut. Why could she not face the life she would be forced to lead without him?

She tried to sit upright and carry her guilt, her regret, her sorrow, but she couldn't. The pain was too heavy. Her chin quivered, her head sank onto her chest. And then she cried. Violent sobs wracking her insides, so fierce she feared her heart would splinter.

CHAPTER 14

Mandat tsera tai kater o Del mai but te avenge tumenga.
From me a little money, but may God give you plenty.
Romany saying

*A*cutely aware he was little more than an obedient soldier in another ceaseless war, James fought bravely throughout the long, dark nights. The siege on Ciudad Rodrigo was over, the fortress' walls were blasted by heavy artillery, and the fortress was successfully stormed. He boarded a British Squadron gunboat from Spain to England, then retrieved his horse. On his ride back to Ipswich, he stopped at a nobleman's townhouse, Lord Stephen Standish, in London. He was immediately offered a bed, clean clothes, and the invitation to stay as long as he liked. There was a party that evening at another nobleman's house up the road, and James spent the time socializing with the dazzling and pompous upper class. He'd forgotten how boring they were, prattling about the petty dalliances of the rich and privileged.

Brazen, lavishly dressed ladies approached him to express their condolences over his late wife's death. They all looked alike with dainty hands and fair complexions. They all dressed alike in their absurdly elaborate gowns. They all talked alike in persnickety, ladylike lilts.

No one had honeyed skin. No one had sparkling emerald eyes, nor tantalizing retorts to his teasing questions. Because no other woman was Valentina.

Leaving the party, James paced the corridors, decked with evergreens. He stared out the mullioned windows at the banks of the River Thames, blanketed in a cold, wintry fog. Heavy clouds rolled overhead, successfully blocking out the moon.

He tossed back his wine and glanced impatiently at his watch. He'd leave tomorrow afternoon, a day earlier than he'd planned. Wryly, he rebuked himself for acting like an infatuated schoolboy, driven by an unreasonable keenness to see Valentina again.

What a stubborn woman she was, refusing to give him an answer to his marriage proposal. By now, she'd probably listed several more reasons why she couldn't marry him. His gorgeous, spirited Gypsy woman.

He knew, by the way she responded to his kisses and caresses, that she desired him.

And he desired her.

When he returned, his only desire was that she would love him as much as he loved her.

Love? He frowned into his empty goblet. Then, with a lengthy, sardonic sigh, he acknowledged the truth. He was in love with Valentina.

* * *

THE FOLLOWING DAY, James politely admired the family portraits hanging on his host's walls. Preparations were well underway for the evening dances and masqued entertainment. The ballroom would quickly fill for a second party, reminding James of his own Christmas Eve banquet, dancing with an audacious and laughing Valentina.

He stood in the drawing room, avoiding the crush in the ballroom, when Lord Dermot, a dignified, older man, caught his gaze. The viscount had been a longtime acquaintance of James' family.

"So good to greet you again, Colchester," Lord Dermot said with amiable geniality.

Not happy to be taken away from his reflections of Valentina, James sipped his heavily spiced wine, hoping to quench his thirst for her. He swished the wine in his mouth, swallowed and grimaced. He'd never liked the taste of nutmeg and cloves. He liked his wine dark and bitter.

"And you, Dermot." He set the silver goblet on a nearby tray, grabbed a slice of syrupy apple, and dismissed an overbearing server hovering near his elbow.

Lady Dermot minced toward them, taking pretentious steps past the wide expanse of eight bay windows that overlooked the street. When she arrived, her ample chest heaved from the exertion of her short promenade. "So sorry, Mr. Colchester, to hear about your late wife's untimely death. A terrible disease, this influenza. Once it gets hold, it seldom will let go."

James raised her gloved hand and kissed it. "'Tis a pleasurable greeting, Lady Dermot, that I, too, extend."

"How is your son? Still deaf as a post, I presume. He must miss his twin sister terribly."

Lady Dermot's genteel accent seemed too cultured to be asking such unintelligent questions. And her eloquently arched eyebrows were raised a tad too high.

A persistent, irritating cadence drummed in James' temple, and he gave a not-so-subtle shake of his head. "Thankfully, he's in good health. Still, I must take offense. My son may be deaf, but his affliction doesn't restrict him."

He wouldn't be lured into discussing Jeremy nor eyeballed by Lady Dermot's pitying stares, and he wouldn't tarnish his precious daughter's memory by speaking her name aloud.

"Because your children were twins, they were surely quite close," Lady Dermot said.

James replied with a cool semblance of politeness. "My son thrives in the country. The forests are fresh and clean, not tainted by the filth of the London streets."

Lady Dermot fanned her rapidly reddening face. "Good heavens, our city is clean."

"You reside far from civilization, Colchester." Lord Dermot clapped James on the back. "London offers the finest food, wine, and women. You cannot mourn your wife's death forever, although I can understand—"

"I assure you, Dermot, I do not mourn my late wife." James half-smiled as Lord Dermot's condolences died on his lips.

"Our city physicians are most skilled and may be able to treat your son's deafness," Lady Dermot inserted in a helpful tone.

Nobility and wealth, James decided, was not a true indicator of class.

"I do not believe my son needs a physician. However, I will consider your advice." James pretended to give the matter some thought by tapping two fingers on his chin and looking pensive.

He nodded absently to stray servants as they strolled past him carrying silver trays laden with neglected food. He glanced at the half-eaten hard-boiled eggs and discarded pomegranate seeds. His gaze fixed on the elaborate marble staircase, envisioning Valentina descending the stairs in her colorful Gypsy clothes as a regal princess, looking heart-breakingly gorgeous.

Why was she so wary of becoming his wife? She was proud, yet so fearful of wagging tongues.

He wanted to begin a new life with her in Wales, on his secluded Welsh estate—far from the prying eyes of the English aristocracy. He wanted her to be a mother to Jeremy.

Not in a month, or a year, or however long it might take her to come to a decision.

He wanted her now, because he was tired of waiting.

In his heart, affection and tenderness erupted, the feelings so strong that they staggered him. He cleared the odd lump in his throat. She was smart, selfless, brave, and bold, and he couldn't wait a moment longer to return to her.

He regarded the last trace of wine from his goblet and set it on a nearby tray.

"In a hurry, Colchester?" Lord Dermot inquired.

James forced a polite grin. "I've been gone from Ipswich far too long."

He turned and strode through the hallway, passing several pairs of hastily raised oval spectacles. He ignored the greetings as he passed. He was too busy trying to calculate how many hours it would take to reach his estate if he rode all night.

CHAPTER 15

Gadje Gadjensa, Rom Romensa.
Gadje with Gadje, Rom with Rom.
Old Romany saying

*L*ord Standish had encouraged James to ride escorted, but James declined and rode on alone. He didn't want anyone with him, questioning the stop he intended to make, and he didn't want to be slowed by another rider. Besides, Albern, his horse, provided perfect company. He understood James' commands and didn't speak.

As he rode, his thoughts returned again and again to Valentina.

Sensual and breathtaking, she was a natural beauty. She had the curves of Venus and the mischievous grin of a cherub, although it was her inborn charm and grace he most admired. Her witty intelligence and impertinent humor were so much like his. When she sparred with him and met his banter with a sharp quip, he laughed out loud. And it felt good to laugh again.

What made her deny the attraction that he knew she felt for him? Each time he held her in his arms, her body would quiver as she unconsciously molded herself to him. What stopped her from accepting his offer besides her inflexibility to accept him—her preconceived notion that just because he was a gadje, he wouldn't respect the Romany culture? As a member of English society, he was certainly class conscious, although his Christian beliefs negated prejudice. The Bible passage from Galatians went through his thoughts: "There is neither Jew nor Greek, there is neither slave nor free, there is no male or female, for you are all one in Christ Jesus."

Riding northeast toward Ipswich, James made his way through an intricate maze surrounding a nobleman's house on the outskirts of London. Bathed in an icy landscape, a fountain in the central courtyard sat silent. Precise configurations of plants, flowers, and shrubs sat dormant under a thin coating of snow. Several gardeners gathered fallen twigs, apparently taking no notice of him.

Before he'd left for battle, there was much he'd wanted to settle with Valentina—including

their move to Wales in the spring. He'd willingly accept the inevitable shock from his peerage because of his marriage to a Gypsy woman. Nonetheless, he had to think of his own happiness, and the well-being of his son.

He grinned at the image of her submissively complying when he demanded an answer to his proposal from her. Perhaps, he'd need to persuade her so she wouldn't refuse. First, he'd kiss her until her breathing centered only on him. Then he'd bury his face in the intoxicating fragrance of her silken hair. And then she would say ... aye.

By nightfall, he watched for the Gypsy encampment he'd spotted when he'd ridden weeks earlier, finally catching a glimpse of a campfire through a thick patch of forest. He crossed a stream, his horse's hooves muffled by the slush of melting snow.

When he reached the camp, he pulled back on his horse's reins and stared.

At the center of the camp, a group of Gypsy women danced on the frozen grass. With a devil-may-care attitude, they swayed their hips in time to rattling tambourines and their quickening tempo. James drew a lengthy, shaky breath as he imagined Valentina dancing like this for him —privately.

Four Gypsy men were seated around the campfire. They studied James with wary expressions and narrowed eyes. One woman tended to a rabbit roasting on a wooden spit. Her hand froze in midair while she subjected James to unblinking scrutiny.

"We're not causing any harm, sir," an elderly man with a grizzled white beard said.

All the men exchanged inscrutable glances. James understood that a gadje riding into a camp didn't bode favorably for a tribe of Gypsies.

One of the men stood. "Is anyone riding with you, sir?"

James had no intention of giving the men the impression he rode alone. He surveyed the destitute campsite, dismounted and tethered his horse's reins to a gnarled tree. "I'm here to ask some questions, not to cause unease. My men are not far behind me."

Keeping a prudent watch on the Gypsy men, James retrieved a coin from his cloak. He approached the campfire and handed the coin to the elder who'd spoken first. "I'm willing to pay for the answers I seek."

The man stuffed the coin into his torn shirtsleeve. "Happy to oblige, then. Drink first, questions later."

As if by an unspoken agreement, the tribe relaxed. Several

men shared a jug of brandy and gestured for James to join them. He accepted their offer and took a swig, then lifted the jug in a gesture of friendship.

After the jug had been passed several times, James sat back and regarded the group. These people were Valentina's people. Independent, humble and determined.

He kept the thoughts close and said, "A Gypsy woman of my acquaintance is to be married. Are there any special rituals for a betrothal?"

A dark-bearded man broke the stunned quiet. "Aye, although first the man must pay for the honor of marrying the bride. *Lowe k-o_vast, bori k-o grast.*" He laughed and translated, "Money in hand, bride on horse."

"How much money?"

"As much as a man can afford. Isn't that always the way when courting a woman?" The bearded man howled with glee, slapping his knee at his own jest. "Some women are worth more than others," he continued. "The groom pays the bride's parents after he haggles for the best price. All parents want the most money they can get for their daughter, although the groom wants to offer the least. Otherwise, the marriage won't be profitable for him."

One younger woman, wearing a swirling orange and red embroidered blouse, and opulent headdress, shook her head in feigned disagreement and tossed her glossy ebony hair behind her shoulders. She bent and tasted a fatty broth cooking over an open fire, licking her fingers and sneaking quick glances at James. The aromas of fennel and spicy garlic, of sweet licorice and foreign spices, reminded him of Valentina, and how much he wanted to get back to her.

Gazing at the campfire, he asked quietly, "Suppose this woman's parents are both dead?"

"The next male relative would speak for her," the elder replied. "If everyone agrees about the wedding, then we have a *pliashka,* a betrothal ceremony. First, the groom's father takes a bottle of brandy and wraps it in a handkerchief."

The man beckoned the young woman. "Miriah, give me your ribbon." He grabbed the moss-green satin ribbon the woman pulled from her hair. "To this, we attach gold coins and make a necklace." He turned to James with a smile that displayed two rows of decayed teeth. "Do you have any extra coins to spare, sir, so I may show you how to make a *pliashka?*"

"Aye." James dropped the gold coins he carried into the man's palms.

The man polished them between his aged fingers. "Miriah, get a needle and thread and attach these coins to the ribbon."

Without a word, Miriah took the coins and ribbon and disappeared into a tent. She came out in a reasonably short time and handed the elder the necklace as he was explaining other Romany wedding traditions to James, including the fact that although Romany men were allowed to marry outside their culture, Romany women were not.

"Because 'tis the women who keep the Rom culture alive for the next generation," the elder explained, shoving the jug aside and grabbing the necklace from Miriah. "The future bride wears this necklace, which symbolizes the bond of marriage."

"I'd like to give her this necklace for the betrothal," James said.

The elder's forearms ticked beneath his mismatched sleeves. He exchanged glances with the other Gypsy men still seated on the log. "Who is this woman, sir? Does she have merit?"

"Of course, and she's very beautiful." James glanced around. It dawned on him that the murmurings of the Gypsy men had risen.

"All Romany women are beautiful," the elder replied.

A pair of capricious feminine eyelashes fluttered. Miriah bent to brush away the mud sticking to the bottom of one bare foot and smiled at James in much the same way Valentina did when she worked in the herb garden.

"Beauty is least important," the elder was saying. "Romany men judge a woman by her health, her stamina."

"This particular woman fears nothing and is very strong."

"Be warned. The stronger the woman, the stronger her temper."

James answered with an appreciative chuckle. "Of that, I am fully aware."

"Men like a woman with a little fire, aye?"

James gave his riding cloak an emphatic shake and stood. "To whom do I pay the bride price?"

The burliest man in the group rose, and several women who had peered from their tents grabbed children by the shoulders and pulled them to the fringes of the camp.

James' heart pounded in double time. In his restless preoccupation to learn more about Valentina's heritage, he'd let down his guard. Glancing around, he fingered the sheath of the knife concealed in his cloak.

"This Romany woman who is to be married—is she someone we might know?" The elder held out his outstretched palm and indicated to each man to do the same.

"Nay." James kept his tone friendly as he assessed the men.

More men, emerging from their tents for the first time, sauntered toward the fire, encircling it. Not even on the battlefield had James witnessed such menacing hatred directed solely at him.

"Do you have a coffer full of gold to make a finer neck-lace?" the dark-bearded Gypsy asked. "Gold can aid us in hiding yer secret of this mysterious bride, *Mr. Gentleman.*" He grabbed a branch from the ground and snapped it at James. Mouth hard, glare deadly, he spat, "We recognize you high and mighty gadje anywhere."

James reached for his knife. *Nay.* He didn't want to fight these men.

"Don't do anything you'll regret," he warned.

"We're protecting our own against the likes of you." The largest man with thick sausage-like fingers struck James in the chest, knocking him to the ground.

Furious contempt at his foolishness pushed James to his feet. He thrust a rock-hard jab to the man's fleshy nose. The Gypsy rubbed his nose, now bent to the side, and his eyes widened at the blood between his fingers. He grabbed a heavy branch, heaved it over his head, and swung. James ducked and grabbed hold of the man's thighs, forcing them both backward.

A rickety tent collapsed beneath them, the wooden frame shattered. The man's eyes rolled up and he twitched as he fell unconscious.

James' stomach bottomed, his breathing a shouted curse as he fumbled for his knife. It eluded his grasp, and he willed himself up.

The other Gypsies closed their circle around him. Years on the battlefield kept him upright and alert. He launched forward and connected with a vicious pair of cannonball fists.

"Ain't used to fighting with your hands, *sir?*" a man shouted. He yanked James' arm with such brutal strength, a shooting pain crippled his wrist.

His thin, chastising breath came with the same whispers. *Valentina. Valentina.*

Infatuation had distorted his reason.

One of the larger men kicked and kicked and kicked and kicked and kicked.

James' mouth choked with mud. Stop. He wasn't dead. Pray.

He prayed silently, on and on, holding onto a sense of control and peace.

* * *

JAMES KEPT HIS EYES CLOSED, aware of the angry pain mushrooming in his skull. Groggy images floated and blackened, and his mouth sucked in breath after squalid breath. He felt the weight of a heavy pendant around his neck. Whenever he tried to touch it, it swung out of reach.

Squeezing his eyes shut to control the pain, he staggered to his feet. Blood ran down his throat. Overhead, a murky stream of stars obscured the nightmarish twilight. He wobbled, fell back into the slushy snow, and vomited. Making his way to his horse, he tried to mount Albern, but the effort was too much. Wrapping his cloak around him, he collapsed into the snow.

He woke as dawn broke, and he could make out a group of men riding toward him. He expected the ghostly images to disappear, for they were familiar men.

Geoffrey reached him first and dismounted. "Mr. Colchester?" Peering up at his face, James noted that Geoffrey's gaze had dimmed to cautious shadows.

"Do I look as bad as all that?"

"Worse."

"Help me stand."

"Tell us who did this."

His men weren't moving. They remained on their horses like silent statues.

"What is it?" Apprehension sparked inside him like an untended fire, leaving him burned and weak. Grateful for

Geoffrey's steadiness, James tried to hold his body erect. "Have you all lost your tongues?"

Geoffrey cleared his throat. "Tobias and I agreed that you needed to come back to the estate immediately." He lifted his palms, ever so slightly, attempting a shaken explanation.

"Is someone attacking us?" James struggled for a semblance of understanding. "If so, then why aren't you there protecting the estate?"

"'Tis not who, Mr. Colchester, but what." The elder man's fingers dug into James' arms. His gaze sobered. "You see, the wretched influenza ..."

James tried to swallow the dried lump in his throat, rancid where the dirt stuck, tiny trickles of blood threatening to choke him. "Is anyone dead?"

"Roland."

James shook off Geoffrey's assistance, conscious of a roaring in his ears overtaking all rational reasoning. "Jeremy is safe?"

Geoffrey wet his lips. "Aye."

"And Valentina?"

"She is also safe," Geoffrey stared at James' throat, then at the ground. The expression on his leathery face changed from a guarded mask to one of disbelief, causing James to flounder for the pendant around his neck.

Several gold coins swung from a ribbon. He felt the coldness of the coins, the smooth satin of the ribbon.

Then his knees buckled.

CHAPTER 16

Mashkar le gajende leski shib si le Romenski zor.
Surrounded by the gadje, the Rom's tongue is his only
defense.
Romany saying

*B*ooted footsteps and distraught whispers
resonated throughout the front hallway as
servants scurried and announced Mr. Colchester's
homecoming.

Valentina sat on a high-backed chair in the nursery and
rocked Jeremy, suppressing the urge to race down the stairs
and greet James. Jeremy snuggled closer—an encouraging
sign he might sleep through the night. She waited several
extra minutes, then eased him onto his bed. Tucking him
under his favorite blanket, she kissed him good night.

She tiptoed out of Jeremy's chamber, her gown brushing
against the carpeted floor. The downstairs hall had hushed
and she went directly to the privacy of her chamber. Too

tired to take off her gown, she slipped into bed. Lying on her side, she propped two snowy-white pillows behind her, pulled her knees up to her chest, and stared at the low fire burning in the grate.

At daybreak, she would tell James about the fortune-telling and be done with it once and for all. Aye, she'd tell him at daybreak. Dead tired and grateful for her comfortable bed, she burrowed beneath her wool coverlet and closed her eyes. James had returned. All was well.

* * *

SOMEONE WAS WATCHING HER.

Valentina tried to peer beneath her heavy lids and force her mind to focus. The weight of a sleep-deprived haze dragged her back into unconsciousness.

She awoke a second time, dimly aware of a strong hand sliding along her cheeks, outlining her mouth. She rolled onto her side and inhaled a whiff of dirt and sweat and ... dried blood!

A scream surfaced in her throat and she clutched the wool coverlet to her chest. Blinking in bleary bewilderment, she stared at a familiar, handsome face. In the flickering fire-light, James' battered face peered down at her.

"James." She raised her hands to stroke his cheeks. "What happened?"

He shoved her hands away. "I haven't given you permission to touch me."

"Permission?" A twist of tension took root along her spine.

"Of course, you've never asked permission to do anything in your life." He seemed to be speaking to himself. "What could I possibly be thinking?"

"Are you foxed?"

"Not as much as I'd like." His tan breeches, linen shirt and waistcoat were ripped and grimy, damaged beyond repair. He gestured to his clothes, as if by way of an explanation. "I returned earlier this evening."

"I—I know."

"Yet you didn't come downstairs to greet me."

"I planned to seek you come the morrow."

"Were you waiting until then to inform me that influenza has already killed one of my men? Or that some of my tenants have run off in a panic?"

She fixed her stare on the silver-white canopy above her bed.

He gripped her hands. "How did Roland contract influenza?"

Her throat worked to find air. "Are you mad? Release me!"

"I must be mad to listen to a fortune-teller." Pointedly, he wrenched his hands from her and stepped back.

She bolted out of bed and darted for her chamber door, intending to place as much distance as possible between herself and this bruised stranger who'd taken James' place.

His swift strides echoed behind her, and she whirled to face him.

A storm brewed in the depths of his silver eyes. Then his features softened. "You're trembling."

"You're scaring me."

"I'm sorry." He wobbled back toward the bed and stepped on the untied laces of his boots. He tripped and landed on the bed with a groan.

"Have you been in a brawl?"

His sharp laugh ended with a grimace.

"Did you quarrel with …Were your battles difficult?" She rationalized that he was undoubtedly exhausted, prompting his unreasonableness.

"If the battles were difficult, I assure you, I wouldn't be here."

"How were you hurt, then?"

"I received a message from your 'kindhearted' Gypsy kinsmen."

"What message? Why?"

"Because I rode into their camp with an inquiry."

"Why?" she persisted as she moved toward him, her questions coming so rapidly she scarcely shaped her words. "Did you attack them?"

"Do I look like I attacked them?"

"The Rom would never strike a gentleman unless provoked. We all know the punishment—a lifetime in an unforgiving English prison." Her chin lifted. "You must've threatened them."

"Am I such a threat to a tribe of Gypsies who far outnumbered one man?"

"My people are fair and caring and ..." Two dozen denials skirted through her mind. She fumbled for answers, anguish cramping a warning in the pit of her gut. "Dear heavens, they did this to you?" She lifted her fingers to stroke his face.

James flinched and jerked away.

Brushing back tears, she scrambled to the washbasin to fetch a linen cloth. "What were you inquiring about?" Her real question, the one unspoken, ricocheted through the chamber: What were you inquiring about *in a Romany camp?*

She kept her back to him. Her conscience took the lead in blaming herself for the danger he'd faced.

He lifted a hand. "I don't need you to tend to my wounds, Valentina."

"I insist." She wrung cold water from the cloth and swallowed a frayed, futile sigh as she turned to him. "Can you please tell me what happened?"

"I rode out of London alone and into a Gypsy encampment. You are asking a lot of questions tonight, and I have questions of my own."

He continued to perch on the edge of her bed, swinging one leg much too casually.

"James, I must tell you something," she blurted. She paused and swallowed. After taking this monumental step to finally initiate this conversation, she couldn't stop now. When she read palms, she was an expert at telling people what they wanted to hear. She was a master at outsmarting an unsuspecting farmer and stealing all his chickens. Why couldn't she speak up now when it mattered most?

Be brave and meet his gaze.

She dug her fingernails into the cloth. No words came, only a blur of tears.

You've rehearsed this a thousand times. Say "I loathed you when we first met. Now all I want to do is love and protect you." Speak. Say the words.

He expelled a ragged breath. To her shock, he began the conversation for her. "That first night, when I asked you to read my palm, I had reason to believe you were a fortune-teller of merit. In hindsight, I never should have disregarded my religious beliefs. Why did I want to take a shortcut and not believe God?"

Heat wicked up her face. Aye, she was good—very good, at reading fortunes. And it had all been a game to her to fool the gadje. However, what mattered now was honesty and integrity. Where once she had fiercely intended to hold onto her Romany way of living, now all she wanted to hold onto fiercely was him and a humbling God.

"The future is God's to know, not us." She glanced at James' hard jaw line and spoke rapidly. "God decides every-thing in His own time. So, if you wanted to see your future, you should have gone to your chapel and prayed directly to Him for guidance, not ask me."

"I did ask Him. He hasn't answered me since Beatrix died."

Neither resignation nor anger showed in his expression, only sorrow. And the sorrow broke her heart.

Filling her lungs with air, she squared her shoulders and stepped from the washbasin.

His eyes closed. The muscles in his arms knotted. "Don't," he ordered.

She gazed at his pale, tortured features and closed the distance between them. *Please let me touch you,* she silently pleaded. "Your wounds need to be washed," she said aloud, "and you know I don't obey orders well."

He didn't protest. She stripped off his slate-colored waistcoat, unlaced his muddy shirt and slid the shirt down his back. His wounds had been bound with strips of cloth, which she carefully removed. Trying not to put too much pressure on his gashes, she kept her motions careful and measured.

His breath was shallow and quick on her fingers; his heart thudded hard and fast.

Using light strokes, she wiped the moist cloth along his bearded neck.

He grimaced and stretched his legs out on the bed. His salty sweat pervaded her nostrils. She lowered her hands, slowly, to wash his chest.

He caught her wrists. "I went to my son's chamber tonight and watched him sleep. He's unharmed by all that's happened?"

"Aye."

James expelled an infinite breath. Deep lines etched around his mouth. "I try to protect him."

"He's had a difficult time without you. I've had … a difficult time … without you."

In her secret heart, Valentina had the irrational hope that James would whisper reassurance and encouragement, assuring her he'd had a difficult time the past few weeks without *her*.

Instead, he dropped her wrists, rubbed the bruises on his forearms and groaned. "Sometimes, I don't understand your culture. I want to understand. I try …"

This proud man who'd bravely returned from battle—her kinsmen had hurt him so much.

Unable to keep the choked sobs from her voice, she asked, "May I tell you a story while I wash your wounds?"

Slowly, thoughtfully, he answered, "Aye."

Her throat ached, her vision blurred. Determined to continue, she drew a breath.

"Many years ago, Daj taught me a cure for influenza." A poignant kaleidoscope of images floated in Valentina's mind's eye—her little brother, her mother and her father.

"My late wife died from influenza," he stiffly informed her.

"I'm sorry."

Unemotionally, he observed her. She gazed at him in her darkened chamber, feeling a need for him so intense she could scarcely catch a breath. He was so superb, so handsome, that if he'd added a slight smile, she would have clung to him and pleaded for understanding because she'd wronged him.

Her hands were shaking as she tried to concentrate on washing his wounds.

"Daj tried to save my little brother, Stevo, from the disease. She attempted many Romany remedies, all without success."

A cool nod from James was all she needed to continue.

"One rainy afternoon when we'd camped near London, Daj brought me and my brother and my father to the edge of our camp. She chose a sapling and told my brother to shake it."

Valentina glimpsed James' flat gaze and tripped over her words. "My father ordered my mother to cease and argued that her cure was hopeless. I cried and blocked my ears. A few hours later, Stevo died." Valentina fingered the edges of her mother's diklo. "I stood next in line as a drabardi, and my mother said I needed to learn the ancient ways of the healer. Instead of assisting, I ran and hid like a coward."

More memories, the ones she couldn't share. Vulnerable, afraid, and alone, she'd been found by Troka, and he'd raped her in a deserted London alleyway. Her body had gone cold, her limbs lifeless. Profound sobs shattered inside her, a young girl screaming mutely to an earless world, a woman washing the wounds of the man she loved.

In the years following the rape, she'd buried her wretchedness under a dazzling bravado. She summoned that bravado and met James' steady gaze. "Luca found me the next morn."

"You weren't a coward. Your parents were arguing."

She was so tormented by her remembrances, she couldn't pinpoint when James' hand came to hold hers, or when he'd begun gently, supportively enfolding her fingers in his.

"And your mother's peculiar remedy?" he asked.

"It sounds superstitious …" James sent her a skeptical half-smile, and her sadness lightened. "Romany believe if you shake a tree, the fever will pass from the person who's suffering to the tree, and the sickness will be cured."

"Stevo died," James reminded softly.

She pulled her fingers from his and huddled her arms to her chest. "I blamed myself for not being brave enough to help my mother save him."

"None of it was your fault." James swung his legs around the bed and sat up. He braced his head in his hands, then studied her.

"Yesterday," she said, "when I dug some herbs from the garden, I recalled Stevo's death."

"'Tis a sad memory." Grunting with the effort, James came to his feet and walked toward the door. "Forgive me. I've had my fill of Gypsy superstitions for one evening."

She grabbed the bedpost for support. "Don't leave me."

He turned, one hand on the brass latch of her chamber door. Standing on the edge of her decision, she advanced a step.

He shook his head, although his gaze wouldn't let her go.

The dying embers of the fire licked red shadows onto the ceiling. She tried to pull air into her throat, enough for her constricted voice to speak. She waited for a minute, remembering the way he'd wrapped his arms around her in the stable and asked her to be his wife.

A muscle twitched in his jaw. His eyes flickered. Silver moonlight streamed through the window lighting his bruised and handsome face.

Two more paces. Tentatively, she massaged his shoulders.

He closed his eyes and leaned back against the door.

Straight and proud, she waited until his gaze met hers. "The night you left for battle, you told me to miss you."

His body stiffened. "And?"

"I missed you more than I ever dreamed."

Infinite seconds ticked by, while he looked away, an attempt to distance himself from her. When he gazed at her again, he said quietly, "I missed you too."

"Then will you please put your arms around me?"

His taut expression eased. He embraced her, and she wrapped her hands around him so tightly, her fingers bit into his back.

He devoured her with scorching kisses, a possessive act of ownership, staking his claim. He murmured her name into her mouth, her hair, her neck. She responded with all the passion in her heart. Eagerly, she kissed the bruises on his chest and inhaled all of him, his sweat, his wounds, and his maleness.

"My beautiful cariad, my sweetheart," he murmured. He whispered other words, Welsh words she didn't understand.

Tears ambushed her eyes. Her throat clogged.

He kissed the wetness from her lashes. "Amidst the cries on the battlefield, only thoughts of you held me together. When I saw my comrades fall—"

Hot tears streamed like silent waterfalls down her cheeks. She rubbed her palm along the coarse hairs of his beard and whispered, "Please don't let me go."

His fingers kneaded the small of her back as he kissed her tenderly, lovingly.

"Do you realize how gorgeous you are?" he murmured.

She shook her head in denial as he reclaimed her lips.

"You're the most magnificent creature in the world." He kissed her birthmark, steadied her face in his large hands and grinned. "Remind me to get thrashed more often."

"Don't speak of such things."

A velvety chuckle resonated from his body. "You're allowing me to kiss you because of my charming appearance."

She covered her face with her hands. "You do look dreadful," she admitted, opening her fingers to view him. "However, 'tis your impeccable manners—beginning with the way you crept into my chamber and frightened me—that was the ultimate charm."

His delighted laughter filled the room. She laughed with him.

Standing by the door, talking to him in the shadows, his arms wrapped around her, gave her a joy she'd never known. How secure it felt, this unforeseen gratification of belonging.

He sprinkled kisses on her forehead. "I didn't expect to

come home to this—influenza and panic. I apologize for my anger. My thoughts were unclear."

"Will you please explain what happened between you and the Rom?"

"Someday." He smiled down at her. "Come the morrow we leave for Wales."

"Wales? In the middle of winter?"

"Aye. 'Tis the reason I visited your chamber tonight, to inform you of my plans. I've instructed the servants to pack their baggage."

"A journey clear across England will be difficult in the coldest months."

Amusement flickered in his eyes. "We'll mark any young trees along the way in case we need to shake them." He jested before becoming serious again. "Jeremy is stronger and must be kept safe. My estate in Wales is even more remote than Ipswich, rugged and untamed. My hope is you'll grow fond of it and one day come to love the countryside as much as I do. In fact, Wales reminds me of you."

"I remind you of a country?"

"Wales is tempestuous, wild and unpredictable. *Cymru*, the land of the comrades." He smoothed her hair behind her ears and brushed two soft kisses on her birthmark. "And very, very precious to me."

She laughed at the comparisons, somehow appropriate. She drew a solitary breath and glided her fingers up the span of his powerful chest.

Tell him about your half-truth. He'll forgive you.

"James, there's something else I must—"

He strode to the mantel and lit a candle. Then he returned to her to hold her again, cradling her close to his heart.

Tell him.

He'd never regard her in the same way again.

151

Valentina inhaled a long breath, reluctant to release it.

She'd always been a coward.

"I shall regale you with battle tales as we travel," he was saying.

I won't be with you to hear your stories, nor see your beloved Wales. But I will hear your voice in my dreams and picture your rugged country in my mind. You'll be there, caring for your son, riding in the hillsides. Without me.

"I imagine your home is quite fancy," she said aloud.

"'Tis comfortable. Several neighbors are noblemen, although you wouldn't want to be a part of all that."

"Because I wouldn't fit in?"

Of course, she wouldn't. She was nothing more than an uncultured sham.

His fingers traced the curve of her lips. "You wouldn't want to fit in, although your presence would add a sparkle to every home."

"'Tis wrong for me to imagine myself as a wife to a gentleman."

"Only wrong for you to think otherwise." He sprinkled kisses on her temples. "I've been wrong too, you know."

"Wrong about what?"

"Wrong about thinking you wouldn't accept my proposal of marriage." He gave her a smoky male smile, and his lips found hers. "I hope you plan to get used to this."

She gloried in his smile and stroked his handsome, bruised face.

Ves'tacha.

Beloved.

CHAPTER 17

Devlesa avilan.
It is God who brought you.
Old Romany saying

*A*fter James left her chamber, Valentina meandered in and out of wispy dreams. Hours passed, daylight neared. Propping a pillow behind her, she lit a candle on her night table.

He'd bathed her in complimentary words. He'd told her she was dear to him. He'd told her she was exquisite. But he'd never said he loved her.

She stared at the lone candle. Superstitions and Romany spirits weren't real, and no palm reading was needed to tell her future. Without James, it loomed empty and desolate. And that was real.

She rose, tied her mother's yellow diklo around her neck, then slipped a plain woolen gown over her head. She blew out the candle, then scurried from the chamber, cautious not to rouse the household.

The long hallway was illuminated by one flickering oil lamp, and she eased her way in near darkness to Jeremy's chamber. She unlatched his door and stepped inside. Noiselessly, she hovered by his bed. He resembled an innocent cherub, breathing quietly though his small, turned-up nose and pink lips. Faint, short hiccups punctuated his dreams. His favorite nubby blanket lay twisted at the foot of the bed.

She pulled the blanket snugly over his shoulders. "Your father will take good care of you. He loves you dearly." She wiped heavy tears from her lids. "I must leave, little man. A decent man deserves an honest woman as his wife."

One last farewell kiss, and Valentina headed to Yolanda's chamber. She rapped, then hit the latch.

"Yolanda, wake up," she whispered.

Yolanda sat up in bed and her eyes widened. "Valentina. What is the hour?"

Valentina lit a candle on the night table. "'Tis almost morning. I came to tell you I'm leaving."

"Before dawn? Why? Mr. Colchester is back. Did you quarrel—"

"Aye. Nay. Well, maybe at first."

"Was he angry when you confessed your reading?"

"I didn't tell him." She covered her mouth to catch a sob. James' scent lingered on her fingers.

Yolanda wrapped her arms around her legs and rested her chin on her knees. Her shiny dark hair tangled in waves down her back. "Why not? Were you too foolish or too proud?"

"A little of both. He's leaving for Wales today."

"I know. I've already packed." Yolanda nodded to a small knapsack by the door.

Valentina's heart sank. "I've decided to rejoin our tribe. You wouldn't want to come with me, would you?"

Yolanda swung her legs off the bed and smoothed her muslin nightdress. She grabbed her tunic and draped it over the nightdress, taking the time to tie each lace perfectly. When she looked at Valentina again, her eyes took on a rounded sadness. "Where do you suppose our tribe has gone?"

"Luca said somewhere warm, near the sea. Brighton, I believe."

Resignedly, Yolanda shook her head. "I can't leave Reginald."

Valentina watched her sister and let a silent beat pass. "I'll go alone, then."

The candlelight spilled across Yolanda's pensive features. For the third time in as many minutes, she sighed. "The nights are long and cold, and 'tis too dangerous to cross the footpaths on your own. I'll accompany you."

She stood and evened the rumpled sheets. "I will need a few minutes to explain to Reginald. He's an understanding man, although not *that* understanding."

Valentina flew to her sister and embraced her in a grateful hug. "Thank you, my darling sister, thank you."

"Don't cry. You're the brave one," Yolanda whispered. "We'll take the back stairwell. 'Twill be deserted at this hour."

Yolanda dressed, blew out the candle, and threw on a russet wool cloak. She assumed the lead and led Valentina down the back stairs and along a narrow passageway.

Valentina paused and scrutinized alternate doorways, trying to place where they were. She turned, about-face, and walked down a different passage.

"Valentina, you're going the wrong way!" Yolanda's tone echoed heavily in the darkened hallway.

"We must fetch Daj's dagger in case we're forced to

defend ourselves while we're traveling, and I know exactly where 'twill be hidden."

James had relocated his sleeping quarters closer to hers a few nights after she'd arrived. His former chamber was in the north wing.

Yolanda lagging at her heels, Valentina creaked opened the door to James' former bedchamber and her mouth dropped. His chamber was much different from what she'd imagined, especially compared to the grandiose chambers she and Yolanda enjoyed. Beyond the neatly made bed and mahogany bureau, the chamber was furnished with only a high table and chairs.

She braced her arms on the doorframe and tried to catch her breath. His presence filled the air, so compelling she felt like she could see him walking through the room. A pair of his worn black leather boots, shined to perfection, stood propped against the bureau.

Shaking aside his image, she hurried into the room and opened the bureau's top drawer. "The dagger must be here somewhere."

The double-edged dagger sat in the bottom drawer, meticulously waffled between two of James' linen shirts. She tied the dagger and its sheath to the inside of her cloak.

The sisters pulled the door closed, then quickened down another set of stairs and through the pantry. They sped past the herb garden and across the darkened cobblestone courtyard.

Yolanda raced to the stables. "Reginald will assist us. He sleeps with the horses." She hoisted open the stable door. "Although he despises them."

"A blacksmith who sleeps in a stable and despises horses?"

"A horse bit him when he was a boy. He's never been able to forgive the entire breed, yet the smell of hay and leather helps him sleep."

The women entered the stables and weaved around bales of hay. Despite the darkness, Yolanda found her way to the corner where Reginald slept. She nudged him awake.

He chafed his hands through his matted blond beard and heaved himself to his feet, grinning at the unexpected sight of Yolanda.

"We need your help," Yolanda began, but was interrupted by his kisses. When he lifted his head, the glower he shot toward Valentina was caustic. "I'm not sure if I should be thrilled to see Yolanda before dawn, or very, very worried."

"Mr. Colchester has returned and plans to depart for Wales today," Valentina began.

"Aye."

"And Valentina cannot travel to Wales with him," Yolanda said.

Reginald's heavy blond eyebrows gathered into one ominous line. "But you will come with me to Wales, Yolanda?"

"I won't abandon my sister."

"Are you both mad?" Reginald all but shouted. "Mr. Colchester would never approve. Tell Valentina you're staying here where you belong."

"She's right in front of you. You tell her. I must go where I'm needed, and for now, my place is with my sister." Yolanda caressed his face and nuzzled his bearded chin, her expression one of pure innocence. "Valentina and I must leave before daybreak and we require a good horse."

Reginald swore as a horse kicked from the next stall. "Absolutely not."

"I'll wait in the courtyard." Valentina paused and offered her sister a silent plea—*convince him*—before leaving the stables.

Outside, she alternated her pacing with staring at the wide stable door that muted the argument within. Finally, a hulking Reginald and a petite Yolanda emerged leading a shaggy, saddled chestnut mare.

Yolanda beamed up at Reginald, and then turned a heartening smile on Valentina.

Reginald's actions confirmed what Yolanda had said the first day she'd met him. He was a brave man with strong morals, and he was proving it by endangering his livelihood to assist them.

And he loved Yolanda.

When they reached the end of the path leading away from the stables, they reached an old stone wall near the river. The mare snorted and thumped Reginald with its front leg. Reginald dropped the reins, swore at the horse, and enveloped Yolanda in his arms.

"Is the mare always this temperamental, Reginald?" Valentina asked.

"Only around me."

Reginald and Yolanda conferred, and Yolanda answered his brusque questions with quiet reassurances. Clearly in no hurry to release her sister, he directed terse instructions to Valentina. "Guide the horse to swim across the river."

Valentina scanned the lightening horizon. "Beyond the cliff, the water runs shallower."

"No one ventures near the cliff since Beatrix's death. In winter, any attempt to scale it would be near suicide. I won't allow you to place Yolanda's life, or your own, in peril. Here, the river is crossable."

Yolanda inspected the water, slapping against the banks, a shimmer of golden black in the pale predawn light. Her pallid face was painted in terror. "I can't swim across that river. Valentina, you know I can't."

"You won't swim." Using the stone wall as a mounting block, Valentina put her foot in the stirrup and eased up and over the mare, settling in the saddle. "The horse will."

"When Mr. Colchester is settled in Wales, I'll come for you." Reginald lifted Yolanda's slim body and settled her on the mare behind Valentina. "Please be safe."

"We'll travel to London first," Valentina said. Uttering the name of the city she hadn't seen since the rape did nothing to settle her nerves. "A Romany caravan will be camped somewhere near the city's outskirts. From there, a *vurma* can direct us to our tribe."

Noting Reginald's puzzled squint, Valentina explained. "Romany have no addresses, so we rely on a vurma to help us find each other. A vurma is a Romany woman who knows where everyone is located when our caravans are traveling."

She clicked her heels into the mare's flanks. The mare obediently stepped into the river, and murky water rose to her knees. Reginald stood on the riverbank, his smile forced, the last of the moonlight revealing lines of worry on his hard-set face.

Valentina held her breath and grabbed the horse's mane. The water deepened.

Yolanda squeezed her arms around Valentina's ribs. "I'm so afraid."

"Bite your lips and close your eyes. The mare is strong and can swim." Valentina's long gown swished and sloshed and swilled. She blinked through splashes of water, her cheeks wet, her eyelashes spiked. Frost clung to the skeletal branches of blackthorn trees, giving the landscape an eerie, wintry glow.

Yolanda's body was shaking uncontrollably. "Soon the water will be over our heads."

Valentina squeezed Yolanda's hands reassuringly. "Dry land is near." She held the reins tighter and guided the mare out of the water. Only then could she exhale, sending noiseless white clouds of breath into the chilly air. "Yolanda, you can open your eyes now," she said affectionately.

Ever so slightly, Yolanda loosened her knotted fingers from Valentina's ribcage

Valentina glanced behind them. Reginald was merely a speck on the other side of the river.

Her throat tightened until she could hardly breathe. Even a distance away, James' majestic estate formed an imposing silhouette against the sky. The home of the only man she'd ever love.

Keeping the mare headed to the south and west, Valentina urged her through forests and frosty silver fields at a fast pace.

"Mr. Colchester will be very unhappy when he realizes you're gone," Yolanda predicted. "You should have told him you were leaving."

Of course, she should have, except she couldn't because she was weak.

She was hiding behind the fear of being judged by God and by James. She couldn't face his heartbroken gaze when she confessed her deceit. She had prayed, believing that God had placed her with James, exactly where she belonged. Perhaps He had. If so, she was the failure, because she couldn't believe in herself.

Wasn't her fear also keeping her from becoming whole? If she concentrated on herself and not God, she'd end up with scarceness.

Too exhausted to respond to Yolanda's prediction, she said, "Someday, he'll come to realize 'tis the right decision. He and his son will be safe, and he'll live his life in peace."

Call me James.

His voice was so clear, that although she knew 'twas impossible, she looked around for him anyway. He wasn't there. He wouldn't be, yet her foolish heart had hoped. She lowered her head, staring blindly at the ground speeding past, refusing to give in to the agony of her loss.

She fingered a strand of James' dark hair caught in the fabric of her cloak. It broke from her numbed fingers and blew away in the whoosh of an acrid wind.

The Rom believed discarded hair was a guarantee that two lovers would go their separate ways, her invasive conscience reminded.

Romany nonsense.

An owl hooted and swooped across a field, evidently intent on its prey.

Both sisters snapped their heads upward and then exchanged nervous glances. Both were hesitant to say the word aloud.

The owl's cry. *Bibaxt. Very bad luck.*

CHAPTER 18

What bak the divvus?
What luck today?
Kker rya.
I never have any luck.
Romany saying

*S*omeone was missing. In fact, two someones were missing. At least, that was what Geoffrey was droning as he shook James awake.

Groggy from a deep sleep, James rolled to his side and opened his eyes a crack. The pale light of dawn sifted through the thick blue draperies of his chamber. He'd rest a few more minutes, he muttered and shrugged off Geoffrey.

When next James woke, sunlight soaked his eyelids. He kept his eyes closed and imagined Valentina waking him, certainly a more delightful prospect than the insistent Geoffrey.

He'd trace the perfect curves of her face while reassuring

any reservations she had about becoming his wife. They'd discuss wedding plans, for when they reached Wales they'd be married in a Christian church, far from the condemning eyes of London.

At her request, they'd also have a Gypsy wedding. If the tradition brought her happiness, he'd even jump over a broomstick for her, a Gypsy custom she'd undoubtedly tease him about for years. They would be blessed, enjoying a lifetime of joy and serving God. A lifetime of meaning and principles, pleasure and peace. She'd teach him to love and trust again. In return, he'd indulge her with the finest herbal garden in all of Wales. And cherish her.

"Mr. Colchester."

Resigning himself to Geoffrey's presence, James opened his eyes and glared at his steward. "I don't require a nursemaid. My injuries will heal, I assure you."

"I'm sure they will, sir. There's some news, and I'm uncertain how to tell you."

James' eyes flew open. He sat up, straight and rigid, startled to see the sun so high in the sky. They would not make an early start that day. Perhaps 'twould be best to leave for Wales come the morrow. "Tell me what?" he asked Geoffrey.

Geoffrey stepped back, no doubt from the blast of impatience from James' gaze. "Valentina and Yolanda are missing, sir. Although," he added a little too desperately, "I'm sure they haven't gone far."

Before the next second split, James was on his feet. He washed and dressed quickly, then hastened to the window. He didn't see Valentina scurrying about anywhere.

He swung from the window and strode to her chamber, surveying every corner of the room, half-expecting to see her. Perhaps she was assisting the servants in packing for the long journey ahead. Or, he visualized her in the kitchen, boiling dandelions in one of her mysterious brews, perhaps to soothe someone's sore throat. Or perhaps she was at one of the tenant farmer's cottages, tending to an ailing child.

Aye, all plausible explanations. Valentina always thought of others first.

He nodded complacently, his smile magnanimous, certain she would appear by noon.

He envisioned her curvaceous body, her generous smile and full lips. And perhaps again she could come close to him and whisper, *"Will you please put your arms around me?"*

* * *

WHERE COULD SHE BE? Tight-lipped, James shaded his eyes from the midmorning sun brightening the fields. Already far behind schedule, his household readied to depart for Wales.

Hoisting Jeremy onto his shoulders, he searched every dreary nook of his home. He did not find her, and none of the servants, busy with packing and readying the house to be empty for an unknown length of time, had seen her.

In the kitchen, Isabel was ordering the maids about as they packed food for the journey. She suggested Valentina might be in the herb garden.

"Whenever I've seen her in the garden," Wiborow said waspishly from the kitchen doorway, "I've noted that Valentina had a fascination for foxglove."

"Is foxglove another potion?" he asked her, absently patting Jeremy's wiggling knees.

"Hardly, Mr. Colchester. Foxglove, added to food or drink, causes great harm."

James harbored no uncertainties about Wiborow. Her observation was meant to alarm him. Casually, he remarked, "Valentina finds plants that save people." With deliberate, unhurried movements, he lowered Jeremy from his shoulders and waited until his son had dashed off. Then he turned back to Wiborow.

"Now say what you mean," he ordered, "and be done with it."

"The afternoon Geoffrey choked on a pear, my suspicions about Valentina were confirmed. Beforehand, she'd dug through the herbal garden for several minutes."

"She spends many days outdoors in the garden because she's a healer."

With a thread of self-righteousness in her smug smile, Wiborow asked, "Is she a healer or a murderess?"

James pursed his lips. His tolerance lowered. His anger soared. "Your accusations are grave, unfounded and cruel."

"Gypsies cannot be trusted. The day of our midday meal, I suspect she attempted to poison Geoffrey."

"When? She's fond of Geoffrey and eased his discomfort that day by brewing a tonic." Trying to recall the events of that afternoon, James sifted through his thoughts. One of the servants had shouted from the kitchen that Geoffrey was choking on a pear, and the servant had been right. Someone else mentioned the deer meat being rancid—perhaps one of the cooks.

Wiborow crossed her arms. "Might Valentina harbor a reason to hurt you?"

"Nay," he snapped.

"I said my peace." Wiborow positioned her mouth into a somber, dull streak. "Be warned."

He studied her spiteful face and arsenic eyes. "Your observations are completely unfounded. Don't speak of this matter again."

Wiborow gave a curt bow, the stiff, mousy strands of her bun coming undone. A servant who understood no life other than serving the Colchester household, she marched away in a thinly veiled huff.

* * *

As the sun was setting, James strode outdoors to consult with Tobias about the readiness of the horses, wagons and carriages that would transport his household. A pinch of sunbeam danced off the river beyond, then disappeared behind encroaching grey clouds. The day had been cool and he spotted Jeremy sitting on a fallen tree trunk, spinning red and black checkers. He clapped eagerly each time the checkers collided.

James bent to smooth Jeremy's white frilled collar over his heavy cotton jacket.

The boy stared up at him. "Val-en-tina?"

"I don't know where she is, son." James cupped the boy's chin so Jeremy had a better view of his lips while he spoke. "However, I'll tell you a secret. She and her sister better have an excellent excuse for disappearing."

Once the afternoon waned and turned to evening, James' mood darkened. Like a lion confined to a cage, he paced his home with feverish impatience. Valentina wouldn't be able to travel far alone, he reasoned. Sooner or later, she'd reappear, most likely where he least expected her. Yet as the hours since her disappearance grew, so did his suspicions.

Maybe she and her sister didn't want to be found.

Nay. She'd never leave without telling him. Never. He commanded himself to take slow, deep breaths and banish that ridiculous thought from his mind. His chest grew empty even thinking such thoughts, much less speaking them aloud, because he loved her with an urgency he hardly fathomed. She must have developed feelings for him, too, in all the weeks of their shared quips and lively conversations.

Certainly, she had more fortitude than anyone he'd ever known. He recalled how she'd met his eyes unflinchingly the night before, as she'd walked across her chamber to him, like a trembling yet proud queen.

"Have you seen Valentina, Geoffrey?" he asked when he went into his study where his steward was sorting through estate paperwork.

"Not since the last time you asked," Geoffrey replied.

James gestured at the papers scattered on the desk. "Instead of dealing with such inconsequential ledgers, use your time wisely and find the two women. And find them quickly, because I'm going to talk some sense into Valentina when I see her."

"And Yolanda?"

"I don't think for a hare-brained minute Yolanda is to blame. She's afraid to put two sentences together if the words might lead to her being reprimanded." Worry growing inside him for the women, he stared at Geoffrey while his insides split and his heart weighted heavy. "Where can they be?"

"Perhaps the women are packing their belongings in their trunks—somewhere obscurely."

Both of the men knew the women had no belongings to pack, nor trunks to stow their lack of belongings in.

Geoffrey couldn't ignore years of ingrained respect and kept his features politely downcast. "I believe you ... ah ... visited Valentina's chamber last evening. Therefore, you were the last person with her."

"No secrets of my whereabouts?" James asked.

"Not a one."

Spinning on his heels, James strode from the room, calling for Tobias to organize a search party. As he and a dozen men met with torches by the stables, he disregarded the meaningful glances the men gave one other, the concern furrowing Geoffrey's white brows. When he stopped thinking about the sound reprimand he'd give Valentina when he found her, he worried some accident had befallen her. She might be hurt, alone, in a barren field, or submerged at the bottom of the swollen river.

Fear and alarm rocked him, and he mounted his horse and galloped with his men to the river's edge. He'd given her explicit orders to stay away from the river the day of Yolanda's near drowning. And Valentina had promised, murmuring aye between blue lips and chattering teeth.

His breath trapped in his throat. The familiar agony of losing someone he loved sapped his strength. He stared at the river, unmindful of the frozen drizzle sticking to his cloak and coating his cheeks with tiny icicles. He turned away and ordered Tobias to take half the men out to the pastures where the tenant farmers lived. He, Geoffrey, and the others set off toward the hills.

"How long do you plan to delay our departure? Geoffrey asked. "Influenza might reappear at any time."

"We will find them," James said, holding his torch high, probing the ground for clues and misguided footsteps.

Geoffrey nodded. "Even if Valentina has some sort of Gypsy magic, two women don't vanish. Unless they had help from their so-called spirits."

"She doesn't believe in Gypsy spirits anymore."

Even so, in her most vulnerable moments he'd detected a sense of urgency—a single-minded purpose to tell him something. In all their afternoons spent together, he'd never given her the chance, too intent on bending the conversation toward his own gains. That was a tormenting thought and he swallowed, tasting a firm upbraiding at himself.

James and Geoffrey returned to the courtyard where Tobias and his men waited. Tobias reported that there had been no sign of the women and asked when they would leave for Wales. "All of the supplies are loaded onto the wagons."

"We'll depart within a couple of days." James swung off his horse with such suddenness, Tobias jerked back.

* * *

AN HOUR LATER, James was trying to make sense of the ledgers that Geoffrey had left on his desk, when Tobias knocked on the door. Stepping inside, he cleared his throat and examined the wall behind James with rapt concentration.

"One of the mares is missing," he said.

James scratched his jaw. The bristling of a neglected beard crackled beneath his tense fingers.

"Surely, you have something better to do than report on a horse."

Displaying a brilliant imitation of a man who was about to say something he didn't believe in the slightest, Tobias said apologetically, "The mare may be grazing in an outer meadow. We checked everywhere, although you can never be sure—"

"A horse is missing," James repeated. "One horse, only one, decided to gallop away."

In the space of a hairsbreadth, the realization staggered him. He jerked back his chair and stormed past the open-mouthed man with lengthy, purposeful strides.

"Mr. Colchester, is it possible the Gypsy women rode that little mare right off the grounds of your estate?" Tobias called after him.

Of course they did, because any other possibility was a coincidence.

James's strides increased to a run as visions of Valentina clouded his eyesight.

Her beauty. Her laughter. Her deceit.

His mind screamed, refusing to believe. How could she leave him without a word?

Tobias ran after him, reaching him as he strode toward the stables. He bent his head to his knees, gasping. "Mr. Colchester, 'twould be remiss if I didn't mention—"

"Go on." Tobias' hesitancy strained James' overstretched nerves.

"Were you aware Yolanda and Reginald were seeing each other?"

James' sigh was loud and volatile. "I'm aware now, Tobias."

He headed toward the stables to confront a wayward blacksmith. Geoffrey, Tobias, and some of the other men formed an invisible column behind him.

Reginald was at his forge outside the stables, clanging his ironwork, preparing to shoe a horse. In stark contrast to the blasting heat of the open fire, the wind blew wintry flurries upward. So close to the fire, he wore only a shirt and breeches beneath his leather apron. His space blistered with the remnants of charred metal.

"Reginald," James began, pleased he was able to control his voice, "it has come to my attention that you and Yolanda have become close."

Reginald plunged a horseshoe into a bucket of water before looking up. "Aye, Mr. Colchester."

"When was the last time you saw her?"

Reginald wiped shaking, sooty palms on his blackened apron. By the blood-red firelight, sweat formed a riveting stream down his forehead. "I cannot place the exact hour, Mr. Colchester. I'm sorry."

"I find I cannot believe you." James stepped closer. "Where did the women go, Reginald?"

Reginald shook his head. "I have nothing to say."

And by not saying, James learned two facts. One, Reginald was far bolder than most of the men on James' estate, which didn't particularly interest him at the moment; and two, Reginald had assisted Valentina and Yolanda in their flight, which interested James a great deal.

"Your actions may condemn them to a frozen death," he said shortly.

Reginald's expression closed. He screwed his thick lips, raised his mutinous gaze to James and then turned back to his forge.

James stormed back to his house where he found Geoffrey waiting for him in his study. He accepted a glass of wine from James, then said, "It occurred to me that upon her arrival, Valentina mentioned returning to her mother's burial site. Perhaps 'tis the reason why the women ran off."

James grabbed the thin back of a wooden chair to steady his frustration. "You refer to occurrences happening months ago. Why would she leave now?"

Quick to acknowledge James' excellent choice of wines on the sideboard, Geoffrey seated himself by the fire and shrugged. "I wonder, though, that although Valentina was correct when she foretold Beatrix's death, her influenza prediction was off the mark."

Was it? The revelation hit James with such explosive force, he snapped the brittle back of the chair. Aimlessly, he stared at the piece of wood in his hand as if it were a curious oddity.

After a prolonged hesitation, Geoffrey set down his glass and said, "She deceived you."

"When she read my fortune?" James scowled. "Fortune-telling isn't real. Valentina knows this."

"That's not the point," Geoffrey persisted. "'Twas real to her at the time, and she may have seen more than she was letting on. Let's not forget her Gypsy friend Luca made no secret about hating the English. In the end, Gypsies are wanderlust people who can't be trusted."

James shuddered violently. Denial clouded his thoughts. In the recesses of his mind, he wondered if he could stand upright.

What a besotted, ignorant fool he'd been. Vaguely, he wondered if he'd made any rational decisions since Beatrix had died. He'd been anchored in bitterness and fear. And then he'd attempted to cling to a hope, any hope, even a false hope.

He inclined his head toward the door, bidding a blunt goodnight to Geoffrey. After a moment, the steward nodded and quit the chamber.

In three paces, James strode to the window. He pushed his hands into his pockets and uttered, "My steps are ordered by the Lord." He repeated the verse from Psalms over and over in his mind, then groped inside his waistcoat for the moss-green ribbon necklace. He'd intended to give Valentina the necklace when he'd returned from London.

He grasped the delicate ribbon, swung the gold coins back and forth, and let it slip from his fingers. "Good-bye Valentina," he whispered.

He should have felt satisfaction when the coins hit the floor.

Instead, he felt empty.

CHAPTER 19

Jek dilo kerel but dile hai but dile keren dilimata.
One madman makes many madmen and many madmen
make madness.
Old Romany saying

"*I*'m tired." Yolanda slumped lower on the mare. "My fingers are numb and the wind is freezing my toes."

"'Tis better to ride a few more hours and take advantage of the daylight." Valentina turned to her sister, noting the long-suffering look on Yolanda's angelic face. Valentina managed a reassuring smile. "Did I ever tell you that Luca didn't even blink when we stole three chickens from a wealthy villager's farm? We ate well for days."

Yolanda tilted her chin down and scowled. "You've told me that story at least a half-dozen times. When we were children, I often wondered who was more daring, you or Luca."

"Luca," Valentina assured her.

Yolanda laughed. "He's like the wind—completely unpredictable."

"He cares for our elders and has never deserted the tribe."

"You always defend him, and I'm not interested in Luca." Yolanda sobered, adding, "I'm interested in Reginald and I hardly had a minute to bid him a proper farewell." With an audible humph, Yolanda pressed her head against Valentina's back.

"When I rejoin our tribe," Valentina said, "you'll see Reginald again."

"And I'll become a proud and fancy Englishman's wife."

"You act like Reginald is bestowing the crown jewels on your head because he wants to marry you. I had hoped we'd fit into the English world, although now I'm not so sure." All the swallowing in the world didn't relieve the unexpected lump of sadness in her throat. "We can't change who we are, nor the color of our skin. At the end of the day, we're still Romany—strong and proud."

"Little good it's done us," Yolanda contradicted. "We're poor and hungry and resort to thievery."

"You must be exhausted. 'Tis why you're speaking disrespectfully about our people." Valentina scanned the trees, searching for long-hanging, supple limbs. "We can stop here and build a *bender*, a tent, to shelter us for a few hours."

"We'll not need to build anything." Yolanda pointed ahead of them. "A very strange man is coming toward us from the bottom of the hill."

Valentina reined the mare in sharply. Her startled gaze fell on a short, egg-shaped man emerging from the woods. She held the mare's reins steady, knowing she and Yolanda would look guilty if they tried to bolt.

The man hiked nearer. "You wenches are trespassing on Mr. Wellsey's estate!"

Trespassing meant imprisonment.

Valentina stilled her twitching hands, praying her worries were premature.

The man drew closer, squinting at them as he touched his stringy red beard. "I don't recall any reports of Gypsies roaming these lands."

The mare leapt beneath Valentina, and her gaze flew nervously across the empty fields. "James confided that the Wellsey and Colchester families have feuded for years," she murmured to Yolanda.

"His feuds shouldn't matter," came Yolanda's sharp retort. "You left him, remember?"

Valentina flinched, her tormented heart protesting. She half-hoped Yolanda might soften her response, perhaps adding that James would never have wanted Valentina to leave, that he would be searching frantically for her even now.

Yolanda didn't speak anything of the sort. In fact, she didn't speak to Valentina at all. Instead, she said to the man, "Sir, we've been guests of Mr. Colchester."

Valentina glanced back at her sister with a warning scowl as she shook her head.

The red-bearded man fingered the mare's reins, and the horse gave a panicky lurch. "If you're telling the truth, then Mr. Wellsey will want to meet you and extend his pardon."

There was no time to think. Things were moving too swiftly, and images of what might happen rushed across Valentina's mind. She did not trust this man, nor did she trust that she and Yolanda would find a warm welcome at the Wellsey estate. Yanking the reins free from the man's loose grip, she wheeled the mare around in a tight circle and then urged it into a charging gallop.

The man expelled a violent oath and called for help.

The breeze tore at her long hair, tossing it riotously about. She threw a glance over her shoulder. The man ran after them uselessly, and no one else was about. He was no match for the mare. The women bolted along a stream, then tore over a low stone bridge. She focused on the mare, speaking encouragingly. As they neared a sharp bend, she sensed that the mare was tiring. As the mare rounded the next curve wide, Valentina saw the heavy limb jutting from an oak tree.

A swell of panic volleyed through her. She held her breath as time slowed.

"Yolanda! Lower your head!"

Valentina felt the blow to her head as both women were unseated from the horse. Then her world went black.

CHAPTER 20

May kali muri gugli avela.
The darker the berry, the sweeter it is.
Old Romany saying

A peculiar shout. Rushed footsteps.

"Mr. Colchester!"

James awoke to a distressed shriek and rubbed his hand over his face.

Wiborow stood in the doorway of his study, staring at him, and yet not appearing to see him. She seemed to be attempting to speak, although she stuttered.

Between his worry about Valentina and her sister, and then needing to get up early to see many of his household servants off on their journey to Wales, he had barely slept the night before. When he'd retreated to his study after the last wagon had disappeared, he had fallen asleep at his desk. The strange shriek and Wiborow's appearance jerked him up from his chair. An idle fire burned low in the grate.

Trained for battle, he yanked his knife from his boot and raised the blade. Then he blinked and scanned the room. He saw no danger.

He focused on Wiborow's ashen face. Wiborow never cried, yet tears poured down her cheeks. He raced to her, grabbing and shaking her bony forearms.

Eyes wide, she sputtered between mispronounced words, nearly incoherent. "Jeremy! You're cursed, Mr. Colchester!" She looked around. "First Beatrix, now Jeremy—"

"Jeremy? Cursed?" James' breath pierced his lungs. He couldn't say any more.

He tore past her and leapt the stairs two at a time. *His legs. His legs were too slow. When had his balance become so pitiable?*

Seconds later, he stopped at the open door to Jeremy's chamber and froze. Jeremy thrashed on his small bed. Sweat matted his hair and trickled down his flushed cheeks.

His son. Sick. Here in England. Impossible.

James let out a cry that couldn't be contained and brought a shaky hand to his temple.

He plunged toward the bed.

Elspeth wiped a linen cloth over Jeremy's forehead. "He's not well, Mr. Colchester."

He waved her away and leaned against the bed frame. Continually, he shook his head. "I should have taken him to Wales weeks ago."

"Tad?" Jeremy stirred beneath a pile of blankets.

James's chest tightened. He couldn't breathe. Despair submerged him—the same heaviness he'd felt after Beatrix's death. He'd never have the strength to emerge a second time.

He sagged to the floor by his son's bed and clutched Jeremy's small fingers. "Stay awake, son. I'm here." *Calm, calm, calm, for Jeremy's sake.*

The boy gave a ragged huff, his eyes fluttered, opened, closed. "Sleep ... y."

"Nay! Don't go to sleep!" Powerless, he clasped his son's hands tighter, and prayed. "Dear Lord, I put all my faith in you."

Through the morning and into the afternoon, he recited verses from the Bible—from Proverbs and Psalms—and words from hymns. When Richard, the vicar, stepped into the chamber, he blessed Jeremy and sat on the floor next to James.

"We can do nothing for him, Mr. Colchester. Influenza, as we've experienced, must run its course." Richard kept his gaze downcast, his drooping shoulders giving little hope. "We must seek God for our answers. Everything is in His time."

James nodded, wordless. Jeremy lay fitfully on his bed, moaning, his face flushed with fever.

Clare hesitantly entered the chamber, keeping her head down. "Mr. Colchester, might we attempt Valentina's cure? She spoke to me about shaking a sapling—"

"Nay." Looking past Clare, he noted Tobias and Geoffrey, and wondered how long they'd been there.

"Pardon us, Mr. Colchester." Tobias made an exaggerated show of fumbling for something in his waistcoat. "One of the tenant farmers said they've located Valentina and Yolanda."

"Alive?"

"Aye, and ..."

James exhaled slowly. "And?"

"And not far from here. Apparently, they were crossing Mr. Wellsey's estate when they had an accident. Valentina suffered a blow to her head, but no broken bones far as anyone can tell. Did you want me to bring her back here?"

James sank his head onto his chest, shaking it back and forth. Nay. Nay, nay.

His shriveled heart refused to beat. His mouth felt so dry. The women had been only a few miles away? He'd imagined they were halfway across England by now, while he'd wasted all of a precious day and night searching for her. A day and night when they could have been far from here, traveling to Wales, away from the influenza.

"I'll accompany you."

"Mr. Colchester," Clare said, "Valentina cared for my aunt Dionise, so perhaps—"

He raised a hand. "Please, no talk of supposed Gypsy cures." He rubbed his fingers against his son's damp cheek and kissed Jeremy's burning forehead. "I won't be long, son," he whispered. "I'll return within the hour."

"What exactly do you intend to do, once she's back here?" Geoffrey asked.

"I'm not a fool, Geoffrey. However, if she's hurt, I'll not abandon her."

Several minutes later, James and several men drove their horses into a full gallop amidst a shower of mud and grinding hooves. A gathering of starlings scattered in the courtyard, their wings flapping in noisy agreement.

CHAPTER 21

Nashti zhas vorta po drom o bango.
You cannot walk straight when the road is bent.
Old Romany saying

Frozen leaves crackled under a horse's galloping hooves, and a sharp wind peppered Valentina's ears and cheeks. She winced, biting her lips to stifle the moan. Wisps of consciousness faded as shifting rays of sunlight penetrated her closed eyelids. A nightjar's song frittered in the trees, chirpy and cheery, hunting for moths.

She leaned back, luxuriating in the strength of a hard chest. Her body settled into the percussive rhythm of the powerful horse beneath her. She sniffed, catching a whiff of worn leather.

She opened her eyes and twisted in the saddle. *James.*

His heavy cloak swirled around them. His unkempt beard darkened his chin. Puffy, dark circles dragged under his eyes. He stared ahead, solemn and silent, his gaze refusing hers.

She had thought she'd still been dreaming, only dreaming, when he'd appeared like a spirit and lifted her onto his horse. When he'd mounted behind her and closed his arms around her, she'd rested against him without hesitation and fallen asleep.

"Yolanda?" she asked, grimacing. Her head felt as if it were exploding.

"Riding ahead with Geoffrey," came the terse reply.

She strained past shadows of fatigue and spotted her sister's russet cloak whirling about her slight frame. She drew a relieved breath. "Thank you. We had—"

She thought he swore under his breath, and she stared down at her bare hands. She didn't want

to close her eyes again because her mind might swim with memories—of her time spent with James, her emptiness without him, the pain from her fall.

She focused on the stark branches of oak trees speeding by in ever-changing outlines.

An oncoming limb rushed at them, promising to dislodge them both from the saddle if they didn't bend their heads. This time she ducked quickly.

She hardly remembered the earlier fall and what had happened after. Eventually, she and Yolanda had wakened to find the mare had run off and they were both chilled and wet from lying on the ground. She had lost all sense of direction, but some instinct told her which way lay James' estate. She and Yolanda walked for hours, and as darkness fell they saw a light from a cottage in the distance. 'Twas the home of one of James' tenant farmers and his wife and children. Too exhausted to do much more than sip some broth, the sisters had fallen asleep by the fire. Since James had found them there, she assumed the farmer had gone to the estate to tell him where she and Yolanda were.

Should she provoke the cold man whose chest she was leaning on, or talk rationally with that same caring man who'd carried her so gently onto his horse? She'd seen the worried, bleak light draw off his face when he'd bent over her and realized she'd been hurt. She thought of the day he had proposed to her in the stable, the way he'd tenderly kissed her in the rose garden when he'd reassured her that the hand of God was on her.

She knew James cared. However, he was angry because she'd left him without an explanation.

"Thank you for rescuing us," she whispered.

"I hope I didn't thwart your carefully laid plans. Reginald finally confessed that you and your sister were on your way to London."

"I'm sorry. 'Twas wrong."

"Did your spirits advise you to sneak off in the middle of the night?"

"You know spirits aren't real."

"I don't know what to believe and not believe anymore."

Heartbeats passed, and they galloped across the final acres bordering James's land. Valentina drew in a sharp breath. Her body hurt everywhere.

As they approached the main house, her first thought was that the house looked the same as it always did. Candles flickered in paned glass windows, oil lamps were lit, and smoke meandered from the kitchen chimneys. However, as they rode nearer, she realized that the front courtyard and all the outbuildings were strangely quiet, devoid of any person or activity.

The horse slowed.

"Your home is defenseless and could be in jeopardy.

Where is everyone?" Her thoughts marched through her mind in tense formation. "Suppose you were attacked?"

With deadly composure, James replied, "An enemy worth half his salt would throw himself off London Bridge before he attacked an estate struck by influenza."

Fear trickled through her, and she forced herself up straight.

They rode across the courtyard, and James reined in his horse. He dismounted, handed the reins to Tobias, and helped her down. Once her feet hit the ground, James was quick to release her.

"Thankfully, Yolanda wasn't injured." Valentina pointed toward her sister who was rushing already toward the stables. "She must be searching for Reginald."

James began striding across the lawn.

"Slow down," Valentina shouted as loudly as her tortured lungs allowed. "I said, Yolanda is searching for—"

James turned. His somber stare he gave proved far more furious than reassuring. "Yolanda won't find her blacksmith in the stable nor the forges. Reginald departed for Wales, along with most of the servants."

"James, wait. There's much I need to explain."

"Not now."

"Thank you for coming for Yolanda and me. The mare ran off and—"

At first, he ignored her. Heated, silent fury reined. He exhaled slowly, a nerve in his jaw vibrating with fury. He met her stare once more and replied curtly, "Don't thank me again."

She had to reach him. She had to go back to the beginning so he'd understand. She spread out her hands, an attempt at an explanation.

His gaze raked over her. "Knowing you were injured, I came to extend my help. Fortunately, you weren't far away."

He paused a second too long, although not before stark, bleak heartache ripped across his face.

"James, what's the matter?"

He folded his arms and looked past her. "My son is sick."

Jeremy. Nay. Her mouth opened and closed. She could find no words. She pressed her hands to her temples to calm the dizziness ringing through her skull. "How sick, James? How sick?"

He closed his eyes, and she knew.

Influenza.

Jeremy. Sweet and kind, gentle and innocent, the precious child she loved.

She leaned over, her hands on her thighs, and pulled in a tortured breath. "What can I do?"

"I'd appreciate your prayers."

Abruptly, he pivoted and strode up the wide stairs to his home. She caught up with him as he started for the hallway stairway, matching his swiftness, stride for stride. "Did you attempt my Romany cure?"

He rubbed a hand through his dark hair, his expression bordering between frustration and sadness. "I've come to believe shaking trees requires only your clever Gypsy skills. And, as we've both acknowledged, your Romany remedy didn't work."

Tenderness welled in her heart. A wrench of compassion made her lips shake. "May I pray with you?"

"Aye." He mumbled something in Welsh. "I lost one child, I cannot lose another."

"You won't lose your son," she vowed. "God will listen to our prayers." Valentina hoisted her gown and girded her loins. She'd become a prayer warrior, fighting for Jeremy's life.

CHAPTER 22

Te na khutshos perdal tsho ushalin.
Try not to jump over your shadow.
Old Romany saying

With Yolanda behind her, Valentina edged into Jeremy's cramped chamber. Richard, the vicar, was there, along with Elspeth and Clare. Valentina pressed her palm against Jeremy's flushed forehead. "How are you feeling, little man? Your father said you're unwell."

His over-bright gaze fixed on hers. "Mam?"

For the child's sake, she steadied her shaking hands. Sinking onto the bed, she swabbed his sweaty brows with slow, careful massages across each tiny hair. The image of her brother's dark Romany face merged with Jeremy's light, cherubic features.

She rested her head on the mound of pillows by Jeremy and prayed. It wasn't enough, she knew, although she was learning that God's grace was enough.

Hours passed, and inky-blackness deepened the chamber. The handful of servants who remained kept hovering in the doorway.

"Jeremy is afraid of the dark. Beatrix was afraid too." James' impassive statement belied his words, making them all the more frightening because they were filled with desolation and despair.

"'Tis a natural fear," Valentina said. "Everyone is afraid of the dark on occasion."

She recalled Luca's warning whenever their caravan camped near a new town. "We are safe for now, although beware of the dark."

"My son cannot speak," James was saying. "Who will help him if he cried out?"

"You will. I will. For as long as he needs us. Believe in a miracle."

"A miracle," James repeated quietly.

Minutes went by. A sliver of moonbeam lit the dark sky and streamed into Jeremy's chamber.

Valentina and James spent the remainder of the night pacing the floor on either side of Jeremy's bed. Jeremy kicked off the covers when fever burned or clambered for blankets when his teeth clicked. He was a fighter, though, Valentina assured herself. Tough, like his father.

His slight body became a shivering cocoon. He tossed in his sleep.

But he was alive.

She closed her eyes to shut out the slightest distraction—the sputter of the curling flames in the fireplace, the mumbling of servants in the corridor, the grating creak of the carpeted floor beneath her footsteps.

James stared out the window at the night sliding past.

"Jeremy, there's so much I want to show you. Wales. Do you remember our home there, and the sea? I can hear the drumming of the waves against the shoreline, taste the salt ..." His gaze darted to the bed, his face spoke of panic. "Don't leave me, son."

Valentina studied the tall, enigmatic man standing across from her. Desolation filled his haunted features. Slowly and surely, he was being crushed by a sadness he couldn't control.

Other men might fear him in battle, but in this chamber, James was only a desperate father who'd sacrifice everything for his son. And his anguish ran as deep and shattering as her own.

He strode to Jeremy's bed and held his son's small hand, an attempt to infuse his strength into Jeremy's weak body. "I'll not allow you to die. You can't hear me, but God can."

Valentina approached and stood behind James. She wanted to touch his back, clasp his hand. Ordinary acts of kindness she knew he'd never accept from her. He kept his focus on his son and didn't acknowledge her. If the muscles in his forearms hadn't tightened, she might have thought he hadn't even noticed her nearness.

* * *

THE DARKEST HOURS of night slipped by.

With a weightless rap on the door, Geoffrey entered. "Mr. Colchester, I can watch over your son so that you may rest for a few hours. Sir?" Geoffrey raised his voice, for James seemed not to hear him.

"You expect me to leave my son?" James asked, as if he hadn't understood Geoffrey correctly. "I left Jeremy alone countless times when I was away at battle."

"You're of little use to anyone if you're exhausted. You haven't slept in days. Perhaps if you rest for a while—"

"Easy answer. Nay." James shook his head, allowing no room for argument.

With a heavy sigh, Geoffrey threw his hands up in the air. "Very well, sir. I'll be in the hallway. Yolanda and Clare are keeping watch also." Geoffrey retraced his steps and latched the door shut behind him.

Valentina stared at James until he made eye contact, keeping her tone firm. "*I*, however, will continue to stay."

"Stay. Go." He shrugged. "It makes little difference."

The chamber was shadowy, and the flickering fire in the grate burned low, mimicking the pensive mood of the room. Valentina sat on the floor at the foot of Jeremy's bed. James settled a feather pillow beside her, shaking his head when she opened her mouth to thank him.

She watched while he kept his vigil, his lips uttering prayer after prayer, although she didn't know all the words. What she did know was that the fever needed to break, and soon, or Jeremy wouldn't recover. And neither, she knew with the same certainty, would his father.

She knelt by Jeremy's bedside and prayed the same prayer countless times: "Please Lord, come into this chamber and take away this little boy's illness and pain. Let us feel your guidance and grace. Guide us, Lord, we praise you. Amen." She couldn't start with the way things were, so she focused on how He was a triumphant God who performed miracles.

At some point during her prayers, she pressed her fingers to her temples to dull the headache she'd suffered since her fall and felt herself dozing.

* * *

THE DOOR RATTLED. Valentina squinted at the first rays of dawn lighting the chamber. The aromas of warm ale and yeasty bread floated to her nostrils.

James bent to set a tray of food on the night table beside her. "There's little left to eat. Our supplies are low." He inclined his head away from her, preferring to restlessly pace the chamber than sit by her.

"Because the servants have left for Wales?" Blinking in confusion at how long she'd slept, she reached for Jeremy's bedpost and stood.

"Aye."

She clutched the folds of her gown while she attempted to drag enough air into her lungs to dispel the heavy knot of guilt. "How many hours did I sleep?"

"Not many." James added wood to the fire and settled his gaze on his son.

She had vowed to be strong, for Jeremy's sake. Bravery and faithfulness, she reminded herself. Between her and James, they had an abundance of both.

"You, little man, are going to fully recover." She busied herself with tucking the woolen blankets around Jeremy. "James, he seems more comfortable." To illustrate her point, she lifted a finger to her lips and stood quiet, noting Jeremy's raspy breathing had calmed.

James walked toward the bed. "I thought the same."

She shook her head. "I shouldn't have slept so long."

"We all need sleep."

"You don't."

"And in our many years together, since he was a young boy trying to escape the schoolroom, Mr. Colchester required a minimal amount," Geoffrey provided.

Valentina spun.

Standing in the open doorway, the elderly man acknowledged her with a slight nod.

"Geoffrey, you were so quiet I didn't realize you were here," she said.

He strode to the bed and assisted her in tucking the blankets around Jeremy. "Think of me as a guardian angel, silent and ever-present. I've stood in the doorway for a while now, despite Mr. Colchester's insinuations I should hang about in the hallway."

"Some things never change," James murmured. He leaned over and pressed the back of his hand against Jeremy's forehead. With a stiff nod, he swung back to the window and stared out at a colorless dawn.

Valentina hid a slight smile. "A guardian angel is a pleasant idea, Geoffrey."

"Excellent, because you have one also." Geoffrey turned a conspiratorial half-grin toward James, who stood with his back to both of them.

Another insistent knock broke the silence. Clare entered, curtsied, and kept her gaze nailed to the floor. "Mr. Colchester, Tobias insists he must speak with you, sir. He said 'tis urgent."

James scowled and strode from the room. Clare followed him.

Valentina assumed James' earlier position on the right side of Jeremy's bedside. Scattered fragments of sunbeams filtered through the window.

She bent and rubbed her cheek against Jeremy's forehead. His face wasn't as warm. Hope surged, filling her heart.

"Don't give up on Mr. Colchester," Geoffrey said. "He needs you."

She glanced bleakly in the direction of the doorway. "You couldn't be more wrong. He blames me, and for that I must bear his cold manner."

Geoffrey pulled up a stool. "Are you a person who enjoys stories, Valentina?"

The tiniest note of dread whispered between them before she answered. "Aye. Who doesn't? My mother spun many a tale."

"Good, because 'tis necessary you hear this one."

She pulled up a high-backed wooden chair beside Geoffrey. "What kind of story?"

"A story about the people you love."

She braced her hands along her thighs and took in Geoffrey's tight mouth, his sad eyes, his bowed spine.

He beckoned her to lean nearer. "When Jeremy and his sister were born, Mr. Colchester wasn't present for their births. While we were fighting on a gory battlefield, the babies came early."

Valentina gripped her hands in her lap, knowing this story's ending was plagued by grief. "His wife must have been frightened to birth two babies without her husband near," she murmured.

"Aye, and when we returned, Alyce ailed for months. She blamed Mr. Colchester for everything—the fact he was at war and not with her, the hard childbirth, and Jeremy's deafness. She took little interest in either baby, most notably Jeremy."

Geoffrey paused to gaze out the window at the somber treetops, groggy with tiredness, preserving the weariness of the night. Compassion etched his hard-worn features.

"And Beatrix's death is spoken about only in whispers," Valentina said.

"Beatrix was perfect." Geoffrey dropped his voice to a whisper and kept a guarded gaze toward the door. "She resembled her mother, all shiny blonde hair and violet-blue eyes. Unfortunately, the child was too curious for her own safety."

Valentina held the breath in her throat, afraid to exhale, afraid to disturb the fragile memories. Mumbles from the corridor grew louder, followed by James' voice giving rapid directions. Lightly, she touched Geoffrey's arm, encouraging him to continue.

"The day of the accident, Alyce insisted on leaving Jeremy at the main house and taking Beatrix for a walk. Elspeth offered to accompany them, although Alyce refused."

"Perhaps she wanted to spend the afternoon alone with her daughter," Valentina offered.

"Nay." He shook his head. "Beatrix loved sniffing the white roses growing wild along the hedgerows. Perhaps she went looking for them while her mother was otherwise occupied. She didn't realize the child was missing until later that day." Geoffrey concentrated on Jeremy's chest rising and falling beneath the bedcovers. "You see, Alyce met her lover. He is Mr. Wellsey's brother."

"So that's what this feud was all about," Valentina murmured.

Geoffrey paused and rubbed his temples. "And Alyce went into quite a state when no one could find Beatrix, although by evening, she'd confessed her tryst. Mr. Colchester searched all night for his daughter. I've never seen such crazed agony in a man. His frenzied search resulted in the horrific find of his little girl's body the following morning. She'd fallen to the bottom of the cliff."

Tears coursed down Valentina's cheeks. "A nightmare for him, for everyone."

Geoffrey reached into his waistcoat pocket and offered her a linen handkerchief, which she appreciatively accepted.

"As he often does, he blamed himself and grew quieter as the weeks passed. I saw him pray often and watched as he experienced it all—grief, anguish, anger, and a sense of desperateness." Geoffrey shifted, hesitated. "Are you aware Beatrix's death had been foretold a few months beforehand?"

"By whom?"

He let the question hang in the shallow breaths between them. "By you."

Valentina shoved back her chair and stood with a jerk. "Me? When?"

"The Colchesters had visited a traveling fair in a nearby village, Lowestoft, as I recall, where you read Alyce's palm."

Slowly, Valentina sank onto the bed beside Jeremy. "I remember. A distinguished woman inquired about her twin babies and insisted I read her palm. And a man stood a few feet away."

From the furthermost sealed corners of her mind, realizations rushed to the fore. Arms crossed, his back propped against a tree, a tall man with grey eyes had caught Valentina's gaze with nonchalance before letting go.

"Oftentimes, I worried that Mr. Colchester would never recover from Beatrix's death, and his wife carried on for months afterward," Geoffrey was saying.

"Surely she loved her daughter, and her son."

"In her own way, perhaps. Jeremy tried to be close to her. She acted ashamed of him, perhaps resentful because of Beatrix's death. One never knew for certain what Alyce was thinking. The boy clung to his mother. But the harder he tugged at her sleeves, the harder she shook him off."

Valentina's chest felt compressed as if in a vise. She clutched Geoffrey's handkerchief and dabbed at her eyes. James had assumed that Beatrix's death was proof that Valentina's predictions were accurate, and that was why he'd trusted her, despite his belief in God. Her heart broke at his desperation, which she'd betrayed without a care.

Geoffrey went on. "Mr. Colchester believed he should have been able to prevent the accident because of your frightening warning, even though he was skeptical of Gypsies. We all were, although we'd begun to—"

"If you're finished whispering, Geoffrey," James said abruptly as he strode into the chamber, "you may leave."

Geoffrey's sentence trailed off into silence. Stiffening, he stood. "I'll wait in the corridor, sir." With a loud humph, he quit the room.

"You shouldn't speak so curtly to your closest friend." Valentina swallowed to clear her parched throat. "He's concerned about you."

"No need for refined trivialities. Geoffrey knows me well enough." James removed his waistcoat and hung it by the door. He looked leaner than she remembered. His wrinkled linen shirt outlined the contours of his hard chest; the thin morning sunlight accentuated the ache flashing across his handsome face.

How would she ever understand this man? She veered between wanting to shout at him for the distance he'd effectively placed between them or sobbing her regrets against the sweat-stained sleeves of his shirt. She did neither, easing Jeremy's damp hair off his forehead instead.

Aye. The boy's skin was definitely cooler, the color returning to his pallid cheeks. Her hand stopped in midair. "James, the fever is gone."

Two strides brought James to the bedside. He clasped Jeremy's hand. "Are you certain?"

"Aye." Valentina kissed Jeremy's frail fingers through his father's strong ones.

James held her gaze. "Valentina, I've heard your prayers this past day and night, and you've heard mine. Will you join me? Prayers of thanksgiving are greater when said together."

"I've just begun learning your prayers."

"Then you know the words are simple." His hands closed over hers and he bowed his head. "God, please look upon my son with favor. Guide him to adulthood, so he may enable others to live a giving and full life. We pray for thy everlasting mercy." He squeezed her fingers before releasing them. A tear leaked from the corner of her eye. She could fight his anger, but his kind-heartedness would be her undoing.

"I prayed this prayer more times than I could count," he said.

"You display such a strong sense of faith."

"'Tis when I need the most encouragement. And I had a revelation while I prayed. There are some things that my own irresponsibility and despondency created, and I kept searching for a reason—someone to blame. Then I realized God is still with me, through my good decisions as well as my poor ones."

"Your beliefs never falter."

He studied her before he replied, a flicker of disquiet in his eyes. "Nearly never."

His convictions and integrity ran deep and wondrous, and he acted on them, his word true. And she'd never loved him as much as in that moment when he stood so near, yet so removed.

"Keep up your courage, for all of us." Tentatively, she rested her hand on his forearm.

His muscles tensed. "Perhaps you should rest awhile? You're still recovering from your fall." He didn't physically move, although she felt him retreat.

With a sigh, she let go of his arm and touched Geoffrey's handkerchief to her temple. The headache had abated. "Aye, for a few minutes," she agreed.

She stepped toward the door, changing directions for one more peek at Jeremy. The woolen blankets on the bed stirred, and his face peeked out from underneath.

Valentina stood mutely, one hand on the door latch, the other hand splayed across her heart.

"Ver-y …" Jeremy wiggled into a sitting position. His smile seemed to light up the entire gaping chamber.

She hurried toward the slender boy, enveloping his body with hers. Warmness healed everything inside her that had earlier been cold.

"'Tis so good, so good, to see you smile."

"God was listening and answered our prayers, son." As she released Jeremy, his father hugged him, holding him so fiercely she wondered if he'd ever let him go.

She dabbed at her tears with Geoffrey's already damp handkerchief. "Our God is a God of faith. His presence in this chamber gave me purpose."

"Because praying works." For the first time since she'd returned, James smiled.

"Hungry." Jeremy pointed to his stomach and scrambled beneath his father's grasp.

"There's plain bread and warm ale." Valentina frowned at her forgotten tray of food. "Surely I can find something more appetizing for him in the kitchen." Thrilled at the healthy color already returning to the boy's face, she studied his father's haggard one. "He'll recover fully, James."

He wiped at his eyes. "Thank God."

Her chest lightened. She wanted to fling the tray to the ceiling, then wrap her arms around both James and Jeremy, kissing them with all the elation in her heart.

"He's with us wherever we go," she said.

"Emanuel." Joy flickered in James's gaze. "He showed up in the middle of despair."

"And He is here now."

CHAPTER 23

Patshiv tumenge Romale.
This song was offered as a gift to worthy men.
Old Romany saying

*J*ames hardly noticed the amber-tinted sunlight filtering through the clouds lighting the winter landscape. Since Jeremy's recovery, he had spent the days tallying his accounts. Trade was paralyzed because of the influenza epidemic and rural England was hard-hit. However, a shortage of necessary supplies had forced his hand, and he was preparing to depart for Wales before the end of the week.

"Tad!"

James looked up from his seat behind his desk in the study. He gazed out the half-open window as his son ice skated across the lawn in his boots. Valentina ran close behind him.

Jeremy broke off his carefree wave to concentrate on his

balance. "Eeek! Uh-oh." He fell into the slick grass with a squish.

"Jeremy!" James sprang from his chair, bounded down the hallway and darted outdoors.

Valentina had already hoisted Jeremy upright, sweeping the snow off his royal-blue cloak. "Your son wanted to learn how to skate on the snow." Her mouth creased into an easy smile and she dabbed at her wind-lashed nose.

"He did? Or you did?" His amused gaze flitted over her. Her gown matched the crimson of her lips, as rich and vivid as the vegetable rouge English women wore on their cheeks. She looked so attractive it took him several seconds before he could look away.

She laughed. "'Tis a splendid day and too agreeable to stay indoors. The physician said Jeremy is completely recovered."

"Aye. The remaining servants have burst into euphoric activity, readying for the journey to Wales."

"Euphoric?" she teased with a grin. "Still using fancy words, Mr. Colchester?"

She didn't call him *James* anymore, he noted. How long had it been?

"Are you impressed?" he asked aloud.

"You should speak in Welsh or learn a few useful phrases in Romany."

"Thanks to you, I've learned a number of colorful Gypsy curses. At least, I think they're curses. Is that a start?" Their smiles connected, and he was tempted to continue their friendly banter. He even debated asking her to join him for supper.

Nay. Never again. He silenced his tongue. His grin slipped away.

She licked the last trace of snow from her bottom lip. "You're doing it again."

"What?"

"Staring at me and scowling. Do you think I'm too old to play childish games in the snow?"

"On the contrary, I thought to join you. However, there's much I must attend to before departure."

"Some other time, then," she called out to him as he returned to his much-too-large home and endless responsibilities.

He inclined his head, neither agreeing nor disagreeing. It was easier this way—simply enjoying his son's devotion to her. Their squealing joy should have lifted his spirits. Their happiness should have been contagious. Instead, the emotions left him with impossible obstacles, bringing a genuine sadness to his chest.

Just when he thought he could walk two steps without thinking of Valentina, lyrical Gypsy songs floated across the fields to resonate vivid chords in his heart. When he caught her expressive eyes staring at him, his heart lurched, his stomach tightened. And then he remembered her deceit—her deceit with her fortune-telling and how she had run away.

He paced his chamber each evening, any semblance of restful sleep evasive. Valentina had always stripped him of the skill to act reasonably. Why should these final hours be any different? He knew the servants were impatient to embark on their journey to Wales, but he told himself he had to be certain Jeremy was well enough to travel. However, that wasn't the only reason he waited. He was delaying telling her.

Truth be told, he was delaying telling himself.

* * *

JAMES AND GEOFFREY dined together at midday, carrying their sparse meals up to James's private chamber. As he did every day, Geoffrey spread a woven tablecloth over the decorative wooden table and set their bowls on top.

"What I wouldn't do for a tankard of sweet Welsh ale and fresh venison," he said.

"Include a loaf of laverbread seasoned with bacon fat and a fistful of honeyed almonds while you imagine a perfect meal." James seated himself across from Geoffrey, eyeing the dirty smudge on his spoon before stirring the suspicious broth in his bowl. "Anything is better than what we've eaten lately."

Geoffrey picked at his half-cooked goose and took a tentative bite. He scowled, pushed the plate to the side and loosened the ring of his black leather belt to better fit his stomach's wide girth.

"No doubt Valentina will enjoy Wales," came his unasked-for observation.

James' spoon slid into the broth and disappeared. "I believe we were talking about food, not Gypsies."

"Our food may be inadequate, but our conversation can still be entertaining."

"Entertaining or disagreeable?"

"I only speak with your permission."

"And when did this start?" Getting up, James strode to a table in the corner and poured himself and Geoffrey a generous goblet of wine. "Please—eat, drink and speak your mind."

Geoffrey gave his best imitation of looking contrite, then shrugged. "When you were away, the household panicked after Roland's death. Your son was beyond himself with fright, and Valentina comforted him constantly."

James held the heaviness in his heart. "My place was here with my son, not on a battlefront fighting a war for an impetuous king."

"You had no idea influenza would strike while you were gone."

"Because I wasn't paying attention. Memories, sad memories, had taken hold of my heart. And because I was too interested in a Gypsy woman who dominated my every thought." James gazed through the window and surveyed the sweeping view of his estate, along with the emptiness of the late January day. The leaded glass pane lent a blue tint to the ringlets of smoke streaming from the kitchen chimney across the courtyard.

"Sometimes, the greatest gift comes from the greatest regret." Subjecting James to a brief perusal, Geoffrey added, "No disrespect intended, Mr. Colchester. However, you look like you haven't slept in a month."

James brought their goblets back to the table. "Has anyone ever mentioned that tactfulness is not your forte?"

Amusement glinted in Geoffrey's eyes before he turned his attention back to extracting a hunk of meat off the bone. Failing at the attempt, he sat back and downed a tidy swig of wine. "Valentina has capably reassumed her role as Jeremy's caretaker."

James took a long swallow of his drink. "Thank you for your astute observation, Geoffrey, although I already employ Elspeth, a calm and thoughtful nurse who has attended to him since his birth."

"Aye, she's a lovely woman, though as ancient as Merlin the magician, and she's not Jeremy's mother." Geoffrey raised his goblet. "Every child needs a mother."

"His mother is dead."

"A mother is a woman who loves a child and will sacrifice everything for him. A woman who is also an equal partner for the child's father. Someone who's unselfish and gentle and ..."

Half-listening to Geoffrey's droning, James pondered a

number of ways to politely dismiss his steward. Before the afternoon faded, James planned on confronting Valentina, and the afternoon was fading rapidly.

"Mr. Colchester, have you heard a word I said?"

"Aye. You refer to Valentina, and two months ago, I would have agreed with you." James grimaced at the whiff of a vinegary vegetable he didn't recognize. He fished his spoon from the broth and shoved the offensive food toward Geoffrey.

Sitting forward, Geoffrey inspected the broth with genuine interest. "And have you noticed—"

"I wouldn't want to deprive you of your two favorite pastimes, saying whatever is on your mind and eating."

Geoffrey made no attempt to cloak his grin. "Have you noticed Valentina's expression whenever you're around her?"

"As always, her tongue is tart and her manner insolent."

Her sparkling laughter had shimmered beneath his skin on one too many occasions of late. His body's reaction to her had blindsided him, a reminder she wielded power.

"She regards you with respect and admiration, oftentimes when you're not looking. And she sings every morning in her Gypsy language no one understands except Yolanda. Do you enjoy hearing Valentina's songs as much as I do?"

James started from his chair, then sat back down. He debated about whether to reply to Geoffrey's rhetorical question. No response at all might be taken as agreement. He gave a low whistle through his teeth. "I hear little else."

"She told me the melodies and words were lullabies from her childhood. Her voice is lovely."

"Aye." James lifted his goblet as if in a toast. "Lovely voice, lovely eyes and a lovely face."

"You cannot live alone forever."

"Your directness is laudable, Geoffrey. However, my son is perfect company."

"He's a child." Geoffrey blithely ignored James's unwavering frown. "You need a strong woman by your side, because a man like you will want more children."

"One surviving child is a blessing."

Images of olive-skinned toddlers with flashing grey eyes and tangled black hair skipped through James' mind. Wishful notions, forever intruding and invading. He swallowed hard and cut them off.

Geoffrey kept his steady gaze on James. "You prefer the Welsh countryside to England. 'Tis isolated, and few people would give a second look to a Gypsy woman."

A beautiful Gypsy woman would draw stares wherever she went. Still, James found no reason to dispute the finer points of the discussion. Once Geoffrey formed an opinion, he held onto it like a cat that scurried around its owner's feet until it was fed.

James drained his goblet and grimaced, belatedly remembering how much he disliked sweet wine. "Have you forgotten what she did? I made one misstep in marrying a dishonest woman, and I won't make another."

"Valentina spoke a half-truth in foolishness and desperation."

James laid down his spoon and scraped back his chair. "Surely you don't expect me to forgive her?" Try as he might, James couldn't read Geoffrey's answer, well hidden in the depths of his steward's clouded blue eyes.

"Perhaps—"

James surged to his feet.

Geoffrey, on the other hand, remained relaxed in his chair. "You don't believe in Gypsy superstitions and fortune-telling. Forgiveness will release your heart from rage and resentment. Or you will grow to be an unreasonable old man."

"Like yourself?"

"I never regretted my decisions. Nonetheless, I'd loathe

seeing you live your life alone, knowing 'twill be filled with sadness and regret."

"I will live in peace."

"A lonely existence is no life for a man in your position."

James leaned over the table to peer at Geoffrey. "Do you believe for one moment I didn't consider marriage to Valentina? I have thought of little else, my friend." He chafed his fingers against his temples. Memories recurred of the meal Valentina had offered to prepare for him. Pickled porcupine, or some such Gypsy dish, seasoned with hot black pepper. For a wedding, a Gypsy wedding, a feast comparable to any the English aspired to.

Geoffrey met James' stare with bullish determination. "Even a strong emotion is better than none."

Noncommittal, James hedged for a beat. "No emotion is best."

Geoffrey seemed to form his next words cautiously. "Will Valentina and Yolanda accompany us to Wales? Yolanda is eager to see Reginald. She inquires incessantly about him whenever I pass her in the halls."

"Reginald is a good man, despite his disloyal efforts."

"He displayed more courage than I ever suspected he had in him." Geoffrey sat straighter. "What *are* your plans for the women?"

James stared past Geoffrey, regarding the frost gathering outside the mullioned window. "Need I mention the fact I prefer silence over your insistent, prying questions?"

To James' annoyance, Geoffrey simply finished his goose and reached for James' broth. He skirted the broth out of Geoffrey's reach, then strode to his chamber door, opening it so wide the hinges whined. "My friend, you must be pondering the numerous preparations for our departure, and I won't delay you any longer."

Geoffrey grunted to his feet. "I've been more than ready

to depart for a fortnight. In any case, I trust you'll come to the right decision." With an affectionate slap on James' shoulder, Geoffrey quit the chamber.

As Geoffrey's footsteps lumbered down the stairs, James sat back down in his chair and propped one booted foot over the other.

Valentina expected to travel to Wales come the morrow. He'd pretended not to see the quiet anticipation in her eyes, the questioning glances whenever he mentioned their upcoming journey. *'Twas easy to fake ignorance.*

Once, he'd believed her a woman of spirit and compassion, kindness and empathy. Instead, she'd misled him, all the while obediently complying with the rhythm of his household. Believing him an idiot.

Forgiveness. Remember Colossians 3:13. "Bear with each other and forgive one another if any of you has a grievance against someone. Forgive as the Lord forgave you."

A grudging laugh, a shake of his head. Nay, he couldn't, not this time. Valentina had taken away his expectations and dreams, and his disappointment ran too deep. Alyce had taught him well. He'd lost a valuable part of himself that he couldn't risk losing again.

He brought his rigid shoulders forward and stood. As if his legs were made of wood, he strode to the window. Hesitant, he slid his fingers over the cold glass and opened the bottom pane.

Valentina's laughter trilled upward. "Jeremy, you're thirstier than a lake with no rain. And nay, I won't go with you to visit the falconer because I loathe those awful birds. I'll walk through the garden and see if any herbs remain that I can salvage for the journey."

Jeremy chuckled before scampering off like a skylark. She'd probably made one of her absurd, silly faces.

At the vision, a streak of unanticipated joy flowed through James. In spite of his trouble-filled heart, he smiled.

CHAPTER 24

Kay zhala I suv shay zhala wi o thav.
Where the needle goes surely the thread shall follow.
Old Romany saying

A few minutes later, James donned a heavy cloak and headed to the herb garden. For months, he'd thought of the herb garden as Valentina's garden. They'd strolled its flagstone path numerous afternoons when he'd overseen her planting efforts. Wheelbarrow in tow, she'd doubled the size of the herbal beds. The beds, arranged in neat, rectangular rows, stretched from the kitchen garden to the far side of his home. By June, sage, parsley, and thyme would bloom.

At least, that was the plan.

A whisper of wintry air tiptoed across his cheeks. He blew on his hands and tucked them inside his cloak. He checked on Jeremy first, who was with the falconer. Then, James continued on to the garden.

He stopped short when he reached her. For an infinite minute, he just stared.

Flanked by a garden spade and her yellow scarf, Valentina sat on a decorative iron bench bordered by shrubs. A burgundy velvet pelisse cradled her body and pooled at her ankles, and a large cashmere shawl covered her shoulders. Sunlight warmed her skin to ripe chestnut. Her lustrous hair flowed around her, reminding him of an ebony waterfall.

His breath came quickly. Even at this distance, she captivated him.

A layer of unmarked snow crunched beneath his boots as he approached.

She smiled at him. "Did Jeremy find the falconer?"

"Aye. And I found you."

"I'm not very hard to find these days. Seldom do I wander like I used to. Mr. Colchester … James." She shrugged. "I don't know how to address you anymore."

"I'm the same man."

"Are you?"

"Who else would I be?" He walked behind the bench, unable to resist combing his fingers through her hair. "Address me whatever way you'd like."

She tilted her head back and settled her hands in her lap. "I like *James*."

"James it is, then." Despite his unsteady efforts, her hair crackled beneath his fingertips.

Her head rested on the garden bench, her face turned to the sky. "Why are you smirking?"

"Because you always say whatever you please, regardless of my opinion."

She looked up at him with her laughing, extraordinary gaze. "I try to think before I speak."

"Surely not when I'm near."

"You seem different. You've avoided me since I returned. Are you angry about something?"

"Why would I be angry?" He gave a cracked, hopeless laugh. Was that what this emotion was called—the one making his muscles clench and his face brittle?

Her wide-set eyes sparkled like the purest emeralds, blemished with a yellow speck of hesitation in the center. "Did you come to the garden to comb my hair?"

He smiled inwardly, because she knew him so well. "You may speak first."

"About what? *You* came to see *me*." She rose from the bench and turned to face him, forcing him to release her hair. "I have nothing to say, except 'tis freezing and I'm going inside." She straightened her shawl, lifted the hem of her pelisse, and started walking away.

He grabbed her hand, enveloped her in his arms and pressed her body close.

"I waited and waited," she said, "and I was beginning to think you no longer cared." Her tongue slid over his parted lips. Her hot breath tickled the prickly hairs of his beard. "I miss the walks we used to take together. I miss—"

No man could resist a woman like her, his melting mind rationalized. He kissed her, savoring her sultriness, stamping her skin with blistering, wild kisses.

His conscience nudged. *What was he doing?*

He'd sought to tell her of his decision, not to kiss her.

He dragged his lips from hers and took a rigid step backward.

"What's wrong?"

"Nothing." *She's a trickster. Remember?* Yet when he kissed her, he couldn't feel a trace of deceit in her response.

She folded her arms around his neck. "Thank you for being so tolerant. You're a good, forgiving man. I don't deserve—"

He shook off her hands. She probably hadn't told him the truth since they'd met.

And she'd never accepted responsibility for what she'd done but had blatantly withheld the truth from him. He didn't believe in fortune-telling, although that wasn't the point. A lie by omission … He had to be strong. He'd cared for her so much, fallen in love with her, asked her to be his wife and spend her life with him. Yet now when he gazed at her, he felt conflicted, his anger a constant reminder of her dishonesty. His gut split in thirds as infinite seconds passed. Her captivating eyes bore into his and she leaned in to kiss him.

He hadn't intended this. He'd come to say goodbye.

Recklessness warred with reason as he answered her kiss. His tongue probed. Her delightful mouth opened and gave.

Her moistened lips brushed his throat, and she inclined her head toward the pathway. "Someone might see us."

He kissed her earlobe and breathed in her ear, "We're concealed by the garden wall."

Her fingers burrowed into his back, her mouth feather-touched his. He tried to focus on the sunlight, the snow, the hazelnut trees—anything except her nearness. Her mouth moved urgently against his. Her silky eyelashes fluttered, a surrendering sigh across his cheek.

In the blue-grey glow of the winter afternoon, his tongue explored, voracious, like a starving beggar. "Valentina, I can never get my fill of you. Why? Why?"

Her hands twined through his hair. "Because we love each other."

He reclaimed her lips in one last kiss, branding her with possessiveness so that she'd never forget him. His gorgeous, irresistible Gypsy woman.

Me kamav tut. She placed a light kiss on his chin, marking a path down his neck.

He grasped her face, stopping her. A blistering wind blew across his nape. He shuddered and

waited for the tremor to pass.

Floating silver crystals of snow outlined her flawless face, and her spicy scent heated the coldness around them. The tip of her tongue peeked beneath her lips. "Are we leaving for Wales come the morrow?" Her combination of innocence and sensuality kept him spellbound.

A war raged through him, the battle cry of betrayal. He stared past her, his resolve

slipping, his tidy piece of earth swept to the side.

"Nay."

"When are we leaving?"

"Soon. There's something I intended to tell you first."

"First?" Her expression closed. "Before you kissed me, or after?"

If she didn't look so heartbreakingly gorgeous, if he didn't despise himself, he wouldn't be so torn. Nay, he couldn't be weak. He needed to be in control.

Their gazes met, and for the first time in his life, he wasn't sure how to begin. She seemed so far away. He wanted to touch her again. He didn't. He wouldn't get hurt ever again.

"Unfortunately, all the women I've known in my life seldom speak the truth," he said.

Her fingers fumbled with the edges of her shawl. "My mother was truthful."

The air murmured by, a silent beat after beat.

"Women think they can dupe a man."

'Twas the beginning of a conversation with no end. She'd never understand. His words wouldn't matter to her.

"James." She reached out her hand. "Geoffrey confided about your late wife and how Beatrix died."

"My wife cared little about our daughter."

Stains of color flamed Valentina's cheeks, her emerald eyes shining.

Stay focused. Stay focused. She was a consummate street performer and would use all her feminine tricks to deter him. He grasped a handful of icy snow from the bench, hoping to numb his feelings.

Tendrils of black hair wreathed her face, frozen into wavy curlicues—calling to mind a provocative ice princess from a far-off snowy land.

He drew in the deadened air, tranquil except for ice tinkling against stark tree branches.

"If I'd stayed longer in your chamber that night," he said, "I might have asked where you intended to go once I left."

Her slim fingers tucked her hair under the shawl, exposing her birthmark. Moist with snow, it glittered like a miniature horseshoe.

Worry was overtaking her expression. Why had she deceived him and cheated them out of their love? Why couldn't she have been honest?

"Has the entire night escaped you?" he persisted. "If I hadn't been half dead because of my beating by a misguided Gypsy tribe, I would have woken and heard the creaking wood floor as you departed. Nonetheless, on a midnight breeze and a chestnut mare"—he snapped his fingers—"you and your sister trotted off. Only a person harboring a secret slips away when the hour is darkest."

Her hands fidgeted like dueling swords. "I never intended to hurt you."

"You have a dramatic way of accomplishing your goals."

"Your goals are my goals."

"My goal is to protect my son."

She bit down on her shaking lower lip. "You know I love Jeremy."

"And yet you left."

"If I'd known Jeremy was sick, I never would have left." Her tone rose and sliced the stillness. He recognized that tone. It reminded him of his late wife's high, teary voice whenever she was backed into a corner.

Tapping his fingers on the garden bench, he waited. An intense sorrow hit him at the loss to come, and he had no way to defend himself.

"Why did you leave, Valentina?"

"You're an honorable gentleman. I couldn't let you spend your life with the likes of me." Her expression was so vulnerable he had to physically stop himself from wrapping his arms around her to protect her.

He shoved away from the bench. "Why did you leave so suddenly?"

She snatched up her sodden yellow scarf from the ground. "You're making me feel as though you are peering down from atop your gentlemanly perch—judging and belittling."

"What were you running from?"

"Myself."

Her quiet breathing was sweet, filling the air.

The wind no longer howled. In a desolate garden, the normalness of an ordinary winter afternoon ceased. He counted the number of times she blinked before dropping her gaze. A tiny piece of blue embroidery lined the sleeves of her gown, and she fiddled with the lace at the cuff.

"The night I read your palm," she said, still looking down, "I didn't tell you everything. I'm sorry. Please forgive me. I was wrong and made a terrible mistake."

He gripped her forearms. "Mistake? Is that what you call it?" *She'd broken his heart.*

Tears flowed from her eyes. With a pang of self-reproach, he let her go.

"I'm sorry." She wrapped her arms around herself and wept. "Please accept my apology."

"Why?" He thought he repeated the question aloud, although he could no longer be sure.

Why? The question he'd asked himself countless times.

Because he'd been fastened to sadness and trepidation so long, he'd decided on his own foolish plan, relying on superstition and disregarding God. Because he'd felt God had abandoned him.

James peered up at the thick, sullen clouds, then down at the snow accumulating at their feet.

She lowered her gaze. "I want to be a good person. I try and I fail."

He folded his arms, driven by a need to be right. "What did you see on my palm that first night?"

"You don't believe. I don't believe."

"Indulge me."

Tears glinted. Strange that at this moment he thought of her lashes as luxuriant, velvety fans she could no longer hide behind. Stranger still, she attempted to conceal her tears from him. Most women used tears to their advantage.

Furiously, she wiped at her eyes. "I saw sickness."

He snapped his head to the side, as if she'd actually struck him.

"My son. He loves you." So calm, so numb, some other man must be speaking.

"I love him too. And by reading your fortune, we ventured into a place we shouldn't have gone. My spirits are false because there's only one true God. You knew it before I did, yet you asked."

"You're blaming me?"

Even as he spoke, he knew she was right. He'd been out of step with God, and desperation and fear had steered him far from the truth. He needed to follow God in the right order.

There was no easy answer to his dilemma about traveling to Wales. It took prayer and prayer alone.

Her unmanageable hair clung to her face. He nudged the wet strands away before forcing his

hands down.

"You'll never understand how the rest of us struggle just to survive," she said. "When I first met you, that was my life. I knew no other."

Images flared through his mind, infinite bloody battles. "'Tis the life you're used to, as I am used to mine."

"I was obliged to you for every meal, every piece of clothing."

"You and your sister were welcome guests." Guilt stabbed like needles, numbing his frozen feet. Unnerved, he pushed out words wedged in his throat far too long. "I assumed you were happy with me and my son. Wasn't that enough, sharing a lifetime together? I would have given you everything I own, Valentina. Everything."

"We can still have our life together." Guarded hope shone in her eyes, the hope he'd once had,

that elusive shimmer of happiness. He could never get it back.

"I won't be a fool again." He locked his hands behind him and fixed his gaze beyond her on the bare branches of the trees. "I came to tell you I've made arrangements for you and Yolanda to be escorted to London. My son and I and the remainder of the servants will travel to Wales."

She drew in her breath with a loud gasp.

Life, his life, must go on without her. *Unthinkable. Unimaginable. No other course.*

Terrible regrets assailed him. To control her trembling, and in an insane effort to comfort her, he gripped her arms as if to give her courage against his words, against him.

Face pale, eyes proud, she coolly lifted his hands away from her.

A lonely existence, Geoffrey warned.

"I'm leaving." She spoke to herself, reflective, no longer hearing him. "Influenza may sweep throughout England soon."

"Your journey won't end in London. I've made further arrangements for you and Yolanda to travel to Scotland. You'll be safe there."

"Nay. We'll go where our tribe has settled."

"'Tis safer in Scotland until the influenza epidemic passes." In addition, he'd be tempted to seek her out if she were any closer.

She took a low, shuddering breath. "'Tis so far away."

"Gypsies are resilient. Better to escape an epidemic and be protected from exposure."

"You condemn Yolanda and me to a life of begging and stealing."

He shook his head. "I'll give you both a substantial amount of money to live comfortably."

"You're sadly delusional if you believe we'd ever accept money from you!"

"Your safety will be ensured by me and my acquaintances abroad."

"Are you paying to make amends and atone for your indifference?"

He extended his hands, attempting to explain. "I'm trying to do what's best."

"Yolanda counts the days until she sees Reginald. This arrangement will break her heart."

"There are many hearts broken today, cariad."

"I thought you loved me." Her words came in whispers. "I thought I meant more to you than one of your endless possessions."

Uneasy determination propelled him. He needed to ensure she loathed him so she'd never look back. "Perhaps you'll find another caravan in Scotland. Many men will want you as their wife. Your Gypsy friend, for one." The image of her with another man, any man, tore at his insides. He blotted the thought out of his mind, for 'twould surely kill him.

Ramrod straight, she clasped her shawl tighter. "Once, I believed you were an honorable man. A true gentleman caring for his lands and his tenants. How wrong I was, because you're an unforgiving man. Your son may be deaf, but you're blind."

"What you did—"

"I want to see Jeremy, to tell him I'm leaving and kiss him good-bye."

"'Twill be too difficult for Jeremy to see you weeping. Better he remembers you by your laughter than your tears."

James half-expected the snowflakes to keep falling, harder and faster, leaving them frozen in time. The snow had stopped, though, and a wan sun desperately tried to warm the air before it sank beyond the grey horizon.

"I'll arrange for Geoffrey and Richard to ride with you to London, as I realize you trust them. A servant will awaken you at dawn." Already the gravity of his decision wound around his heart like a shackle, and he feared his feet might root him to the spot behind the garden bench forever. A lifeless, ice-covered statue that had once been a man.

She rolled her yellow scarf between trembling hands. "Once I depart, don't try to find me. I'll disappear."

"Rest assured, I will not seek you, cariad."

An infuriated sob broke from her throat. "I'm not your sweetheart."

He didn't expect the glorious, defiant woman who raised her gaze to his. Chest heaving, she almost smiled when she snapped the scarf across his cheek, so sudden his head jerked to one side. She dodged a twisted hazelnut tree as she pivoted and marched through the snow in a flurry of ruined velvet.

He rubbed his sore cheek. "Valentina, if you knew how much ..."

Even from a distance, the slam of the heavy front door rang throughout the deserted garden. He retraced her small footprints across the whiteness of the fresh snow. When he reached the entry, he had the urge to yank the miserable door off its brass hinges.

Hours past sundown, James stood in the shadowy upper corridor of his magnificent home, lashing himself with the sound of Valentina's racking sobs. He leaned against her chamber door, taking in her sorrows, struggling to eradicate her pain. In hopelessness he whispered, "I'm sorry." He whispered over and over, empty words because the person who mattered most couldn't hear him.

She'd endured countless hardships, withstanding her burdens with bravery and grace. No one else he'd ever known had displayed a more splendid fortitude or stronger character. Tougher than any man, she'd been afraid to own up to her mistake because she'd feared his inability to forgive, his massive pride.

I thought you loved me.

He closed his eyes. He'd planned everything sensibly, carefully, wisely, because he was right and she was wrong. He was now free of resentment.

However, he didn't feel very free because he'd lost the only woman he would ever love.

CHAPTER 25

Mutato nominee, de te fibula narratu.
With but a single change of name, the story fits thee quite the
same.
Romany spiritual incantation

*I*t was the last cariad that had done it.

James' final Welsh endearment before casting her out of his life.

The wood fire blazing in the fireplace did little to warm Valentina, nor stop her persistent shaking. She stifled her sobs into her pillow to drive out her grief. Throughout the night, her emotions had spiraled. Then they disintegrated, leaving an empty shadow of a person she once knew.

The first rays of morning prompted her awake.

She rose and shuffled to the basin on her bureau. Survival. Moving on.

She ripped off her muslin dressing gown and flung it to the floor. She splashed cold water on her swollen eyes and lathered herself with a shard of rosemary-tinged soap, the scent of pine burning her nostrils.

Kneeling, she groped through the trunk in the corner of her chamber where she'd kept her Romany clothes. All those months ago, she'd laundered and sewed her scarlet gown. Wisps of black pepper, comforting scents, and the roughness of homespun cotton soothed her sadness. She donned the scarlet gown and smoothed out the wrinkled seams.

Taking a deep breath, she descended the stairway and stepped outside. Blinking back tears, she greeted Yolanda, who wore a full-length coat and carried a beaded reticule, every inch the English lady.

Yolanda answered with a cheerful smile, an attempt to hide the sadness lurking in her deep, soulful eyes. It was everywhere, this sadness, Valentina thought, as Yolanda grasped her icy hands, an attempt to give Valentina a strength she couldn't accept.

Someday she would be competent again, courageous again, consistent again. Just not today.

The lawn spun, and the ice glinting from the peak of James' home grew fainter. Yolanda shouted, although Valentina couldn't understand her because of the roaring in her ears.

"Are you unwell? Here, take my coat." Yolanda secured her full-length coat around Valentina's shoulders. "I'm bringing my jacket also."

Valentina tried to straighten, to act proper and strong for her sister. "Thank you."

The sight of Yolanda's solid expression brought feelings of unabashed pride. Yolanda had abandoned the man she loved to stand beside her sister. If Yolanda held Valentina responsible for taking her away from Reginald, she gave no indication. She only offered compassion and courage.

Together, they gazed upward at James' home.

"No different from any other wealthy landed gentry's home," Yolanda murmured.

A slight stirring shifted the ash-grey light in James' chamber window. Valentina's heart quaked, a flurry of hope he might still be there. He might glance out the window, extend a teasing smile.

Nay. A man like him couldn't love a woman like her. They were from two unlike worlds—poles apart. Hadn't she tried to read what lurked behind his silvery eyes? For an exposed second, she thought she'd glimpsed his pain. Now she realized she'd been mistaken.

I assumed you were happy with me and my son. Wasn't that enough, sharing a lifetime together?

"Do you know how much I love him?" she whispered to Yolanda.

Yolanda gave Valentina's trembling hands a reassuring squeeze. "Aye."

"Valentina."

A little boy called out and Valentina peered through the morning fog.

"Jeremy! Little man, I'm here." Her gaze caught a round red checker jutting from the snow. She bent and slipped the checker into the folds of her coat, a precious keepsake for all she'd lost.

Yolanda extended a questioning glance, and Valentina shook her head, knowing she'd imagined Jeremy's voice. Only the woof of a stray dog pierced the quiet.

Geoffrey rounded the corner of the stables leading an enormous black horse. "I beg your pardon, Valentina. If you're expecting Mr. Colchester, he and his son departed before daybreak. Tobias and the others rode out with them." Geoffrey studied her. "You're so pale. Are you and Yolanda strong enough to ride? We can take one of the carriages."

"Of course. When have you known a Rom to be weak?"

Unable to bear the elderly man's scrutiny, Valentina turned her head.

"I'm certain Mr. Colchester bids you a safe journey." Geoffrey checked the saddle's girth and then patted the horse's neck. Its ears pricked, and its bushy tail swished behind a squared-off body. James obviously had ordered the use of a military animal, one ridden for extended travel.

Her strength of mind rising with her chin, Valentina accepted Geoffrey's gloved assistance to mount the horse. Simple motions required greater effort, and her movements were labored.

Once she was seated, Geoffrey swung up behind her. She clutched the horse's wiry mane and focused on Richard and Yolanda mounting their own black and white steed. Hooves ringing, they crossed the cobblestone courtyard.

The two horses gathered speed. Geoffrey pushed the horse into a gallop, and Richard and Yolanda followed at a close clip. They reached the outer edges of James' estate, then followed a narrow path rather than the main road.

"We're going in a different direction than I expected," Valentina said.

"'Tis a shorter route."

The devastation in her chest broke into an inconsolable sob. James had wasted no time in ridding himself of her. The quicker, the better, he'd obviously told Geoffrey.

Her heartbeat dulled. If the pressure in her lungs ceased, she might be able to breathe.

Geoffrey broke the hush of the following three days by recounting a stream of ceaseless tales, albeit one-sided. He related the history of Mr. Colchester's estate, how many years he'd served Mr. Colchester's parents and the battles he'd proudly fought by Mr. Colchester's side. Carefully, he avoided using a certain man's given name.

Valentina replied to Geoffrey's long-winded epics in

monosyllables. She welcomed their hurried pace since it helped her sleep at night.

Whenever they stopped and rested, Richard offered a tranquil prayer, and Valentina prayed with him. Richard spoke softly, a pious vicar, garbed in a black suit and white cravat. For the most part, Yolanda listened and nodded, as was her character.

On their fourth day of travel, Yolanda's loud exclamation woke Valentina from a fitful sleep.

London emerged, nay, *swarmed,* in front of them, and pigeons flew in scattered paths overhead. Haze cloaked the city's ragged edges, the crooked rooftops and spiked chimneys backlit by the pocket of an amber sun.

Valentina's head jerked up. On these twisted streets, Troka had sated his lust with her.

The sickening waves of horror erupted, as dreadful as that day long ago. She wiped the sweat off her hairline, slowed her breathing to a crawl, and clutched the horse's mane. Why had she assumed the passage of time would bury the memories? How isolated she'd felt, her worth as a person unraveling, along with her honor. That evening, the cold of a winter's night had snuck in, and Valentina had never felt so alone.

And all these years later, she still felt alone, and there was nothing for it now.

She stroked the horse's mane and wiped a strand of hair from her eyes. The awful stench of waste and garbage oozed from packed alleyways. Grimy, underfed children ran alongside Geoffrey's and Richard's horses, begging for coin.

Yolanda fingered the lining of her fine Spencer jacket. Then her gaze darted to a harried man, tugging and shouting obscenities, tugging at a herd of goats. A woman hunched over, gaze dull, dirty white cap untied, carrying a basket of soiled laundry.

All of London looked forgotten and tired.

"We lived here once, like these people, trying to survive each day," Yolanda said.

"We've changed, even if London cannot," Valentina replied.

For the first time since arriving in the city, she noted Geoffrey and Richard exchanging a faint signal. Catching her gaze, Geoffrey offered, "Mr. Colchester arranged for you and Yolanda to rest at an inn for a few days. From what I recall, the Smuggler's Purse is clean and serves a good meal."

"We'll not accept any more tokens from him." Valentina reluctantly commended James for his generosity, although her life and future was her doing from now on, not his.

Geoffrey handed her a generous amount of coin. "He insists."

She didn't argue. Instead, she beckoned to a particularly scrawny boy who'd followed them into the city and decided how best to use James' offerings.

* * *

WHY, James thought, avoiding another thatch-roofed village, did it seem like he'd never reach the Welsh border? He'd led his group through remote areas of England to avoid the influenza epidemic. Unending days of hard riding did little to settle his raging disposition, and his servants struggled to keep up with his breakneck tempo.

For most of the journey, Elspeth and Jeremy rode in a carriage behind him. The nurse sat rigid, stout frame upright, bending now and then to tend to Jeremy's needs. She doted on him, as a good nurse should, heedful of his frailness.

Jeremy's puppy had doubled in size in less than six months. Within fifteen seconds of departing, its continuous barking grated on James's already frayed nerves. The offensive dog had been placed in the carriage with Jeremy, to his acute delight and Elspeth's speechless dismay.

They rode for hours, days, in blessed silence. James used the time wisely—to dwell on his torturous memories of Valentina. Her lilting laugh, her impudent wit, her splendid fearlessness. He took in little of the sparse English landscape nor the icy paths beneath his horse's hooves. When he wished to force himself to the brink of madness, his mind burned with thoughts of her trembling words.

I thought you loved me.

Awash in those particular tormented reminders, he noticed dusk nearing.

He glanced to his left. In the cumbersome coach, his son snuggled beneath a nubby blanket, a wriggling dog on one side, a flustered nurse on the other.

James smiled at the trio, his first smile in days, before self-reproach stole the smile from his lips. He hadn't allowed Valentina to see Jeremy one last time. What had he done instead? Refused her, of course.

He uttered his preferred curse of the day at himself, grinding another spike into his sore joints by recalling her pale, dry lips and hollow expression.

The sky had blackened by the time James halted. In a grove surrounded by fir trees, the servants dismounted. For several minutes, his son ran along the compacted snow while the men built campfires. The hiss of wet wood filled the acrid, smoky campsite and James sniffed appreciatively, oddly calmed by the promise of warmth.

Days before, he'd explained to Jeremy that Valentina wouldn't be traveling to Wales with them. Jeremy had cried and called out for her. Since then, he'd folded his little arms and lifted his small chin in mute blame whenever he caught his father's gaze.

James understood his son's sadness and reassured him at

every opportunity, wanting him to enjoy the naiveté of child-hood. Still, his attempts to kiss Jeremy good night were met with an accusatory frown. Jeremy was neither happy nor reassured.

As a father, James had failed. As a husband, he'd failed. As a man on the brink of finding love where he'd least expected, he'd thrown it away.

Resting on top of a woolen blanket, he clasped his arms behind his head and stared at the silent winter sky. Come the morrow, his group should see the rocky peaks of Wales. To return to his homeland gave him a quiet joy and helped to quell the lonesomeness of his life. Sleep, as usual, eluded him, and his mind traveled to the sole place it cared to dwell—on his green-eyed angel and her beautiful smile.

Had he made the right decision by sending her to Scotland? That was only one of the nonstop questions with no answers that plagued him. After a few minutes of exhausting the same air in and out of his throat, he resorted to the finer torture of recalling her infectious laughter. Especially, he liked to recall those early days when they'd strolled the lawns of his home every afternoon, and she'd dined with him every evening.

All the while, she'd shrouded her love for him under the heaviness of her remorse. Because she'd feared confiding in him, afraid he wouldn't forgive her. She'd never asked anything of him, except his forgiveness.

Coldheartedly, he'd thrown her apology back at her, intent on assuaging his never-ending need to be in control—a cruel maestro. For his beginning bars, he'd interrogated her. For his repeat, he'd belittled her love. For a finale, he'd kept Jeremy from her.

Proof that he was, indeed, the cold-hearted gadje she'd called him on numerous occasions.

He closed his hands over his ears, attempting to block out

the memory of her weeping. He focused on a brooding cloud to stop the sound of her heartache breaking through her chamber door and ferociously burrowing a hole in his heart.

"My brave, beautiful, girl," he whispered. "How did we end like this after the love we found together? I'd been so confident of our impending marriage when I'd stopped at that Gypsy camp before riding back to you."

Mercifully, the steady rise of a silver dawn broke, and James stretched his limbs and stood up. If the snow blowing down on them erased her image, he might be able to find his footing again.

Perhaps in Wales, a pert Welsh woman would make him shout with laughter at her witty retorts, or tempt him with sultry green eyes, a regal tilt of her head.

Any such idea died a quick and effortless death. There'd be no other woman.

Because no other woman tied an absurd bright yellow scarf around her neck, ensuring it never matched any garment she wore. And no other woman teased him about his singing or laughed at herself when she tried to learn the intricate steps of a fashionable and senseless dance.

Because no other woman was Valentina.

James rose, tended to his uncommunicative son, and prepared the camp for departure. He remounted his horse and gave the signal to resume. If they continued at a gallop, they'd see his beloved Wales by midday.

I remind you of a country?

Valentina would have loved the rough mountains and primitive coast of Wales as much as he did. Although she'd never see it, because now she was gone.

CHAPTER 26

It's ushti bak to wellan a Rom,
When tute's a pirryin pre the drom.
When you are going along the street,
It's lucky a Gypsy man to meet.
Old Romany saying

*E*asy.

James planned to immerse himself in overseeing his Welsh estate as soon as he arrived in Wales. A simple plan requiring simple effort.

As he expected, the rugged landscape and wild gardens were neglected. Perfect. He'd engage in grueling physical labor and erase Valentina from his mind.

He rode with his group through a lively rain. He spotted his Welsh flag flying—the red dragon flapping on a green and white background—and the sight was like music to him. Finally, he was truly home.

Lowdie, one of his servants, greeted him.

Little things should've alerted him something was wrong —her skittish eyes, her agitated hands, her white face beneath her whiter bonnet.

The neigh of a Welsh pony distracted him.

He stared at his mansion house, the pockmarks in the stone, the moorlands in the distance.

Dismounting, he smiled. "Did you wish to speak, Lowdie?"

She stared at the ground, her shoes shuffling wet gravel into tiny circles.

Jeremy and his dog darted out of their carriage and slid into the mud, racing side by side. A befuddled Elspeth gasped and panted and scolded. James laughed at the mismatched threesome before directing his attention back to the voiceless servant.

Lowdie curtsied. Standing in the rain, she blocked his path.

"I assume you've been in Wales a while," he prompted, soothing his sweaty horse.

"We arrived days ago, Mr. Colchester."

He nodded and raised the hood of his cloak over his head. Brisk, salty dankness teased his nostrils, and he embraced the turbulent clouds, the scent of rye grass, the gritty soil.

Nearby, the sea's violent tide hurtled against the shore. For an instant, he thought he saw Valentina balancing on the craggy rocks, arms outstretched, a flock of seabirds swooping around her. She gave him one of her surreptitious smiles, followed by an insolent wave.

He almost raised his hand to wave back before he expelled his breath. He brought two fingers downward to glide across his lips and scratch his wet, bearded chin before his gaze returned to Lowdie. "You may speak." His voice rose to be heard above the persistent rain. "That is, if there's something ... anything ... of merit to say."

"Aye."

"Are all the servants here?"

Her unsteady sigh rose with the wind. "Most are settling into the household routine."

"Did Tobias ride into town for our supplies?"

"Aye." Lowdie curtsied again. "Mr. Colchester, 'tis something you must know."

At this rate, he'd never see the inside of his home.

"Speak your mind."

"Reginald is no longer here in Wales. He overheard one of the servants who rode ahead saying that Geoffrey was taking Yolanda and Valentina to London, then sending them to Scotland. There is a rumor in town that Scotland might be imprisoning all Gypsies who enter their country."

"These new laws are frequently discussed and then usually discarded." James handed his horse's reins to a stable boy. "When did Reginald depart?"

"Soon after he heard the rumor. He told Tobias that he intended to ride to London and find Yolanda. The next minute, Reginald saddled a horse and was gone."

The rain picked up, attacking from a black cloudburst. When he reached the front hallway of his home, he didn't stop to admire the beloved furnishings he hadn't seen in years, nor the stucco walls and poplar beams.

He yanked off his soaking cloak and threw it on a carved wooden chair.

He shivered. 'Twas so damp. He'd forgotten about the dampness. It was everywhere, seeping through the walls onto his clothing. He could even smell it.

As his booted footsteps echoed across the slate floor, he prayed the peace he'd hoped to find in Wales wouldn't elude him. He looked around. Little had changed. Even the hallway leading to Beatrix's sleeping-room, the one she shared with

Jeremy, tucked away near their nurse's chamber on the second floor, was undisturbed.

Beatrix.

He fumbled with the chamber's latch, hesitating. The door rattled when it opened. He stepped inside the tiny room and bent his head to avoid striking the slanted ceiling.

Rain buffeted the eaves, a driving staccato. The sound of the sea's stormy waves against the shoreline battered beyond the window.

Jeremy's bed stood on one side of the room. Beatrix's wooden bed stood near the wall, her favorite doll sat lopsided on woolen bedcovers. A picture book lay opened with several pages folded at the corners. Pictures of bedraggled, tawny kittens and lame, purple ponies. Beatrix had always loved to save the forlorn.

Grief and emptiness sliced open a wound in his chest that had never healed. Lightheaded, he leaned against her bed and gazed around the precious chamber.

Something was missing.

Where was her cloth ball, the one she'd played with for hours? She'd arranged her doll and ball together on the bed the day they'd departed for England.

"My toys for Wales, tad. They stay here." Her giggle had filled him with love and unconditional joy.

"Aye, darling," he'd promised. "They'll be waiting for you when we return."

Unsteadily, James crouched and lifted the bedcovers. Clouds of dust burned his eyes. He reached underneath the bed and grasped his fingers around her tiny pink ball.

He stood on trembling legs, letting them guide him to the window. He held the ball close to his face and inhaled a whiff of flowers. Wild roses, fragrant and wistful. Bouquets she'd pinned upside-down in her silky blonde hair, rose petals she'd dropped on the stairs when she'd pretended to be a countess.

"Watch me, tad," she'd call out to him as she skipped across the lawn like a grand lady.

Once more, he breathed in the pure fragrance of white rosebuds and childhood and closed his eyes. She was gone, his sweet baby girl. Helpless with grief, he whispered a psalm of comfort and hope. "Even though I walk through the valley of the shadow of death, I will fear no evil, for you are with me; your rod and your staff, they comfort me."

How can you tell me not to be discouraged, God? How can I be strong and courageous through such sorrow? He couldn't help his feelings, couldn't help feeling overwhelmed with grief.

Although God never said not to be sorrowful. Just because James felt those feelings didn't mean he had to carry his sorrow on his own. Surely, God was with him.

James examined the well-worn ball and squeezed it back into a semblance of its former shape. Ever so gently, he rolled the ball to the bed.

"I will always love you, darling. My perfect angel." He grabbed the wall and sank to the floor. His limbs had changed to sand.

He put his head in his hands and wept like a child.

Hours passed, and the light streaming through the window had colored the walls to a brilliant gold, deepening to purple. The Sleeping-room stood silent, traced in shadows.

Evening neared. James descended the stairs and found his favorite linenfold chair by the blazing hearth in the parlor. The chair creaked when he sat, and he changed positions a number of times never feeling comfortable. An unseen servant had placed a goblet of bragget on a side table. The honeyed Welsh ale beckoned, and a wretchedly empty evening awaited.

"Cheers." He lifted the goblet and saluted the fire. While he drank, he listed the many reasons why his former blacksmith showed an astounding lack of common sense, first and foremost by saddling up a horse and riding off to London.

Still, Reginald had displayed undeniable bravery, which was why James respected him.

He set the goblet on the table, swearing at the silence and lack of any servants about. Somewhere in the sizable house, a shutter banged open and shut, most likely caused by the howling wind. An odious mix of leeks and lamb coming from the kitchen made his nose wrinkle. Grimacing at the scent of *cawl,* his favorite soup up till a moment ago, he proceeded past the kitchen and up two flights of stairs.

When James reached Jeremy's chamber, he found his son huddled beneath woolen blankets, ignoring him, his *father*, and feigning sleep. James opened his mouth to bid his son good night and kissed his hair instead.

"Mr. Colchester, may I get you anything?" Elspeth stood in the doorway and displayed her usual half smile.

"Nay." Unwilling to engage in a second of conversation with anyone, especially his son's anxious nurse, James ascended another flight of stairs leading to his own chamber.

'Twas sleep he lacked. 'Twas why the day had seemed so endless and despondent.

At midnight, James lay awake in the middle of his four-poster bed, a stubborn fire refusing to burn out in the grate, an unceasing tirade of rain pummeling the window. Hands folded behind his head, he studied the cobwebs on the ancient ceiling.

"If I come for you, will you return with me, cariad?" he whispered. "You can teach me your Gypsy customs and I'll teach you about life in Wales. We'll have as many children as you wish, with eyes like emeralds who will speak in gentle Welsh brogues."

Impossible, his mind cautioned. He'd insured she'd hurl every Gypsy curse she'd ever learned straight at him if she ever saw him again. It would be better if she lived with her tribe. Anything was better than staying with him and his wretched inability to forgive.

In an effort to sleep, he tallied the ways he might strangle Reginald.

Each time James added something, memories flowed of Valentina's laughter, her carefree manner of living. Oh, how he missed her. The pure love that was theirs and theirs alone. He couldn't imagine what life could bring without her at his side.

So, what was he doing lying in bed counting cobwebs?

James surged to his feet and shoved on his boots. Quickly, he snatched his cloak and secured a precious necklace into his pocket. It wasn't the loneliness that prompted him. It was time, and he wouldn't lose another minute of it without her beside him. Valentina, he vowed, would never set one shapely toe in Scotland.

He'd been headed in the wrong direction when he'd met her. And then he'd blamed her. Although, in hindsight, he'd needed to meet her to turn him back around. God had had everything planned.

He strode to the window and jammed the iron latch until it opened. Heavy winds lashed an impressive sea against the rocks. Treacherous weather for travel. Perfect weather for travel.

He bounded down the stairs, spotted Clare asleep on a pallet and prodded her awake.

"Mr. Colchester?" Clare's lisp slowed her speech. The blanket she clutched slid through her hands.

James yanked on his damp gloves. "I'm riding to London

and expect to arrive back in Wales within a fortnight. Tell Elspeth to tend to Jeremy. I leave immediately."

By moonlight, a groom saddled James' stallion. James flung himself on and lowered his head to escape the biting rain. Across meadows and mountains, he headed east toward London.

Despite the frantic pace, his shoulders eased. The downpour settled to a drizzle.

He focused on the rising sun, the beginning of a rainbow on the horizon, and laughed out loud.

Aye. He wanted children, four more, with the beautiful woman he loved.

CHAPTER 27

Piri telemosa chi athadjol o kam.
The kettle that lies face down cannot get much sunlight.
Old Romany saying

*A*ll color escaped from Yolanda's face, and she looked as though she'd seen a *mulo*. She skidded to a stop in the midst of a busy London marketplace, crushed her hand to her mouth. Her cry held a note of … jubilation?

Geoffrey and Richard set down their bundles of gingerbread and shortbread and blinked simultaneously. They enjoyed the baked goods in the central courtyard of the inn, watching passengers being let down and horses changed.

Valentina cast a baffled, sidelong glance toward the baker's stand on the lively street corner. "Yolanda, how much white bread can you possibly eat?"

"'Tis not the bread." Yolanda broke into a teary smile. "'Tis Reginald."

Valentina dropped the biscuits she carried and spun.

Reginald rushed to Yolanda and embraced her, unmindful of the stares of passersby. "I feared you'd left for Scotland and I wouldn't find you in time."

"The rumors reached Wales?" Geoffrey asked.

"Aye."

"Rumors?" Valentina accusatory gaze landed on Geoffrey. "What rumors?"

"Richard and I heard the talk as we approached London. The Scots don't want Gypsies in their country, and we couldn't risk placing either one of you in danger."

"So that's why we've stayed in London a fortnight? I was wondering why 'twas taking so long for fresh horses," Valentina said. "Surely you should have told us this before now."

With his customary cordiality, Geoffrey replied, "I was unsure where to go next."

Reginal beamed, a contented man with Yolanda at his side. "When Yolanda and I marry, we'll make our home near Bury St. Edmunds. The lakes are beautiful and several of my brothers live nearby."

Yolanda crossed to Valentina and placed her cold hands in hers. "Reginald and I spoke of our plans often while at Mr. Colchester's estate. Please come with us. Reginald won't mind, will you, Reginald?"

He shifted his weight from one foot to the other. "Of course not."

If Valentina had met her sister's gaze, she might have considered accepting her kind offer. Instead, she focused on two farmers bartering over the price of a sheep. "I promise to think about it."

"I want you to be safe," Yolanda said softly.

"In that case, 'tis settled." Geoffrey shrugged, strode to Reginald and shook his hand. "The women will be well cared for, and Richard and I can be on our way to Wales."

Yolanda and Reginald, arms entwined, attached as twins joined at birth, headed to the baker's shop. Valentina stooped to retrieve her biscuits and wiped the tears from her cheeks. She smiled, an overwhelming clash of emotions filling her chest. Happiness for her sister's prospects; uncertainty about her own future. Although, one night when they'd traveled, hadn't the vicar said that peace might feel far away even when it didn't have to be? The decision was hers.

The wind grew stronger, depositing discarded refuse around their feet. For once, Valentina was grateful for the predictable torrent of rain, providing an excuse to dash back to the inn.

The next morning, she awoke to the indifferent first rays of the sun shining through the window of her spacious bedchamber. She washed and dressed in her scarlet gown and tied her yellow diklo in place. Thinking better of it, her hand stopped in midair. Instead, she gently woke her sister.

Yolanda thrust the bedcovers aside and slid from the bed. "You're up before dawn."

Valentina placed her diklo in Yolanda's hands. "Take this. I'm leaving London, traveling to Brighton and returning to the tribe."

Yolanda's smile faded. Her fingers froze around the diklo. "Mr. Colchester won't be pleased."

"Please don't tell anyone where I'm going." Feeling chilled, Valentina swung her cashmere shawl around her shoulders and blew her warm breath on her cold fingers. Several careful steps took her down the stairs. Bypassing the inn's front room and grimacing as a loud horn heralded the arrival of numerous coaches, she marched out into the light snow of a London morning.

* * *

JAMES ARRIVED four days after Reginald. Tearing through the noisy streets of London, he rode straight to the ivy-covered inn he'd arranged for the women's stay. He dismounted, tethered his horse, and strode inside. The innkeeper and a serving wench collided in their hurry to assist him. He dismissed them with a wave of his hand.

"Mr. Colchester, so good to see you … I think," Geoffrey called from a corner of a private sitting room as James neared. "Are you in London to see some theatre?"

"You must be jesting."

"Are you under the weather?"

"Perhaps from not sleeping since I left England a fortnight ago, only to turn around and ride back." James perched on the edge of a chair near the room's large fireplace. He raised a sardonic brow at the innkeeper, who hovered nearby.

"The Scots might be making rash decisions," he added.

Geoffrey offered a thin smile. "'Tis the reason why Richard and I remained days longer than we intended. We'd planned on departing for Wales come the morrow."

"Glad I caught you before you left."

"Our plans were all sorted out with Reginald's help."

"Reginald is at the inn?"

"Aye. He arrived days ago."

James scanned the front room beyond, over-crowded with patrons. A server in a gathered skirt and low bodice appeared and disappeared with fragrant lamb pies and crisp apple tartes.

"Valentina—is she upstairs in her chamber?" he asked.

Geoffrey sloshed his tankard of ale and watched the foam run over the rim. "She's not here at the moment."

James sighed in grateful relief and removed his gloves. "Where is she? I want to give her something."

With an expression bordering on helplessness, Geoffrey

eyed the diners seated at the next table, then a grease spot on the wall above James. "Reginald and Richard are searching for her. You see, Valentina seems to be missing."

James dropped his gloves to the floor. "How can someone *seem* to be missing?"

The clinking of spoons, the laughing diners, the raucous conversations in the room, all came to a standstill.

Geoffrey went to speak but paused. His blue eyes held James imprisoned, seeming to be appraising what James' next reaction might be. "She couldn't have traveled far. However, for now, she's disappeared."

James strode out of the inn, pushing past a wandering musician playing his recorder in the large cobblestone court-yard. Then he mounted his horse and sped away.

The fruitless afternoon search was a frustrating agony, for there was no sign of Valentina anywhere. When he returned to the inn, he immediately asked for ale, not even bothering to seek out the others. He'd been there only a few minutes when Yolanda joined him.

He stared at the yellow scarf tied around Yolanda's slim neck. Sighing, he averted his gaze. He couldn't, he wouldn't, look at that diklo.

Yolanda untied the scarf and placed it in his hands. "Valentina would have wanted me to give this to you."

"Thank you." He hesitated, gliding the worn fabric between his fingers. He brought the diklo to his lips, inhaling the guileless scent of pine and pepper and promises. He breathed it all in, swathing his face in the sheer heartbreak of losing her.

"She loves you very much," Yolanda said.

"Do you know where she is?"

Yolanda shook her head. "All I will tell you is that she's safe. I know Reginald and the other men want to find her, but after tomorrow, I will convince them that Valentina is secure in her decision and we should leave for our own homes."

"I hurt her because of my pretentiousness. Who am I to judge right and wrong? I've done nothing worthy to deserve her love." Just as it was written in Luke 6:41, he thought. *Why do you look at the speck of sawdust in your brother's eye and pay no attention to the plank in your own eye?*

"Your presence speaks of your devotion," Yolanda was saying. "Don't worry."

He raised his hands, trying to explain, then watched them collapse on his lap. "After she left me, I couldn't forgive her. And then the fortune-telling ... And then Jeremy got sick, and my temper blinded me to reason." James drank more ale, a hard swig.

"Valentina took her role in our tribe very seriously. Without her and Luca, we all would have starved." Yolanda touched a piece of fox fur that seemed to have been hastily sewn onto the sleeve of her fine silk gown. "She didn't want to leave you, although she knew you'd never forgive her. She always described you as an honorable, upright man."

"I was more interested in doing things my own way. I didn't listen to her. I listened only to my pride."

"Valentina is stronger and braver than anyone. Nothing in this world will be cruel enough to take her away from you a second time."

"Please tell me where she went."

A reassuring smile flicked across Yolanda's pretty face. "You'll realize soon enough."

Memories of Valentina, her wittiness, her kindness, rushed over him, and sadly, he smiled. She'd cared so much for him, putting him on loftier ground than he'd ever deserved. Yet her humble principles were higher than his.

Her strength, not his, pushed him to his feet.

At dawn, their group spread across the outskirts of

London. Geoffrey and Richard searched to the north, and Reginald to the south. James combed the bank of the River Thames, riding past tall ships and rich merchants exporting their wool. He searched the inner streets, narrow and crowded, until all the wooden buildings of the alehouses and shops blended into the same brown canvas.

Indeed, Valentina had vanished. He knew that as each hour went by, the sadness he'd caused her would change her love to resentment. And if anything untoward happened to her, he'd never forgive himself.

In the encroaching dusk of a clambering city street, a thought struck him completely unaware. His hands tensed on the horse's reins before he brought his horse to a halt, staring into the bright cold air with a mixture of incredulity and relief.

"We're traveling to the coast, near Brighton," Luca had told Valentina the night he'd snuck into her chamber.

James charged back to the inn to leave word for Yolanda and the men. Nearly colliding with a horse cab, he thundered out of London and headed for the coast.

CHAPTER 28

Zhan le Devlesa tai sastimasa.
Go with God and in good health.
Old Romany saying

*V*alentina pushed open the flap of her tent and leaned on the precariously fragile pole keeping the tent from collapsing. "Luca, you're tending to the fire all wrong. Blow on it carefully or our entire camp might burn to the ground with all these dried leaves underfoot."

Luca tossed a handful of grass onto the slow-burning campfire. "Green damp wood will never burn. Your fire will be useless for cooking. Heap dry branches onto the flames so the fire will get hot."

Valentina opened her mouth to tell him he was impossible, overbearing, and that she loved
him as a true friend.

He pressed his index finger to his lips, his smile broadening. "Just agree with me for once or you'll wake the elders."

"How did you know what I was thinking? Often, I've wondered if you were the drabardi." She lifted a clay pot filled with water, leeks, and parsnips and walked toward the campfire.

"Stop lifting these heavy pots." In a primal show of strength, he grabbed the pot from her and hoisted it over the open fire.

She waved him off. "Don't you have anything better to do than watch a woman cook?"

"I'll be back by dusk with two crows. If I'm lucky, I'll snare a rabbit too. The Brighton townspeople should be setting up their wares soon because 'tis market day."

Valentina tried to disguise her mirth and disapprove, although a chuckle broke out anyway. "They should willingly offer you all their small wild animals to save you the effort of stealing."

"'Tis my responsibility to provide food for our tribe."

She touched his sleeve. "Please be careful."

She might have imagined the undercurrent of desperation in his dark eyes. Perhaps the concern was her own, because Luca never worried about anything. He survived by instinct. She used to be like him, acting on impulse and not caring about the consequences. A long time ago, in another lifetime.

With a mischievous grin, Luca retied the square orange cloth around his head and wiggled his gold hoop earring. In one heartbeat, his lean frame pivoted and blended into the woodlands.

She sighed and stirred the broth in her pot. He might be overconfident and think himself invincible, but he'd handled her mother's burial with dignity and honor and had kept their tribe alive through much of the winter.

Valentina blinked at the whitish sun, rising steadily higher, assuring another day of mild temperatures, even though it was only February. As she'd done for the past several mornings, she walked to the edge of the caravan and kneeled at a small, modest gravesite she'd erected for her mother.

"Daj, I have something special to tell you today. I fell in love with a wonderful man. He's an Englishman, and very generous and fine-looking. He wanted to marry me. Me, can you imagine? We didn't ... because ... Please be proud of me. I've learned a lot about myself and—"

She stopped. How could anyone be proud of her? She'd wronged the very people she'd loved. She tried to continue to speak and decided to pray. Then she cried until her temples throbbed and her throat was sore and she didn't have any grief left to spill.

When the sun sat directly overhead, she stared up at a brilliant blue sky. Strangely refreshed, she wiped her eyes and sniffed a whiff of wild primrose, an assurance of spring. Soon, the wildflowers would bloom, strewing blossoms of yellow and gold along the worn trails. Valentina tarried at the modest gravesite and noted the air. So calm, the oak trees hardly swayed. A sunny day meant she'd be able to hang laundry outside to dry, as well as tidying several unused wagons. The elders would be awake by now and finishing their pots of porridge. She was about to stand when a man spoke.

"Bury me kneeling, for I have been standing all my life."

The deep, familiar voice pervaded the tranquil air, speaking words she recognized, yet out of order. Warm hands stroked the back of her hair, then kneaded her shoulders in gentle, persistent circles.

James.

Her heart tilted. She gazed ahead at the tips of hazelnut trees bordering the campsite. She couldn't breathe. Nor think. Nor move. She clutched her jacket to stop her body from shaking.

Rest assured, I will not seek you, cariad, he'd said while her heart had split in two.

Nay, it couldn't be him. Not here. He wouldn't have known where to find her. No one knew except Yolanda, and Yolanda wouldn't have told anyone.

"Valentina."

She could never turn to him, because she'd never recover from the heartache of seeing his handsome face. If she wished to shout at him, how could she find air to utter the sounds?

"Valentina."

His deep voice was different, his tone strained to a whisper. And something else.

He no longer stood behind her, because he was lowering himself to his *knees* beside her. This proud man who'd never knelt to anyone except their king, who employed countless servants and tenant farmers, had dropped to his knees.

James. Memories squeezed and reminded. *Your presence would add a sparkle to every home.*

Slowly, she opened her eyes.

He held out his arms in a gesture of helplessness. "'Twill be easier if I can hold you."

She never hesitated, moving forward into his embrace because she belonged with him. She inhaled his agonizingly recognizable scents, the worn leather, the raw silk, the scent of fresh air.

He tangled his fingers through her hair and kissed her.

How she loved him. She didn't know how many minutes they held each other. She only knew the sheer delight of his embrace.

"I'll chain myself to you if I need to," he said, "because I'll not let you venture another day from my side." His words were so quiet, she tipped her head nearer. He kissed her with his lips, his eyes, his tender smile. "I'm sorry for all your hurt, all your pain."

Tears welled in her eyes. "I'm not worthy and need God's grace."

"I'm not worthy, either. I need the same grace as you." His solid hands were so gentle, caressing her face. "Please promise to stay with me."

She outlined his forehead with her fingertips. She couldn't bear to see his strong face so broken. "My days of roaming ended when a desperate landed gentry with a noble spirit showered me with more kindness than I ever deserved."

He rose and extended his hand, assisting her to her feet. "I have something I want to give to you." He grinned like an expectant schoolboy, reminding her of his son, a hopeful gleam in his velvet-grey eyes. "I've carried this necklace with me for far too many weeks." He lifted a tattered ribbon from the pocket of his cloak.

She gaped when she recognized the symbol, shiny gold coins hanging from a moss-green ribbon. "Where did you get this? 'Tis a pliashka."

"Aye." He brushed a kiss from her neck to her lips. "So I've learned from a group of Gypsy men who weren't at all happy to see me."

"You carried this necklace all the way from London?"

"I never had the chance to give it to you, although I wanted to many times."

She laughed through a constricted throat and smoothed her trembling fingers along the ribbon. "'Tis so beautiful. Thank you."

He rubbed his thumbs underneath her eyes to catch her

tears. "Marry me and say you'll come to Wales. I asked you once before in a horse stable and waited for your answer. This time, I'm not leaving until you agree. And I have a son who misses you almost as desperately as his father."

"You stole my heart months ago when we stood on a hillside admiring your splendid estate."

"You threw the boots I'd given you into an abandoned field."

She laughed, then grew quiet. This affectionate man, this man with a wry sense of humor, had come for her. She snuggled her face near his chest. "Please keep your arms around me," she whispered.

He squeezed her closer, taking on her sadness. "*Rrwy'n dy garu di.* I love you. I love your bravery. I love your—"

"*Me kamav tut.* I love you." She turned her face up for another exquisite kiss.

"How could I have been so unforgiving?" he murmured. "I'm sorry."

"And I've forgiven you. Now you must forgive yourself and realize you're as imperfect as the rest of us."

He secured the necklace around her throat, then leaned back to study her. "'Tis so unpretentious."

"More eloquent words." She smiled and stroked the silken ribbon. "You risked your life for this necklace."

"An understatement." He grinned wryly. He reached into the pocket of his cloak again and produced her mother's yellow diklo. "A gift to me from Yolanda. I intended to keep the scarf until I found you. Now 'tis where it belongs, with you."

They strolled arm in arm through sprinkled sunlight shining past hazelnut trees, returning to the cluster of ragged tents. Several elders sat on improvised stools and peered at James, their wilted dark faces curious.

James glanced down at his black cloak. "From my limited experience as a gadje, I don't think the Rom like Englishmen."

"Most likely they don't, though they may like Welshmen, so eventually you might be accepted." Valentina stopped at the campfire. She sniffed the clay pot, chiding the solid residue of scorched leeks and parsnips, as if the vegetables were to blame for burning. "We'll have to make do with soft cheese for supper tonight."

"I'd hoped we might enjoy a pickled porcupine for our meal."

"'Tis a roasted hedgehog, not a pickled porcupine. And you'll have to wait until we reach Wales for me to roast a hedgehog, unless Luca manages to charm one from one of the hapless townspeople. 'Tis certain they must roll their eyes when they see him coming."

James frowned. "When I see him, I want to do more than roll my eyes."

Valentina placed her hands on both sides of James' face, forcing him to gaze at her. "No doubts or mistrust must ever come between us. Luca is a childhood friend."

"Who unfortunately has grown up."

She rubbed the ever-present stubble on his cheeks. "'Tis you I love."

He led her to the outskirts of the campsite and spread his cloak on the ground. They settled and she shifted close to him. He lifted her hands, pressing them to his mouth, kissing each finger.

She spoke softly, trying to keep her voice from shaking. "I have something to tell you. 'Tis of great importance."

He linked his fingers with hers. "Have you discovered that you must converse with a tree before you shake it? Or have you found another herbal cure? You must recognize every sprig gracing England."

She laughed. "Nay, although I'd like a garden in Wales." Fairly bursting, she couldn't wait another minute. "I want to get married in a church and raise our children as Christians."

He'd been lowering his head to kiss her. Now he paused. "God's timing is perfect, and so are you."

"I don't doubt that He controls the order of our events." As she gazed at him, a Romany word came to mind. She held the word close to her heart and snuggled into his arms. "I wish Yolanda were here to share our wedding news."

"I left instructions with the innkeeper at the Smuggler's Purse to alert Yolanda and Reginald where I was headed. I wouldn't be surprised if they all show up this evening with Geoffrey and Richard in tow."

"What will we feed them? There's no hedgehog prowling through the brush, and my scorched broth is hardly enough to feed the tribe, let alone four more hungry people."

"As I see it, we have two choices."

She smiled. "Please don't hesitate to share."

He kissed her leisurely and thoughtfully, covering every inch of her face. "We can either ride into Brighton for a meal, or we can stay here. The choice is yours, Mrs. Colchester."

"Let's see how the afternoon progresses, Mr. Colchester."

"Call me James."

Which was when the Romany word drifted to her tongue. The word grew from a chant to a melody, singing through her soul.

"*Ves'tacha*," she whispered, gazing up at the face of the man she loved. She clasped his hands and held them close to her heart.

Beloved.

THE END

A NOTE FROM JOSIE

Dear Friend,

Thank you for reading *Seeking Fortune*. I hope you enjoyed it. *Seeking Fortune* is the first book in my inspirational Regency romance "Seeking" series.

If you loved this Inspirational romance as much as I loved writing it, please help other people find *Seeking Fortune* by posting your amazing review, as well as for the bundle: The Seeking Series.

Seeking Fortune is available in ebook, paperback, Hardcover, Large print paperback, and audiobook.

The Romany Gypsy culture is complex and fascinating. After researching their traditions and beliefs, I wanted to write stories focusing on bigotry during the Regency era.

Valentina Rupa is a feisty Gypsy heroine.

James Colchester, an English landed gentry, is the perfect hero—dedicated to his son, yet conflicted in his search for God's truth.

Amidst a time when bigotry was the norm, the vibrant folklore of the Gypsy people sets the stage during the panic of the influenza epidemic. One brash lie spoken in haste is the catalyst.

My hope is to fully touch and engage you with the story of James and Valentina. It is a story of betrayal, forgiveness and God's unconditional love.

The Romany Regency Inspirational romances continues with Charity and Daniel in Seeking Charity, Luca and Patience in *Seeking Patience,* and Nash and Rachel in Seeking Rachel.

I'd love to meet you in person someday, but in the meantime, all I can offer is a sincere and grateful thank you. Without your support, my books would not be possible.

As I write my next sweet or inspirational romance, remember this: Have you ever tried something you were afraid to try because it mattered so much to you? I did, when I started writing. Take the chance, and just do something you love.

My Spotify Play List for Seeking Fortune is here.

With sincere appreciation,

Josie Riviera

Want more Inspirational romances?

Regency:

Seeking Charity

Seeking Patience

Seeking Rachel

The Seeking Series

Contemporary:

Cherished Hearts: 6 book bundle
Holly's Gift

RECIPE FOR ROASTED HEDGEHOG

According to Medieval experts, the hedgehog should have its throat cut, be singed and gutted, then trussed like a pullet, then pressed in a towel until very dry. Roast and eat with cameline sauce, or in a pastry with wild duck sauce. Note that if the hedgehog refuses to unroll, put it in hot water. The Rom would have dredged the hedgehog in black pepper after cooking.

Although I can't personally verify the results, here's the recipe modified from Medieval cookery:

Method:
Season the meat. Wrap it in long grass, first lengthways,

and then tying more grass crossways to secure the green wrapping in place

Prepare your barbecue and place a large pot filled with water on it. Cook the meat for two hours. Once the meat has cooked, remove the grass, then place the meat back in the barbecue to sear. Carve and serve.

Nettle pudding can be boiled in the same pot and served as an accompaniment.

(Sorry, I don't have a recipe for Nettle pudding.)

Enjoy!

Chapter One
Wales, 1812

"Let's drink to a long and happy life for the bride and groom!"

Charity Weston stood at the edge of a smoky campfire with her Romany Gypsy tribe and raised her tankard of ale. Luca, the leader of their tribe, offered the toast in celebration for a *pliashka*, a betrothal agreement.

Miriah, the attractive bride-to-be, smiled radiantly at her intended groom, who grinned proudly at her. Both sets of future in-laws stood beside them. Miriah's dark brows and eyes dominated her features, accentuated by glossy ebony hair tied back with a vivid red headdress.

So unlike her own copper-colored hair, Charity thought, fingering her unmanageable ringlets.

As the tribesmen hooted and cheered, Charity joined in the chants of *sastimos*, good health, even as her cheeks flushed at the bawdy remarks laughingly called out to the couple.

In the glow of the firelight, she studied the Gypsy men and women assembled in a circle around the couple—the laugh lines etched in the corners of their mouths and the granite determination in their jaws, announcing their decision to live unrestrained from the constraints of 'civilized life'.

Several men with greying beards loudly shared opinions about where they should travel next and that they should leave within a fortnight. They'd stayed in one place long enough. In the meantime, Luca didn't respond as he bent to retrieve a bottle of brandy for the groom's father. The father then wrapped a handkerchief around the bottle as part of the pliashka.

These were the people Charity had grown to love. Their kindness, their traditions, their joy for life. They brought nothing with them when they traveled and simply adopted the traditions of wherever they made camp.

A clap of thunder reverberated, and the heavy wooden

wagons, packed with garments and jewelries, creaked in response.

However, weather changes didn't deter the revelers. Besnik, one of the elders, took up a pipe whistle and began playing, whilst another grabbed his fiddle. Kezia, an elderly woman who was considered the *phuri dai*, someone who resolved conflicts with honor, clapped to the music and sang off-key. The melody was spirited yet emotional. Since the tribe had settled in Wales, their music had taken on a decidedly Welsh, Celtic quality.

Charity finished her ale. Intrigued, she watched as Miriah's future father-in-law secured a necklace around Miriah's throat. Made of a satin ribbon with gold coins, the necklace was a symbol of the matrimony bond.

"Remember." Kezia stepped forward and focused on Miriah, "*Ajsi bori lachi: xal bilondo, phenel londo.*"

Charity grinned as she silently translated: "Such a daughter-in-law is good who eats unsalted food and says 'tis salted."

"Good advice!" A boisterous shout of approval came from the men and Charity gave her head a shake. Despite living with Gypsies for six years, the good-natured commotion and dust and brightly-colored gowns sometimes evoked a dreamlike blur of confusion.

And lately, it also brought a sense of detachment. The setting was so different from the proper English background of her childhood—high-waisted white muslin dresses, formals planned months in advance, country dances with their processional marches and ballet-style movements.

But that was all in the past.

Through a break in the surrounding woods, she peered toward a stone mansion, the Colchesters' grand country estate. The owners, James and Valentina, had invited the tribe to camp on their property. Mr. Colchester was wealthy landed gentry, and Valentina, a Gypsy woman. Despite society's rigid rules, they had fallen in love, married, and moved to Wales.

And it was marvelous here, Charity mused, scanning her surroundings. The rugged Welsh landscape alive with summer color, the sounds of the sea crashing to shore, the bright open sky shining at night with pinpoints of bright stars.

Why, then, could she think of little else than her former English home?

Lately, Wales induced a longing for her childhood she couldn't explain. She had spent many a summer in Norfolk by the sea when her mother was alive, she reasoned. Perhaps 'twas why these remembrances came with more and more frequency.

As the last of the tankards were emptied, she set down her own to refill an empty flask with more braggot, a honeyed Welsh ale. She handed the flask to Luca, who poured some into a tankard for himself, then offered the flask to the others. Grabbing a slab of bread, he glanced at her, a smile crossing his dark tanned features.

"Thank you, Charani."

As always, he called her by her Gypsy name.

With a nod, she turned, planning to assist the younger women roasting a hedgehog on a wooden spit.

"What is troubling you?" For such a commanding presence, he had the ability to move quietly and quickly. He'd come up behind her, and she hadn't noticed until he spoke. "This past fortnight, you are preoccupied."

She shrugged her bright-pink shawl tighter around her shoulders. The temperateness of summer promised another month of welcoming days, although the chill of a sea breeze hung in the air.

"'Tis nothing," she said.

He studied her face. "I watched you during the pliashka. Are you missing someone? Mayhap a man from a neighboring tribe? I saw you conversing with Petshah the last time we went to market."

"We met once and are only friends. Besides, isn't he at least thirty years my senior?"

And so heavy he could crush her. She didn't add that part.

"Age doesn't matter."

"Perhaps." She waited for Luca's response. She was twenty years old, and would soon be labeled a spinster if she didn't wed.

"He's made it known he's interested in you," Luca said.

She shook her head and didn't respond, knowing she was no match for the bristle in Luca's deep tone, nor his persistence. She picked up a stick to turn the meat and began a casual conversation about the passing of summer and of Romany customs, particularly the pliashka.

Thankfully, the subject of spinsterhood wasn't mentioned, but her good luck didn't last. With a determined gleam in his dark eyes, Luca repeated his earlier question. "What troubles you, Charani?"

She turned her attention away from the hedgehog and faced Luca squarely. "Sometimes ..." Her voice dropped to a whisper. "I don't know where I belong anymore."

There. She'd blurted it, becoming more like a Gypsy every day. Gone were the days of well-bred protocol, the soft tone of an Englishwoman schooled to never share her opinions aloud. Conversely, within the tribe, she could speak her mind.

Luca nodded slowly, his gaze understanding. "I know the feeling."

The emotion in his admission struck her heart, making

her ache all the more for things left behind long ago—a lavish home, a soft mattress, and sparkling clean bed linens.

Nay, she admonished herself. She was unappreciative for even thinking such thoughts. Luca's tribe had been benevolent, accepting her after the first Gypsy tribe she joined had moved to Scotland.

"How would someone like you, a Rom, know anything about not belonging?" she wanted to ask, although she said nothing. He was the head of the tribe for a reason. While brash, he took an interest in every tribesmen, listening intently, offering advice whenever asked. And although she'd heard rumors regarding his parentage, his past was never questioned.

He took several sips of ale and then lowered the heavy tankard. "Have you met Valentina?"

It was a strange change in subject, although Charity was grateful.

"Nay. Have you?"

"Aye. She was a childhood friend. Earlier this afternoon, I met her at the stables. She assured me we were welcome to remain as long as we wished."

"She's a proper lady now, married to landed gentry."

He shrugged. "She'll always be one of us, a Romany at heart."

Us. So Luca regarded Charity as a Gypsy. Noteworthy, because she looked nothing like them. Her skin was pale, her eyes a crystal-blue, the opposite of the tanned skin and piercing brown eyes of Luca and the others.

"Valentina is kind to allow us to camp on her husband's land," she said.

She waited for Luca's response. The smoky smells of wood campfires, cooking odors of fennel and garlic, hung in the air. Inside a crude stable, a spotted Welsh pony, small and sturdy, whinnied.

As always, Luca took his time, retying the green sash around his waist, running a hand along his buckskin breeches. It was his way, deliberating when he had something important to say. Years earlier, he had assumed the responsibilities of caring for the mostly elderly tribe without complaint, although he was only a young adult male himself.

"Would you like to meet her?" he finally asked.

"Valentina?" Charity scarcely noticed the encouragement in his tone, his voice nearly drowned out by several of the men near the campfire calling for more ale. "From the tales I've heard, she's a *drabardi,* a fortuneteller." She shook her head. "I don't want my fortune told. The Rom have taught me how to live in the present and trust myself and my instincts."

Although when she was younger, she had relied on God to carry her through the rough patches.

Nay. She corrected her thought. God had carried her through every patch, whether rough or smooth. When had she lost the faith she once held so strongly?

"Valentina is no longer a drabardi," Luca was saying. He sipped his ale, took a bite of bread, before continuing. "Valentina told me one of Mr. Colchester's acquaintances is looking for property in the area. She's invited them to stay for a fortnight."

"And?"

"And you can join them for a meal, or a game of whist, or whatever the English do to while away their time." He shrugged. "More important, 'twill give you an opportunity to converse with English men and women."

"I'm happy here with the Gypsies."

Firmly, he shook his head. "'Tis exactly what you need to bring pink color back to your cheeks. You've grown paler this season, despite the sun." Another sip, another bite. "Certainly an English lady like yourself grows weary of our Gypsy customs."

She frowned, reflecting on all he'd said. "I don't know Valentina."

"I'll introduce you."

"I haven't been invited."

"You will be."

"I won't fit in." She regarded her vivid orange gown. "I haven't conversed with any Englishmen besides shop owners in years."

"You'll like Valentina. She's adapted to the English ways and no longer believes in spirits."

"I don't believe in spirits, either."

"Mr. Colchester is a devout Christian and Valentina has followed suit," Luca continued. "You are a Christian too, aye?"

Aye. Once. Long ago.

Since arriving in Wales, she heard the peal of church bells every Sunday. She had contemplated attending services, but always quelled the thought. She was a Gypsy woman now, and she'd enough of her tyrannical father's heavy hand, all in the name of God.

"Although I don't agree with Valentina's interest in Christianity," Luca added, "they are happy, and I am glad for them."

Charity couldn't be happy or sad for the Colchesters because she didn't know either of them, but she appeased Luca by agreeing.

A grin touched his lips. "So, you will consider my suggestion?"

Wrapping her arms around herself, she stared at the grand estate in the distance, the smoke billowing from enormous chimneys, the torchlights lit, the flickering light of beeswax candles through the windows.

"Of course," she replied. Inwardly, she'd already made up

her mind. She couldn't attend a fancy dinner in such a grand house. Not wanting to spoil the pliashka with a disagreement, she decided to wait and tell Luca her decision come the morrow.

He surveyed her, apparently considering her reply. "Good. 'Tis settled." Abruptly, he swung around to rejoin the merriment by the campfire.

Immersed in her thoughts, she stared into the camp firelight, the festivities forgotten. Memories best hidden broke to the forefront. When she had run away from home, she had vowed to never look back.

She'd even changed her name to be doubly sure no one from England would ever find her.

* * *

A few hours later, long after she'd gone to her tent to sleep for the night, Charity awoke to a nightmare. Her eyes snapped open. Her heart beat heavily in her chest, her breathing quick. Something had brought her from a sound sleep to acute awareness.

She shot upright on her floor mattress. Judging from the angle of the moonlight spilling through her canvas tent, 'twas the middle of the night.

She flopped back, trying to get comfortable. With the sharp, chopped straw poking at her, comfort wasn't something that came easy. Still, she was safe, and in her familiar tent, the tent she had lived in for the past six years. Relieved, she swallowed. Her mouth was so dry.

She rolled onto her stomach and scanned the shadowy possessions she'd come to treasure. A small washbasin sat in a corner beside a water pitcher, a wooden stool placed nearby. A basket of blueberries she'd picked earlier in the day perched on a bench.

Her gown was draped on a table made of rough-hewn wooden planks.

She planned to wear it to market. Luca intended for the tribe to pick up supplies, which meant haggling for fresh vegetables and eggs whilst the boys and girls from the tribe stole jewelry from unsuspecting rich ladies to sell for coin.

Although Charity didn't condone stealing, she understood the necessity when supplies were low and jobs for Gypsies were nonexistent. Perhaps someday, the attitude toward Gypsies would change. The Colchester marriage was certainly an encouraging beginning to ending all the bigotry in the world.

Sweat gathered on her brow. Understandable, she rationalized, considering the close air in the tent. But it was more. The nightmare had jarred her dreams, and more memories of her upbringing invaded her thoughts.

Why now? Wales had brought her great joy, yet the remnants of past fears sat on the edge of her consciousness. After all this time, she still felt her father's firm fingers pushing her down onto the cold stone floor of the linen closet. She still felt his hand strike her with such force, the air was knocked from her lungs.

When he punished her, which was often, her mind had gone over and over her mishaps.

Why was she being punished? Was she really that bad?

She did ride her horse for hours, but that wasn't a reason to be disciplined.

Daniel Hayward, a longtime friend from her village, oftentimes accompanied her on his horse. Those were carefree, happy times, she thought. Indeed, her father must have realized she and Daniel oftentimes lost track of time, laughing and racing each other through the woods and pastures that surrounded their respective homes.

She smiled, her heart swelling with the heartening

remembrances. She and Daniel had talked endlessly of their childhood dreams and childhood pursuits.

Where was he now? she wondered. When she had left, he'd been eighteen, four years older than she. Despite that age difference, they got along wonderfully well together, although she sometimes overheard gossip in the village. Even Daniel's sister told Charity she made a fool of herself when she was with him, especially since she hunted him down to come riding with her.

That wasn't true. Daniel had always sought her, and he had clarified that fact on more than one occasion with his sister.

However, it *was* true that Charity couldn't help glancing at him whilst they rode. He was tall and good-looking, possessing the easy charm of the affluent, well-bred gentleman. She'd seen him grow from a lanky boy to a man, his shoulders broadening, his muscular legs clearly outlined in tightly-fitted leather breeches. And his eyes—a soft silver-grey, frequently sparking with mirth. He was handsome and self-assured, and she developed a crush for him. Although, of course, he never knew, for at the age of fourteen she was plain-featured, overly tall, and self-conscious.

She sighed. Hadn't they vowed to be best friends forever? She wondered if he remembered the day before she decided to run away. It had been her birthday, and she had chosen to spend part of the day with Daniel, riding horses and enjoying a picnic with friends and several chaperones.

After they returned to her home and before he left for his, Daniel leaned against an oak tree, so close to her she was afraid he could hear her pounding heart, and teased her that he'd beat her fair and square whilst they'd raced home.

"Please never forget me," she suddenly said.

"Why would I?" He raised his dark eyebrows. "You're not intending to leave me, are you?"

How had he known?

She hadn't answered, gazing up at the face she knew so well, hoping she could memorize it forever.

Lightly, he'd touched her cheek. "Where are you going?"

Away, she thought, briefly squeezing her eyes shut. *I don't want to leave you, but I must.*

On impulse, she stood on her toes and kissed him. In response, he'd stepped away and joked about how he would always beat her when they raced. She'd responded to his bantering with laughter.

At that point, her memories went from good to bad as she recalled her "transgressions," as her father labeled her wrongdoings. Oftentimes, he caught her dozing in church. When accused, she argued her good reasons because the vicar droned on for hours. Certainly her father would understand.

But he never did.

Instead, he forced her to kneel and recite Bible passages. Hadn't he known that by forcing her to recite a beloved verse, she would turn away rather than toward God? Hadn't he known she missed her mother as much as he did? She saw the telltale sorrow crossing his face whenever her mother's name was mentioned.

And her mother's name was also Charity. Many people commented on their resemblance. Charity had her mother's same unaffected beauty, hair color, and fiery, headstrong nature.

She pushed a strand of her unruly hair from her face. That was where the resemblance ended because, unlike her mother, Charity was an independent woman, relying on no one but herself.

Resolutely, she turned her thoughts from anything having to do with the English and her former life among them.

Closing her eyes, she courted sleep. A passage from Proverbs came, uplifting and encouraging.

"'Trust in the Lord with all thine heart; and lean not onto thine own understanding. In all thy ways acknowledge Him, and he shall direct thy paths.'"

She hadn't recited that particular Bible passage, or any Bible verse, in many years. Yet somehow, the prayer had drifted easily to her lips.

*** End of excerpt *Seeking Charity* by Josie Riviera
Copyright © 2019 Josie Riviera

Read the rest of Charity's story.
Pick up your copy of Seeking Charity.
Free on Kindle Unlimited!

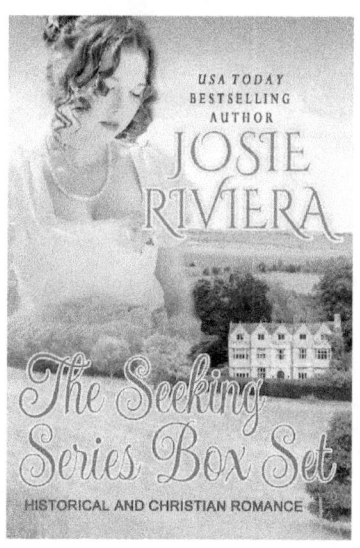

The Seeking Series
Savor the magic of the Romany Gypsies with this collec-

tion of Regency Christian romances in my exclusive boxed set.

Find out why readers are falling in love with The Seeking Series & staying up all night reading! These sweet and Christian romances will warm your heart.

Free on Kindle Unlimited!

ABOUT THE AUTHOR

Josie Riviera is a *USA TODAY* bestselling author of contemporary, inspirational, and historical sweet romances that read like Hallmark movies. She lives in the Charlotte, NC, area with her wonderfully supportive husband. They share their home with an adorable shih tzu, who constantly needs grooming, and live in an old house forever needing renovations.

To receive my Newsletter and your free sweet romance novella ebook as a thank you gift, sign up HERE.

Join my Read and Review VIP Facebook group for exclusive giveaways and FREE ARC's.

To connect with Josie, visit her webpage and subscribe to her newsletter. As a thank-you, she'll send you a free sweet romance novella directly to your inbox.
josieriviera.com/

ACKNOWLEDGMENTS

An appreciative thank you to my patient husband, Dave, and our three wonderful children.

ALSO BY JOSIE RIVIERA

Valentine Hearts Boxed Set

1-800-CUPID

1-800-CHRISTMAS

1-800-IRELAND

1-800-SUMMER

1-800-NEW YEAR

Irish Hearts Sweet Romance Bundle

Holly's Gift

A Chocolate-Box Valentine

A Chocolate-Box Christmas

A Chocolate-Box New Years

A Chocolate-Box Summer Breeze

A Chocolate-Box Christmas Wish

A Chocolate-Box Irish Wedding

Chocolate-Box Hearts

Chocolate-Box Hearts Volume Two

Chocolate-Box Double Hearts

Recipes from the Heart

Leading Hearts

New Year Hearts

SENIOR HEARTS

A Summer To Cherish

Summer Hearts

Romance Stories To Cherish Volume Two

Cherished Hearts

Christmas in the Air

A Very Christian Christmas

The 1-800-Series Volume Two

The 1-800-Series Complete

Christmas Tails of the Heart

Cocoa's Christmas Love

Pawfect Christmas Hearts

Pink Coral Island

Most books are available in ebook, audiobook, paperback, Large Print paperback and Hardcover.

Many are FREE on Kindle Unlimited!